Rough Edges: Volume 2

ROUGH EDGES
BOOK TWO

J.C. ANDERSON

Rough Edges - Volume #2

By J.C. Anderson

ISBN-13: 978-1-967473-14-4

Contents

Chapter One

Sarah

The sun was shining brightly over the manicured lawns of the Pine Grove Country Club, the perfect setting for another day of leisurely indulgence. I, Sara Donovan, formerly Miller, leaned back in my chair, crossing my legs elegantly as I sipped from my flute of mimosa. Around me, the sound of clinking glasses and muted laughter filled the air, blending with the soft rustle of tennis balls being volleyed back and forth on the courts below.

I adjusted my oversized sunglasses, catching a glimpse of myself in the reflective surface of the glass in front of me. Perfect as always—blonde hair immaculately styled, skin flawlessly tanned, and not a single wrinkle or blemish to mar my appearance. The sundress I wore was designer, of course, something understated yet sophisticated, the kind of outfit that screamed wealth without being gauche. I was the very image of the successful, well-kept wife, and I knew it.

"Another mimosa, Sarah?" one of the women at the table asked, her voice sugary sweet.

I glanced over at the woman—Maggie O'Connor, if I remembered correctly. A relatively new addition to our little group, Maggie was slightly older, with a few more lines around her eyes and a thicker waistline than mine, but still attractive in that matronly, motherly way. Maggie had the misfortune of overly caring about her family, particularly her three children, whom she doted on endlessly. It was a trait that I found more than a little tiresome, especially when it meant listening to endless stories about school plays, soccer games, and the trials of motherhood. It was like she didn't have a life outside her kids.

"No, I'm good, thanks," I replied with a smile that didn't quite reach my eyes, waving off the offer. I had enough for now. Besides, I didn't need alcohol to prove my superiority to these women.

Around the table, the other women—Nancy, Rebecca, and Julia—continued their chatter, mostly about the latest sales at Saks and the upcoming charity gala they were all expected to attend. I only half-listened, my mind wandering as I watched my husband, James, on the tennis court with a few other men. He was losing, as usual. The man had many talents, but tennis, or really anything athletic, was not one of them. Still, he was persistent, if nothing else.

"So, Sarah," Maggie began again, her tone bright and pleasant as she leaned in slightly, "how are your girls doing? Are they enjoying their Spring Vacation? Have you heard from them or their father?"

I resisted the urge to roll my eyes. Here we go again. I was already annoyed by the line of questioning. Women like Maggie were always so eager to talk about children, as if they were the most fascinating topic in the world.

"They're fine," I replied dismissively, taking another sip of my drink. "They're up in the mountains with their father right now. Camping or hiking or whatever it is they do up there."

Of course, I knew what they were doing. They did the same thing they'd always done. They went to Ethan's family's spot on Salom Lake and enjoyed the outdoors, but these trolls didn't need to know that.

Besides, that was my old life. I had a new life that did not include camping, bugs, or days on a lake with no amenities.

"That sounds lovely," Maggie said with enthusiasm. "It must be nice for them to spend some time outdoors, away from the city. Do you get to see them much? I cannot imagine being away from them for an extended time is easy on you."

I couldn't hide the slight curl of my lip as I responded. "I don't see them as much as I'd like," I lied smoothly, knowing full well that I was happier without them underfoot—not all the time, of course. But the social season was much easier when the girls weren't around. "James and I have been so busy with social obligations, and the girls... well, they don't get along with James very well. It's difficult."

Maggie's brow furrowed slightly, concern evident on her face. "That's too bad. It must be hard for them, being away from their mother so much. Have you considered getting them a therapist? I know it has worked wonders for my Ruth. She was having a hard time in school last year, and it really helped."

I waved off the question, my tone light but dismissive. "They're kids, Maggie. They're resilient. They'll be fine. Besides, they love their father, and he enjoys doing all those outdoor activities with them. It's good for them to spend time together."

But Maggie wasn't so easily deterred. "It's just that, well, I remember you saying that they've had some difficulty adjusting to your new marriage. Have things gotten any better?"

I sighed inwardly. Why did people like Maggie always have to pry and make assumptions? It wasn't my fault the girls didn't like James, and honestly, I didn't much care for the tension between them, either. But James was my husband, and he provided me with the life I wanted —a life of luxury, comfort, and status. That was what mattered. The silly thing was if the girls could simply let go of their attachment to their father, they could have had the same. Then it would have been perfect. I had actually suggested it originally when I first divorced Ethan—having

3

James adopt Maya and Lily—but James wasn't having it, so I had to let that go. Besides, James' son from his first marriage was around, and James loved the boy, and he had not dealt well with James leaving his mother.

The cow.

Madeline Spencer was a portly woman, with dirty brown hair and a fat backside. She was so far below my league it was like comparing t-ball to the majors. She did have one major point in her category, however. The Spencers were rich. Like crazy rich. It had been James' marriage to Madeline that had helped James' family business get to the next level. It had been quite the scandal when we got together.

It was for the best, of course. James wanted opportunities and photo ops, and I was much better for that than his disgusting ex-wife. Still, the fact that I had two children, had left my husband, and started my relationship with James in a scandalous way did not help our position. For two years now, I had told James that adopting the girls would help with the legitimacy of our relationship, but he simply couldn't disappoint his son again. So, I dropped it.

For now.

I still needed to answer Maggie.

"Things are fine, Maggie," I said, my tone a touch firmer now. "The girls just need time. And honestly, they're old enough to understand that life isn't always perfect or clean. They'll get over it."

Nancy, sensing the tension in the conversation, quickly changed the subject. "Did you see the new collection at Dior? They've got the most amazing new handbags. I picked up one boasting a new type of leather, some sort of bison hybrid—very exclusive, you'd love it, Sarah."

Bison hybrid? That didn't sound right. Whatever.

Grateful for the shift in focus, I smiled and leaned in, eager to talk about something more pleasant. "Oh, I did see those. Absolutely gorgeous. I was thinking of getting the black one with the gold chain in the Hunters collection. What do you think?"

And just like that, the conversation moved on, leaving behind the uncomfortable topic of my daughters and their less-than-perfect relationship with my new husband. The conversation did bring up thoughts that had been bothering me. James had stalled out a bit. It made me wonder how I could further our position. If I wanted that house on the Italian Riviera, without his family's approval, I needed James to kick it up a notch. I watched him trip on the court and squawk like an injured bird.

I sighed.

The truth was, I didn't love James. I never had. He was convenient, wealthy, and obsessed with me. He was easy to control and lived for action in the bedroom. A little sexy time, and he'd do just about anything I wanted. He was ready and willing to give me and my daughters the life we deserved—one of privilege and position. James could give it all. Why didn't the other people in my life who were supposed to care about me see that? That thought made me think of Maya and Lily.

They were probably fishing on the lake right now, and it made me sigh. I loved my girls; I was their mother. I carried them, birthed them, and took care of them in their young years. They were important to me, but they were a complication—a lingering connection to my past. People in this world didn't have kids from other relationships, or if they did, they had sole custody and didn't talk about the other spouse. James didn't like having my kids near us, and he found it hard not to show it, especially when Peter, his son, was around. I'd always thought that it was because even if Ethan wasn't wealthy, he was big, handsome, and just powerful.

I involuntarily tensed a bit at the thought of Ethan. Ethan was primal, in almost all senses of the word. If only he had money and real ambition to make more. He would be, well, perfect. But Ethan didn't need much. He was almost too nice most of the time. He did have the killer instinct, especially when the situation required it—someone in danger or trying to right a real wrong. Really, he could be a beast. Oh, he could be a beast, in the bedroom especially, and every once in a while when he unleashed the beast, it was... magical.

I felt my face flush a bit. I needed to calm down.

I righted myself in my chair, ignoring those at my table, and listened to the conversations around me. Patricia, a petite blonde with a perpetually perfect blowout, despite being at the next table, could be heard clearly. "So, Emma's ballet recital last weekend was absolutely lovely," she said with a satisfied smile. "You wouldn't believe who we ended up sitting next to—Wesley Andrews, the CEO of that new solar tech startup. Yes, the one on the society page. He and his wife are looking at sending their daughter to the same school as Emma. Tom's already planning a dinner with them next week to discuss some potential partnerships."

Murmurs of approval rippled through the group. Patricia had always been good at turning casual social events into networking opportunities. I was not a fan. Patricia had grown up in high society and looked down on people like me who married into it. The two-faced hag.

Another woman, Miranda, who was tall, striking, and known for her sharp wit, chimed in. "Oh, absolutely. It's incredible the connections you can make through the kids' activities. Just last month, at Jackson's soccer game, Bill ran into one of his old college buddies who's now a VP at a major investment firm. They've been working on a joint venture ever since."

"Kids really do open doors," Patricia agreed. "The actual education at these private schools is good, but putting them in the right circles is even more important. The people you meet at these events... you never know where the next big opportunity might come from."

My attention sharpened as I listened to them trade stories about the influential people their children had connected them with. I had always thought of my girls' activities as just that—activities. A way to keep them busy and out of my hair. But listening to these women, I realized that I had been missing an opportunity that was right in front of me.

There was so much more to it. The right connections, the right schools, the right friends—these were just as valuable as any single business deal or opportunity.

It was Miranda who unintentionally drove the point home. "Honestly, sometimes I think the kids are our best investments. I mean, look at how many doors Jackson has opened for us just through his sports. And with everything being so competitive these days, it's those personal connections that really make the difference."

I nodded along, though my mind was racing. James wasn't exactly a business guru—he'd coasted on his family's wealth, his ex-wife's connections and investments, and his brother, Nathan. Nathan was the real talent. He was also a bit more handsome and way better in bed. Plus, his wife, Marcia, was a total bitch. She was like Patricia; she looked down on me. Which was crazy because she was a cow just like Madeline. One of these days, I thought I might show Marcia the movie I made with Nathan, but that would have to wait. Right now, I needed to develop opportunities to obtain the level of status I wanted. So, the brother being good or bad in bed was hardly a factor at the moment. What Patricia was saying made sense, the snotty bitch. What James and I needed were connections—the opportunities that could only come from being in the right circles.

After all, since James wasn't exactly flourishing in business (he was always chasing after his brother's shadow, and everyone knew it), maybe this could be the edge we needed. Perhaps my daughters could be the ticket to the kind of connections James had always lacked.

With a calculated smile, I drained the last of my mimosa and mentally started drafting a new plan. It was time to take control of the situation. I would simply need full custody from Ethan. He was an amazing father, and less time with his daughters would kill him. But this was for my future. He would have to understand. He would make a fuss, but he didn't have any money. He would not be able to fight me.

"Oh my goodness," Nancy said, her voice barely above a whisper. "Is that...?"

The other women at the table turned their attention to her, curiosity piqued. Nancy held her phone up, showing them the screen. The photo was unmistakable—two young girls, smiling brightly as they posed with an *exceptionally* striking woman. She had long, wavy dirty blonde hair that fell effortlessly around her shoulders. Her eyes were a captivating shade of hazel green, bright and expressive, with a depth that could draw people in. She had high cheekbones and a sharp jawline that complemented her symmetrical features. There were also several pictures of an elegant woman with black hair and fetching icy blue eyes. It was like looking at the open ocean. Despite being probably 15 years apart, the two women looked somewhat alike.

I stared at the phone. What the actual hell?

"4 million likes. Wow. So posh. Is that Lady Harrington? And... Samantha Harrington?" Maggie exclaimed, her eyes wide with shock. "Those girls... they look just like..."

"Those are your daughters, aren't they, Sarah?" Julia chimed in, her voice a mix of disbelief and awe. "Look, yes, that's Lily and Maya; she names them in the caption as well as your ex-husband."

My heart froze like ice. Indeed, they were my daughters, looking far too happy in the company of Samantha and Lady Harrington. The caption under the photo read something about a "day out with new friends in Silver Ridge; don't we look like a family?" and it was clear from the comments that the post was quickly going viral. There were millions of likes, hundreds of comments, and shares were pouring in, with people fawning over how beautiful the girls were and how stunning Samantha and Lady Harrington looked.

And how handsome the man was. Ethan. My man. At least when I wanted him.

It was effortless for them. The pictures weren't even special. Just them hanging out in Silver Ridge. The most liked comment was from a woman named Olivia Montgomery.

As in the actress, a complete A-lister; she was a Hollywood hot girl.

"A family, with moms like you and Lady Harrington, I don't know who would be luckier, Ethan or the girls! Love you!"

Ethan couldn't be with one of them, could he? And certainly not both of them. Wasn't Lady Harrington married? That would be a huge scandal in those circles, the absolute highest rungs of society. They were top-notch. James' money went into banks. Lady Harrington's money bought banks. And Ethan couldn't be in high society; he didn't have ANY money. Besides that, he was too unruly and uncultured. Sure, he looked good and was a beast in bed, but he just didn't know anything about the important stuff. What the hell was this Olivia woman playing at?

"Wow, Sarah," Rebecca added, her tone a bit sharper, "I didn't know your daughters were hanging out with actual royalty and supermodels. When did that happen? That's... quite the connection. And good lord, is *that* your ex-husband?"

All four women, including Saint Maggie, looked at a picture of my ex-husband. They gawked at it. Then me. Then the picture again. Julia apparently couldn't contain herself. "You said you left him?"

I gritted my teeth. "Yes, we married young, and it wasn't working out. I left him for James."

Julia exchanged glances with the other women. "Didn't you say that he wanted you back? Was always begging for another chance?"

"Yes. He still isn't over me, unfortunately." I sighed dramatically. "Always wanting to get back together."

All four women stared again at the picture, their faces going pink. They looked skeptical, like there was no way that Ethan would want *me* back.

"And now he hangs out with Samantha and Victoria Harrington?"

Nancy asked. The implication was obvious. Nancy did not believe that Ethan was *not* over me.

I forced a smile, trying to keep my cool even as I felt a surge of irritation rise within me. "Of course not. He doesn't know Samantha Harrington. You know how it is," I said dismissively. "The girls are spending some time with their father, and he's always taking them on these little adventures. He has some family land outside of Silver Ridge, which they use as a retreat. They must have gone into Silver Ridge for something and ran into Samantha and Lady Harrington. No big deal."

The women exchanged glances, clearly not buying my nonchalant attitude. Maggie, ever the sympathetic one, leaned in closer, her brow furrowed with concern. "It's wonderful that your girls and ex-husband are doing so well. Divorce is really hard on children, and they look really happy. Does your husband spend much time with celebrities?"

My forced smile grew tighter. I was losing patience on this topic. "Ethan is basically a handyman and has a criminal record. Even if he is handsome, he does not spend a bunch of time with celebrities." I replied, my voice edged with forced politeness. "You all know how Silver Ridge is. You can't toss a rock there and *not* hit a celebrity, and you know how cute my girls are. I am sure they simply charmed them into taking pictures."

Before any of the women could press further, I rose from my chair, smoothing out my dress as I did so. "Excuse me for a moment, ladies," I said, my tone clipped. "I just remembered I need to check on something."

Without waiting for a response, I turned on my heel and walked briskly away from the table, my heart pounding in my chest. I could feel the stares of the other women on my back, the whispers that would no doubt start the moment I was out of earshot. But I didn't care about them. All I cared about was getting to a private spot where I could think.

Once I was a safe distance away, I pulled out my own phone, my hands trembling slightly as I opened Instagram. Sure enough, there were pictures of Lily and Maya, looking radiant and carefree. There were more photos, too—candid shots of the girls with... Samantha Harrington?

Why the hell were my daughters hanging out with a supermodel?

Gorgeous woman. Effortlessly so. Looking at her was enough to irritate me.

Samantha, Lily, and Maya laughing and posing, apparently having the time of their lives acting like they were part of some glamorous family.

I scrolled through more pictures. Samantha was with her aunt, Lady Harrington, who was a Countess of... oh, I forget. I am not much for politics, excluding the occasional intrigue to help James's company. (Yes, that includes sleeping with some politicians.) But even I knew Victoria Harrington. Very British, very posh, very rich, and like 7th in line for both the English and French crowns.

Okay, why the hell are my daughters with a British aristocrat? Has the world lost it?

I kept moving through the pictures. Samantha had uploaded a bunch of pictures and short videos of Lady Harrington, hugging, giggling and horsing around with Maya and Lily. Ethan was in the background smiling and looking content.

That doesn't make any sense. None of it did. How on earth had Ethan connected with the Harringtons? I look through more of the pictures. They really did look like a family spending time together.

I gritted my teeth at one of the last photos. It was a picture of Lady and Samantha Harrington on either side of Ethan, holding his arms, looking awfully cozy. He was smiling. He never smiled. I felt a surge of anger mixed with a pang of something I wasn't used to feeling—was it guilt? No, that couldn't be it. I had nothing to feel guilty about. I loved my daughters, but I had my own life, my own priorities, my own needs and wants. That needed to be respected. That didn't mean I didn't care.

It didn't mean they could be happy without me. And yet, seeing them like that, happy, so far removed from me, it stung in a way I hadn't anticipated.

How dare they? How dare they post these pictures without consulting me first? It was one thing for the girls to spend time with their father, but this? It was fine that he took care of them when I needed them out of the way, but this was too much. It made me look like an outsider, like I wasn't part of their lives at all.

My fingers tightened around my phone as I opened up my messages, quickly typing out a furious text to Ethan. I didn't care if he was busy; he needed to understand that this was unacceptable.

> Sarah: Why are you exposing my girls to a bunch of hussies? You have no right to expose them like that without talking to me first. You think you can just parade them around like that and not deal with the consequences? This is ridiculous, Ethan. You need to put a stop to it now.

I hit send, breathing heavily as I stared down at my phone, waiting for a response. This wasn't over, not by a long shot.

As I stood there, fuming, the noise of the country club faded into the background. I called my lawyer. I would make Ethan regret this. He needed to understand his place.

Ethan

I woke up earlier than usual, the first light of dawn barely touching the curtains. Staring at the ceiling, I couldn't shake the events of last night. The fight at the Rusty Spur was just instinct. It was not something I should have done. Not with my past, and I can't afford to get in trouble again.

Luckily, I didn't really hurt anyone. But, it had been close.

The recognition as "Caveman" caught me completely off guard. I wasn't expecting anyone to know that part of my life, much less react the way they did. The attention, the excitement—it made me uncomfortable. I started fighting semi-professionally two years ago, shortly after Sarah left me. I was currently in a less regulated Underground League. It paid pretty well, and I have not *really* gotten hurt yet. I should probably avoid it now. But it was hard to walk away. It was one of the only real outlets I had.

Back after Sarah left and shoved her cheating in my face, I needed somewhere to unleash my rage, and I was not welcome at the dojo—not after what I had done after... after Ryan died. So I started fighting on the streets. I got pretty good at it. I've had 14 fights until now. All won and all by knockout. I actually have another fight coming up in a month and have not been training very well. I need to get my head on straight.

I rolled over and grabbed my phone from the nightstand to look at the messages I had ignored last night. I saw Sarah's text and realized that the same message I had ignored last night had been repeated five times. I also had 13 missed calls. Then I realized that when Samantha was helping with my phone, she had marked Sarah with low priority.

Okay, that was funny.

My thoughts shifted to Samantha. I wanted to talk about everything that had happened, but I hesitated. She'd seen a side of me that I try to keep away from people I care about. I didn't know her or Victoria very well, but... I care about them and don't want them to think less of me.

Strange thought, I know.

And then there was the kiss. It had been a simple, soft kiss, similar to Samantha's thank-you kiss. It was amazing, feeling a woman's lips again after so long. I can't remember the last time I received a kiss from a beautiful woman, and even if it wasn't romantic, when someone as beautiful as Samantha kisses you... well, it sticks with you. Maybe the whole thank-you kiss was a model thing. Like when the French kiss each other on the cheeks.

That's a thing, right? I don't even know.

Hopefully, I didn't offend her. But the way her lips had felt against mine lingered in my mind, making it hard to think about anything else. I didn't want to admit how much I'd enjoyed it, or how much I wished it had been more.

But now, in the quiet of the morning, I wondered if I'd done the right thing. Samantha was incredible, and I doubt she realized the effect she had on people, me included. It was something I hadn't felt in a long time. But even thinking about being more was dumb. Samantha was famous, gorgeous, and rich. Normal dudes don't have chances with girls like that. I am just me—Ethan Miller, a guy with too much baggage, too many wounds, and too little to offer someone like her. Plus, I have two kids; a woman like that wouldn't want to be an instant mom.

Still, maybe we could be friends. I should avoid trying to kiss her again. I don't know the protocol of this friendship kiss stuff, so I shouldn't step out too much. Especially since I kissed her in a way that couldn't be described as friendship. I have friends, and I certainly don't kiss them like that.

Of course, that thought made me blush. Like a 12-year-old. Get it together, Ethan.

I sighed, sitting up and swinging my legs over the side of the bed. I needed to clear my head.

I got up and headed to the bathroom, splashing cold water on my face in a feeble attempt to shake off the lingering thoughts. Staring at my reflection, I saw the same unkempt guy I always saw—tousled hair, a decently kept beard I hadn't bothered to trim, and the same tired eyes that had seen too much over the years.

I rubbed my face. This wasn't the time to get caught up in emotions. I had to keep my focus on what mattered: my girls, making sure they were happy and safe. They were my world, and they were the reason I kept moving forward, no matter how much the past tried to drag me down.

But even as I told myself that, Samantha's eyes—and yes, her incredible butt—flashed through my head.

Shut up, I can think of two things at once.

I shook my head, running a hand through my hair. No, I couldn't go there. I couldn't risk getting involved with someone like Samantha, not when I was still trying to figure out my own life. Besides, she deserved better—someone who wasn't weighed down by a past full of regrets and bad decisions.

I needed to get out, get some fresh air. Maybe a run and a little kata would help clear my mind.

I quickly dressed, pulling on my usual workout gear and lacing up my running shoes. As I headed downstairs, the house was still quiet, everyone else likely still asleep.

I put on a pot of coffee before I left.

I stepped outside, the cool morning air hitting my face and filling my lungs. The sky was just starting to lighten, the first rays of sunlight peeking over the horizon. It was peaceful, and for a moment, I felt a sense of calm settle over me.

But my thoughts kept drifting back to Samantha. The way she'd laughed last night, the way she'd looked at me with those big, expressive eyes—it all kept playing over and over in my mind.

Damn, I need to get a grip. I picked up my pace.

The rhythmic thud of my shoes on the dirt of the trail was usually enough to drown out my thoughts, but today, no matter how fast I ran or how hard I pushed myself, I couldn't shake the confusion swirling in my head.

I rounded a corner while I tried to outrun my own thoughts. But they followed me, relentless, refusing to be ignored. Honestly, I knew what I was really afraid of—getting close to someone again, opening myself up, only to get hurt all over again. It had taken me years to rebuild my life after everything that had happened, after Sarah had left and I'd been left to pick up the pieces. I wasn't sure I had it in me to go through that kind of pain again.

And I was scared because I didn't know how to do well—anything. Sarah and I had Maya young. I didn't really date. I haven't been with anyone but Sarah, and that thought scares me.

I also had to think of my girls. Lily and Maya liked Samantha, and let's not forget Lady Harrington—maybe even more than I did, if that was possible. And if things got complicated between Samantha and me, what would that do to them? They'd already been through enough, and the last thing I wanted was to drag them through my mess.

My girls, Maya and Lily, were the best. They were such little troopers. So kind. So considerate. I know that Sarah hurt them as well. They know what a mother is supposed to act like, and their mother had not acted properly in a long time.

But with Victoria and Sarah, it was like they had two new mothers. I am not even sure the two women realized what they were doing. The motherly instinct was strong with the Harringtons. I don't know if Vicki had children, but I suspect they were damned lucky kids. I wasn't sure of Samantha's thoughts on kids, but she was a natural. Whoever locked her down and convinced her to have a family would be in for a treat. So much beauty, kindness, and passion.

And did I mention her butt? Do not forget her butt.

I sighed. It was almost unfair. If only people knew how special these women were, Samantha and Lady Harrington would never have a moment of rest.

Still, I know my way of thinking was unfair. Mothering isn't all sunshine and roses, and I shouldn't let my expectations subvert reality. Mothering isn't as easy as eating food, watching movies, and spending money—especially when you have it.

And money they had. Geez.

Money, looks, power. They had it all. But was that enough? Who knew if Victoria or Samantha could be what the girls needed in the long run? Not that they had applied for the job. The fact that I am having these thoughts at all about people that I barely knew—and yes, even though I feel connected to them—I still didn't really know them very well. I don't know how I feel about them, or how they feel about me, or if there is anything there beyond... respect?

I am seriously so out of practice.

One thing I knew to be true was that because of them and their kindness, they had given my girls a nostalgic glimpse of their prior relationship with their mom, and the girls had taken to it like bees to honey. And for that, I will forever be grateful.

I slowed down, finally coming to a stop at the edge of a meadow. I stood there, hands on my knees, catching my breath and trying to pull my scattered thoughts back together. I was overthinking all of this. I just needed to take things one day at a time, see where things went without trying to plan every little detail in advance. It was then my phone rang.

The earbuds I was wearing started ringing. Wireless headphones were a new addition—not something I would have bought on my own, but they were one of the accessories Victoria had insisted on, and I had to admit, they were pretty cool.

I answered the phone without looking at who was calling, having a good idea of who it was. I touched the earbud, and without missing a beat, a rather high-pitched voice started talking rapidly.

"Miller! You beautiful son of a bitch! Have I ever told you how much more talented you are than the other hacks I represent?"

I snorted. Represent. Right.

"Hi, Toni," I said, my tone flat. "Pretty sure I told you I was on vacation and not to call me."

Toni laughed, sounding like a broken woodchipper. "That you did, kid, that you did. But that was before you went viral online. Do you have any idea who that girl you rescued is?"

I frowned, caught off guard. "Viral? What are you talking about?"

"Oh, you really don't know, do you? Kid, your escapades at the Rusty Spur last night, Samantha Harrington—nice pull, by the way. I saw the pictures. Her ass looks amazing. Anyway, you coming to the aid of that Hana chick has all the social justice warriors painting you like some sort of god of chivalry."

"Chivalry, Toni."

"Yeah, that's the word. Fight critics are losing it. Some people are calling you the 'Samurai.' It's all over the fight forums. Your old fight videos have received five million views in just a few hours. People are freaking out. And it's not just because you knocked some idiots around —though that helps. Ethan, the girl, the girl you saved is Hana Yamamoto. Her father is a political giant, potentially the next Japanese prime minister. I want you to think of them like the Japanese Kennedys."

"You cannot be serious. All that from a little altercation? Who would care about this?" I blinked, trying to process. "Wait, why the 'Samurai'?"

That thought made me laugh. My *Chinese* kung fu master isn't going to like that.

Toni's voice took on a more serious tone. "It's a mix of things. Partly because of how you handled those guys. But mostly because Hana's background is making waves. People love a good story, and 'Samurai' just stuck when they found out who she was. She is Japanese. You whooped ass like a Samurai or some shit. Who knows? But it's catching on in the fight subgroups, especially with the Asian communities. Some of those groups are getting big, and a few of them have ties to larger organizations. UFC-level interest isn't out of the question, Kid. And sponsors... they're sniffing around too. I've gotten 23 emails since three this morning."

I rubbed the back of my neck, feeling a mix of frustration and confusion. "So, this is all because I helped a girl out of a bad situation?"

"Not just any girl, Kid. *Hana Yamamoto* is practically untouchable —except, apparently, by you. This kind of thing puts you on the map in a big way. You're not just some underground lackey anymore; people are talking about you like you're the next big thing. And that's not all. You were seen with Samantha Harrington at the Rusty Spur. People are buzzing about that too wondering who you are, what your story is. Your relationship status, all that shit. You cannot buy this kind of attention."

I took a deep breath, trying to wrap my head around the conversation. "So, what are you saying, Toni?"

Toni's tone softened. "I'm saying that the whole damned world wants a piece of you, Kid. This is the big time. We need to go make some money while the iron is hot and some shit."

I appreciated Toni's straightforwardness, even if the situation was more than I'd bargained for. "Alright, Toni. Thanks for the heads up. But for now, I'm sticking to my vacation. I'll think about it."

"Kid, don't take too long," Toni replied. "This is the shot we've been waiting for. I am going to gauge interest and see what potential deals might suit you. Deal?"

I chuckled. "You got it. Thanks, Toni."

"My pleasure, kid. Don't exhaust yourself with those world-class asses."

I ended the call and stood there for a moment, the weight of what Toni had said settling in. "Samurai"? What the hell was I getting myself into?

Samantha

I woke up feeling all kinds of confused and, if I'm being honest, a little annoyed.

Ethan kissed me. He kissed ME and then thanked me for being a friend. What the everloving hell?

Friends? Really? It wasn't like I was trying to jump into something serious right away, but did he really have to shut the door on anything else so quickly? It was like he'd instantly thrown me into the friend zone, and I didn't even get a say in it.

This has never happened to me before.

Perhaps I should just jump him in the shower? That wasn't exactly ladylike. But at least that would get my point across—no, that was a bad idea. I don't think I could deal with the rejection.

Rejection? Have I ever really been rejected? Gregory sort of rejected me. But after I told him—

No. I had rejected him first for all intents and purposes. He just made it official.

So Ethan rejecting me would be a real first. It kind of sucks.

What was his deal? Maybe he just wasn't interested in someone like me. I do have my share of flaws. Some guys aren't into women who are strong, independent, and who happen to be in the public eye. That had to be it. He simply couldn't handle this. I also had my share of baggage. I wasn't too proud to admit that.

The thought really pissed me off for some reason. Who was Ethan to just decide I wasn't worth considering as anything more than a buddy? I could take care of him if the damn idiot would let me.

The shower idea was looking more appealing.

I groaned and grabbed my phone, knowing the Harpies would have something to say about all this. I sent a rage text to them right after Ethan and I locked lips the night before. I sent the text and then I crashed. I said I would give them a full update—even a full play-by-play of the night the next morning. Then I promptly fell asleep.

Surprisingly, I slept well.

Sure enough, they'd been lighting up my phone all morning. They must have seen the pictures and videos from last night at the Rusty Spur. I knew they'd have thoughts—lots of them.

I looked at my messenger app; I had a lot of messages to catch up on.

> Olivia: Sam, I saw the pictures from last night. You guys looked amazing on that dance floor! 😍 💃 And who was that girl Ethan saved? There's a whole video of the fight—and all I can say is damn... just damn!

> Grace: Have you seen this? People are calling him "Samurai." That is way better than "Caveman." Who has two nicknames? LOL. The "Samurai" is spreading like wildfire. And get this, the chick he saved is some kind of Japanese princess. Do they still have those in Japan? She uploaded a video about the ordeal. Here is the link @HanaYammoto. Did you see all the comments on your pictures with his daughters at Silver Ridge? Don't forget that. Everything this guy touches is going viral. This is crazy.

> Natalie: Samurai? Caveman? And you said he put you in the friend zone? Are you serious? Explain.

There were a bunch of other texts, but those were the important ones.

I sighed, scrolling through their messages. I tried to get my bearings before I answered.

> Samantha: Yeah. So. I just got up and am trying to get up to speed. We had a bomb time. Best date I've had since…I cannot even say. He's hot. Like stupid hot. But in a I don't know I am hot way. Its infuriating. The boy draws attention like cosplayers at a nerd convention. And he definitely put me in the friend zone. But not before he kissed me. Full-blown a real kiss. It wasn't like a make-out session or anything. But it was good. Yeah, so he kissed me and then thanked me for being his friend. Guys aren't allowed to do that, damn it. I don't know what to think. He's so hard to read. And no, I didn't know anything about this Hana girl until just now. Apparently, I'm the last to know.

Olivia: Holy shit. Ethan's fight videos have gone viral. I just watched one. He is a major badass. And... this isn't the first time he has done this. He beat five college guys several years ago outside a bar, and it was a thing.

Grace: He got in a different fight outside a bar? He's got all this history; you need to dig a little deeper.

Natalie: I'm with Grace. You need to find out what's really going on. And you can't just let this whole "friend zone" thing slide. I hear you on the fight video thing. I just finished his last fight; it was only two months ago, and all I can say is hot damn. There is something visceral about a guy fighting, especially when it's for you. That being said, I would officially like to put in my application for Main Wifey or Mistress One. I don't mind sharing.

I rolled my eyes. No one else was getting that number one spot. Over my dead body.

Uh? What the hell was that thought? Knock it off Samantha.

I kept scrolling though messages and notifications on my social media.

Samantha: What a freaking mess. I don't even know where to start with that. The Samurai?? He got that nickname just from last night?

Olivia forwarded a link.

I opened it, and it led to Twitter, and sure enough, Ethan was all over it.

Samantha: Damn, The Samurai is the number one topic on Twitter… what do you guys think about coming this direction? I may need a bit of backup. I will talk to my Aunt.

Olivia: YES! I love it. I am just finishing up filming in LA. I can be there in 72 hours. We're long overdue for a meet-up. We can help you strategize. Plus, we all want to meet this "Samurai."

Grace: Count me in. This is too big to just leave to texting. And I want to see this guy with my own eyes.

Natalie: Same here. And since I am applying for Wifey, I will bring my A game.

I smiled at their enthusiasm, feeling a bit more grounded. The Harpies always knew how to rally around each other, and this time was no different. If anyone could help me sort through the mess of feelings and confusion that was Ethan Miller, it was them.

Samantha: Alright, let's make it happen. I'll set something up, and we'll get to the bottom of this.

I set my phone down and stretched, feeling a bit more resolved. I wasn't ready to admit anything to myself yet, but I also wasn't about to let Ethan off the hook so easily. He might have put me in the friend zone, but that didn't mean I had to stay there.

With resolve, I stepped to and stood in front of the mirror, staring at my reflection with a mixture of frustration and determination. What exactly did one wear when they were firmly planted in the friend zone by a guy they couldn't stop thinking about?

Ugh, why was this so complicated?

25

I didn't want to dress up too much—after all, I wouldn't want to make my "friend" feel uncomfortable, the big jerk that he was.

But then again... why should I hold back? I shouldn't. I shouldn't change myself just because he couldn't see past his own issues. No, if I was going to be stuck in this ridiculous limbo, I was at least going to do it on my terms.

I rummaged through my closet, pulling out a couple of options before tossing them aside. Finally, I decided on one of my most flattering gym sets—a sleek, fitted ensemble that hugged my curves, accentuating my hips, butt, and bust. It left a couple of inches of my midriff exposed. The deep green color made my eyes pop, and the cut of the top was just enough to be both athletic and alluring.

I pulled on the outfit, feeling a surge of confidence as I adjusted it. It was a little over the top, even I had to admit. Girls that wore something like this wanted attention, not comfort. Though it was comfortable. It didn't matter. Today I was in the mood to push the boundaries a bit. I am NOT going to fade into the background even if Ethan wanted to keep things platonic.

Satisfied with my choice, I grabbed my phone to check Instagram, wanting to see how the posts from the Rusty Spur were doing. The number of likes and comments kept skyrocketing—Samantha Harrington out at a country bar wasn't exactly an everyday occurrence. I had been trying to live down something of a reputation for the last several years. I didn't go out much anymore, so being seen at an actual club was surprising. The candid shots were getting a lot of love, as were the videos of me and Ethan dancing.

We do look good together. Still, what was really going crazy was Ethan defending that Hana girl. Now that I think about it, she called him by name. How did she know him?

Wait... she said something about giving him her phone number and calling her? When the hell did that happen?

I felt my irritation flare as I continued scrolling and heard a knock at the door. Before I could respond, the door swung open, and in walked Victoria with Lily and Maya in tow.

"Good morning, Samantha!" Victoria greeted me with her usual warm smile. The girls, however, looked a bit more lethargic.

"Morning, guys," I said, sliding my phone into my pocket. "What's up?"

"We wanted to know how last night went," Victoria said, her tone casual but firm. "You know, after you left the house."

I saw the curiosity in her eyes, along with something else— perhaps concern? The girls, on the other hand, looked downright expectant.

"Well," I began, trying to find the right words. "It was... eventful. I had a good time, but some things happened that you might want to see for yourself."

I pulled my phone back out and opened Instagram, showing them the photos and videos from last night. Victoria leaned in, her eyebrows lifting in surprise as she watched the video of the fight. The girls huddled close, their eyes wide as they took in the scene.

"Oh my," Victoria murmured, clearly impressed. "Ethan really got himself into something, didn't he? The boy can handle himself. How delightful. Maybe I should hire him... he's more than capable. And then..."

Victoria chuckled. "Oh, the Society Page is going to love this."

She said that last part more to herself than to us.

The girls, however, were not pleased. They exchanged worried looks, and I could see the concern written all over their faces.

"Is Dad okay?" Lily asked, her voice small. "He didn't get hurt, did he?"

"No, sweetheart," I reassured her, giving her a comforting smile. I gestured to the girls, and they fell into me.

It felt good to have these babies in my arms.

"Your dad's fine. He was just protecting someone who needed help.

But I think it might be a good idea to go check on him, just to make sure."

Maya nodded, looking equally worried. "Yeah, we should go find him. I don't like it when he gets into fights."

I glanced at her, surprised. "Maya, Lily, do you know about your dad's fighting?"

They both nodded. Maya sounded emotional. "We don't like it. Dad does it because of what happened to Uncle Ryan and the business. He gets hurt sometimes. It's scary. He does it for money."

I glanced at Victoria. Uncle Ryan? Business? What? She gave me a knowing look but shook her head a bit. She seemed to have an idea as to what they were talking about. Still, that didn't matter. My girls were hurting. I gave them a squeeze.

"You don't need to worry about your dad," I said in a gentle voice. "He's... so strong. Like Superman. He did not get hurt this time. He was a real hero."

The girls held me, and then Aunt Victoria put her arms around all of us.

I made a promise to myself right there and then. Ethan was having money problems. I would find a way to fix that. Ethan isn't going to have to fight.

"Come, girls," Victoria said, wiping away a tear from Lily. "Let's go find your father."

We all headed out together, the girls leading the way with determined steps. As we walked down the hall toward the kitchen, Victoria leaned in close, her voice dropping to a whisper. "I have some things to share with you later, Samantha. Some insights about Ethan... but now isn't the time."

I glanced at her, intrigued but also slightly apprehensive. "Insights? About what?"

Victoria gave me a knowing smile, her eyes twinkling with that familiar hint of mischief. "Ethan is more complex than medieval limericks. But later."

I snorted. "He's definitely not as boring."

Victoria sighed. "You have no sense of poetry."

I nodded and tried not to laugh. I waited, but curiosity gnawed at me. What could Victoria possibly have to share that I didn't already know? Ethan was a mystery, sure, but I felt like I'd been getting to know him better, peeling back the layers one at a time. Still, if Victoria had something to add, I wanted to hear it.

When we reached the kitchen, it was empty, save for the strong scent of coffee. The silly man had obviously brewed a pot. But... Ethan? No sign of him. The girls looked around, their brows furrowing in concern.

"Where's Dad?" Lily asked, her voice tinged with worry.

Maya wandered over to the window, peering out into the yard. Suddenly, her face lit up. "He's outside. I should have known."

Victoria and I moved closer to the window, and there, in the middle of the yard, was Ethan. He was practicing... movements, smooth and precise, almost like a dance. There was punching and kicking and blocking—just beautiful movement. Ethan stepped with grace, power, and a fluidity that made it impossible to look away.

We watched with rapt attention. Then he suddenly ripped off his sweatshirt, tossing it to the side without breaking his rhythm. My breath caught in my throat.

Damnit, damnit, damnit. The man was... well, there was no other way to put it—he was magnificent. His arms were thick with muscle, defined in a way that spoke of strength and control. His white undershirt was an under armor set that was made to be defining and left little to the imagination. With just the undershirt, every movement Ethan showcased flexed his form, showing off the power coiled within him.

And the dude wanted to be my friend. I wonder if he's gay?

Victoria and I exchanged a quick glance, and I could see that she was just as captivated as I was. We were both silent, mesmerized by the way Ethan's body moved, the way the sunlight glinted off his skin as he flowed from one pose to the next. It was hard to tell whether it was the sheer physicality of the moment or something deeper that held us spellbound.

I felt a sudden rush of heat, and before I knew it, I was fanning myself, trying to dispel the warmth creeping up my neck. Beside me, Victoria did the same, her cheeks slightly flushed. The two of us must have looked utterly ridiculous, standing there at the window, watching him like two schoolgirls with a crush.

"Are you okay, Samantha? Aunt Victoria?" Lily's voice broke through the haze of our mutual distraction, her tone filled with genuine concern.

Maya, who had been watching us with a curious expression, chimed in, "Yeah, you both look really red. Are you getting sick—oh. Hehe. Never mind."

Victoria and I snapped out of our daze, both of us straightening up and quickly composing ourselves. I cleared my throat, trying to sound nonchalant. "Oh, we're fine, girls. Just a little warm, that's all. It's, uh, hot in here, don't you think?"

Victoria nodded, though I could see the amusement flickering in her eyes. "Yes, definitely warm. Maybe we should open a window or something."

"Or take off my clothes." Victoria snapped her hand over her mouth. I pretended not to hear her.

Lily looked at us confused. Maya just smiled, clearly not convinced by our weak explanations, but they didn't press the issue. Instead, they returned their attention to Ethan, who was still immersed in his practice, completely unaware of the effect he was having on the two of us.

He really was a big fat jerk. I crossed my arms and scowled.

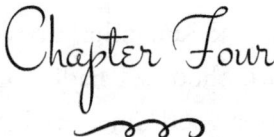

Chapter Four

Hana

The night at the Rusty Spur had started out as just another evening of drinks and casual conversation.

Sort of.

I watched him—the man I had first seen at the grocery store, Ethan —throughout the night. He drew me in the moment I saw him. Tall, muscular, but quiet; unassuming, with a masculinity about him that was hard to ignore.

Really hard to ignore.

I watched him interact with those around him while at the Rusty Spur. He looked at the same time in his natural element but uncomfortable. It was really cute.

I regret to admit that I felt a pang of jealousy every time I saw him with Samantha Harrington. The former supermodel was out with Ethan. Samantha was tall, leggy, with a beautiful athletic but curvy figure. She was almost unfair. Samantha captivated the men around her, and they were in one of the few cities, few places that were used to people like her, beautiful like her.

Well, maybe not completely like her. She was not only beautifully famous but famous for being beautiful.

I am pretty sure I hate her.

The way Ethan looked at Samantha, the way he drew her to him, bothered me more than it should. I had come to the Spur with my friends, intending to have a good time, maybe flirt a little, and yes, to find Ethan. But I spent way too much time watching him. I wanted to dance with him, to feel his strong hands touch me, feel his fingers in my hair and on my backside, move me across the floor. But Samantha was always there, always simping for his attention. Bitch couldn't take a hint.

I'd been drinking, maybe a bit more than I should have, and it made the night blur at the edges. My friends and I were laughing, attempting to have a good time, but my eyes kept drifting back to Ethan, hoping I might catch him looking at me. I admit I may have led myself to his line of sight. It worked too; I even made eye contact with him.

I can see desire in a guy's eyes. I can tell. Men are simple, manipulable creatures. I understand that makes me sound like a bitch, but I am not; it's just the truth of the situation. Beautiful women are a weakness to men.

Plainly put, I am a beautiful woman. More than most, I am a soft ten; sue me.

But Ethan...Ethan was hard to read. The time I made eye contact with him, clearly through my effort, not his; his eyes were warm, friendly, but they weren't burning with desire or passion like most I knew. Like I said, I know how attractive I am. But why didn't I feel that way when I looked at Ethan?

That really irritated me. I am used to being pursued. Ethan did not pursue me. Not sure he totally acknowledged me. The good news is that he wasn't really pursuing Harrington either. They were clearly there together, and it was clear he found her attractive, but it was equally clear that they weren't *together*, at least for the moment.

There was a moment on the dance floor when Samantha and Ethan were doing a bit of grinding. Not like strip club grinding or anything, but more intimate than anything they had thus far displayed.

I watched him closely, and for the briefest of moments, I saw a beast. Something primal appeared. It sent shivers up my spine. Then it was gone.

Who was this guy? How did I not know him? How did he end up going to a bar with Samantha Harrington on a random spring night in one of the most exclusive cities in the world? Wasn't she dating that Roger guy? What was his last name...Pendragon?

Well, whatever.

I am frustrated to say that I did not get a chance to dance with Ethan. Even though I waited. All night! For him to ask me. Besides Samantha, he danced several songs with an Instagram model whose name escapes me. She was short, stacked, and looked totally ridiculous hitting on Ethan.

She annoyed me, as she was mostly boobs and eye makeup. Ethan noticed her chest. THAT really annoyed me.

The night wore on. I drank more than I am used to drinking.

The trouble started with another group of girls. I wasn't even sure what we were fighting about—something stupid, something that didn't really matter. Words were exchanged, insults thrown, and before I knew it, things had escalated. The girl from the other group was in my face, yelling at me, and I was too drunk and too angry to back down. I don't even remember what I said, but I do remember her shoving me, hard enough that I stumbled back a few steps.

And I may or may not have slapped her.

Then, out of nowhere, her boyfriend stepped in. I didn't see it coming. One moment I was yelling back at the girl, the next moment, his hand was swinging toward me, and I barely had time to react. The slap landed hard across my face, the sting sharp and immediate. It knocked the breath out of me, and for a split second, I thought I was going to end up on the floor, curled up in a ball.

But before I could fall, before I could even fully register what had happened, Ethan was there. He moved so fast it was like a blur, and the next thing I knew, his big hand was around the guy's throat. The transformation was instant—gone was the sweet, laid-back man I had been watching all night, replaced by someone fierce, someone dangerous.

I saw rage in his eyes and strength in his arms. I would have been scared if it didn't turn me on so much.

Like. It was bad. I should probably keep that little fact to myself and talk to someone about it.

"You don't hit women," Ethan said, his voice low, but it carried a menace that sent shivers down my spine. Everyone here heard the controlled anger in his words, a promise that this guy was about to regret his actions. With a single, powerful shove, Ethan sent him stumbling back, and it was like watching a predator toying with its prey.

The guy barely had time to recover before he stupidly tried to swing at Ethan. I didn't even have a chance to feel scared; Ethan dodged the punch like it was nothing. He was calm, almost methodical in the way he moved. Then, with a quick, powerful jab, he sent the guy crashing to the ground. It happened so fast that it didn't seem real. It was over in seconds, but to me, everything felt like it was moving in slow motion, every detail burning itself into my memory.

The guy's friends, clearly shocked and out of their depth, hesitated. They looked at each other, trying to muster up the courage to rush Ethan together. For a moment, I thought they might back down, but they made the wrong choice. Ethan was ready. He took them down one by one, his movements precise and deadly efficient, like he'd done this a hundred times before. I watched, barely breathing, as he dismantled them with ease. He was relentless, each blow calculated, each move deliberate.

And just like that, it was over. The four guys were on the ground, groaning in pain, and Ethan stood over them, calm, but with the calm of a city after a raging storm. My friends and I stared at him with wide eyes, unable to fully grasp what had just happened. He wasn't just some random guy from the grocery store. He was... something else entirely.

Ethan turned back to Samantha, his expression softening, his eyes scanning her. "Are you okay?" he asked, his voice so gentle that it was almost jarring after what I'd just seen.

Samantha nodded and laughed. "Are YOU okay? You were the one in the fight."

He shrugged, wiping a bit of blood from his knuckles like it was a minor inconvenience. "I'm good. What he did was unacceptable. I made sure he understands that." There was an edge to his voice, a coldness that sent a chill through me.

Good lord. I think I might need to change my underwear.

My heart was pounding, both from the shock of what had just happened and from how incredibly intense he was. I stepped forward, my voice shaky but full of gratitude. I reached for Ethan's hand, needing to feel that he was real, that this wasn't some adrenaline-fueled hallucination. "Who the heck—who are you? Where did you even come— Thank you," I said, my eyes wide as I looked at him, trying to understand how someone could be so powerful and yet so calm, and of course, I was babbling. I could be embarrassed about that later. "Thank you so much."

Ethan gave me a nod, his voice calm and steady again, like he hadn't just single-handedly taken down four guys. "Just be careful, okay? Maybe avoid drunken fights in the future."

I nodded quickly, still looking a bit shell-shocked, the events of the night swirling in my mind. "Will you call me if I do?" I blurted out, half-joking but also desperately hoping he would.

He chuckled, letting out some of the intensity he'd been holding. "Just stay out of trouble, okay?"

I grinned, feeling a bit of the tension ease. "That wasn't a no."

Before I could say anything more, another guy approached Ethan. He was big, not quite as tall or broad as Ethan, but close. There was something about the way he walked, a confidence that made me uneasy. I, like an idiot, I might add, instinctively stepped in front of Ethan, but he moved me gently to the side, as if he knew this was about to go somewhere.

The new guy stopped a few feet away from Ethan, sizing him up with a curious expression. "Not bad, man. You really handled your business. You got some training."

Ethan shrugged, looking a little uncomfortable with the compliment. "Just didn't like the way they were acting. That's all."

The guy raised his hands, slipping into a boxer's stance. "Hopefully, you don't regret getting involved."

Ethan mirrored his stance, and they watched each other carefully. But then, something changed. The guy's eyes narrowed, and recognition sparked in them. "You look familiar... What's your name?"

Ethan opened his mouth to respond, but before he could say anything, the guy's eyes widened. He took a step back, his mouth dropping open. "No way. No freaking way. Caveman? Are you... you're Ethan, the Caveman, Miller."

He said it loudly enough that it caught the attention of everyone nearby. The name echoed through the crowd like a ripple in a pond. "Caveman! It's the Caveman!"

My confusion grew as the name spread through the crowd. People started buzzing, pointing at Ethan like he was some kind of celebrity. What the heck was going on? Why were they calling him that?

The big guy closed in on Ethan, a huge grin on his face, and offered a hand. "I'm Dan. I freaking love you, dude. I am sorry about my idiot friends."

Ethan seemed to deflate. The intensity. The rage. It all just disappeared with the gesture. Ethan took Dan's hand. "Nice to meet you, Dan. Tell your friends not to hit girls."

Dan nodded. "I will kick his ass later."

I just stood there, watching as people gathered and started shaking Ethan's hand, taking pictures with him, acting like he was some kind of hero. My head was spinning, trying to piece together what I'd just seen and heard. Who was this man, really? And why did they call him the Caveman?

As I stood amidst the crowd, still processing the whirlwind of events, I saw two familiar figures standing amongst the sea of people. My bodyguards, two imposing Japanese men who watched Ethan and then me. After a few more moments of watching, they walked towards me.

Boy...did they looked pissed. They had the right to be. I ditched them on purpose earlier that night.

Daisuke and Hiroshi had been with my family for years, their loyalty unwavering, and while they didn't advertise it, everyone who worked closely with my family knew that these men were more than just body-guards—they were elite operators, trained in ways that most people only read about in martial arts novels.

When they reached me, Daisuke, the elder of the two with graying hair at his temples, gave me a once-over, his eyes sharp and assessing. "Miss Hana, we have dishonored you. We should not have allowed you to go unattended. Are you alright?" His tone was calm, but there was an underlying tension that suggested he wasn't pleased with the situation.

I rolled my eyes. "I'm fine, Daisuke. And you cannot dishonor your-self for leaving me when I ditched you though I noticed you didn't intervene when I was struck."

Daisuke ignored my questions.

Hiroshi, younger and more aggressive, scanned the area, his gaze lingering on Ethan, who was still surrounded by people. "Our training is lacking if the young Miss can so thoroughly elude us. We will train harder."

I sighed. They should be mad at me, and they were, but of course, they would never say that. I am such a bitch sometimes.

Hiroshi continued. "The young man who intervened—he was very skilled." I gave him a strange look. Hiroshi was quiet. It was rare for him to offer an opinion unprompted, which only underscored how impressed he was.

Daisuke nodded in agreement, his eyes narrowing slightly as he observed Ethan's calm demeanor. "Indeed. It's not often we see such... efficiency in a street fight. He was precise, controlled. A dangerous man, if he wanted to be."

I looked between them, feeling a strange mix of pride and curiosity. Ethan wasn't just some random guy who happened to be in the right place at the right time—he was something more. I felt drawn to him, not just because he'd saved me but because of the way he handled everything with such calm authority.

"Let's get you home, Miss Hana," Daisuke said, gently steering me away from the crowd. "Your father will want to know you're safe."

I told my friends I was leaving, not that they really needed to be told. They knew how things worked with bodyguards. I wished I had a chance to say goodbye to Ethan.

As we walked back to the car, I felt the weight of the night's events settling in. The adrenaline was wearing off, leaving me tired and a little shaken. But there was also something else—an excitement, a curiosity that I couldn't shake.

Once we were in the car and on our way back to the estate, I leaned back in my seat, my mind racing. "Daisuke, Hiroshi," I began, glancing at them in the rearview mirror. "From what you saw from Ethan, can you tell me anything about him?"

It was a dumb question, but I felt inclined to ask it.

Daisuke didn't hesitate. "He has either a police or military experience. He's highly skilled. And not just in fighting, but in maintaining control under pressure. That's not something you see every day. Whoever trained him knew what they were doing; he has a background in classical martial arts."

I paused. "What makes you say that?"

Daisuke looked contemplative as he answered. "The footwork and palm strikes looked like techniques from Bajiquan and Wing Chun, but that is not all; I saw several other styles mixed in. Both traditional and contemporary. The knife strike on his last opponent was straight from the US Marines Combat handbook. This man... he is interesting."

Hiroshi added, "He's someone who could be a valuable ally... or a formidable opponent."

I nodded, mulling over their words. I felt it too. When we arrived at the estate, I hurried up to my room, my mind buzzing with thoughts. I quickly changed into something more comfortable and settled in front of my laptop. My buzz was starting to waver. I couldn't shake the feeling that there was more to this story, that Ethan was someone worth knowing.

Honestly, I don't know anything about the guy. Earlier that day, I saw a tall, handsome man in the supermarket walking with Victoria Harrington, and I thought, wow, he's hot. But not like in my type sort of way. He's rugged. Almost down to earth while I tend to date—well, let's just say my last boyfriend was a K-pop star.

Then I watched him a bit as my girlfriends grabbed a salad at the deli.

I don't even know how to describe it. I liked watching him. He stepped gracefully for someone so large. His movements were smooth and deliberate. His interactions with Lady Harrington were also, I don't know, comfortable? It was hard to describe. I decided, hey, let's go talk to him.

So I did and was instantly hit with a curveball. He didn't get tongue-tied or stumble over his words. He looked me in the eye instead of at my chest. His voice was deep but soft. The fact that he didn't have social media, is that a red flag or a good thing?

Naturally, I was curious about his interaction with Lady Harrington, who is famous for being rich, gorgeous, and powerful. (I think my father even has a crush on her.) Even I had to admit, at forty-something, Lady Harrington looks amazing and could easily pass as a woman ten years younger. Her conglomerate has dealings with Japan; I think it has something to do with beef, which is how I know her, though I have never met her directly. Anyway, I found Victoria on social media, which led me to Samantha Harrington's page, where I saw Ethan in a whole bunch of pictures with Samantha, a couple of younger girls who were clearly his daughters, and Lady Harrington. Samantha posted a picture in her outfit for that night with a caption; it was clear they were going out, and that is how I ended up at the Rusty Spur.

I got more than I was looking for tonight, that is for sure. However, I didn't do more than an idle search earlier. It was time to change that.

I opened my browser and started typing: "Ethan Caveman MMA." The search results were immediate and plentiful. Dozens of articles on blogs, fight syndication magazines, forum threads, and even some YouTube videos popped up, all discussing Ethan Miller's past as a former Marine, a freaking war hero, turned fighter. He was known as "The Caveman"—a fierce competitor with a reputation for taking down opponents with ruthless efficiency, and apparently, the guy could take a hit like a champ.

As I read through the articles and watched the videos, I couldn't help it; my intrigue level skyrocketed.

Ethan was impressive. Not just for his skill but for his lack of hesitation. The way he'd stepped in tonight, the way he'd protected me without a second thought—it was as if he had this innate sense of duty, of honor. I am Japanese. Honor. Skill. Duty. Dedication. These traits are drilled into us culturally. But to my surprise, I knew very few people who exhibited them. I have seen men who possess them; some work for my father, but rarely in anyone else.

Then I noticed something else—people online were starting to buzz about the incident at The Rusty Spur. There were a few scattered posts with video of me and Ethan. Wow, the entire incident from different angles. Me. Ethan. My fight with the other girls. Getting slapped. Samantha Harrington. Everything...

I do not come across well in those videos. Even in my stupored mind, I can tell that. My father was not going to be pleased.

Still, Ethan's moves were even more impressive. This was going to blow up. A beautiful girl who happens to be a foreign national. Samantha Harrington, the US's national sex symbol. A man who looked like a bear manhandling four other guys in the defense of another. Yes. It had all the makings of a viral story.

I needed to get ahead of this; control the narrative or someone else would.

Without hesitating, I opened my social media accounts and started recording. I recounted the events of the night, from my perspective, and gave a play-by-play from the moment I spotted Ethan at the grocery store to the way he'd stepped in to protect me.

"I've never been more grateful for someone's bravery. Tonight, I met a true Samurai—someone who embodies the honor and strength of a warrior. Thank you, Ethan Miller, for being there when I needed you most. #Samurai #Hero #TheCaveman"

Was it over the top? Yes. Yes, it was. Do I mean it? Yes. Yes, I did. I hesitated for a moment before hitting the "post" button, but only for a moment. I sent it out into the world.

The response to my video was immediate and overwhelming. The view counter started ticking slowly at first and then faster and faster. Messages flooded my inbox, comments stacked, and within a few hours, the story spread like wildfire across social media. People were captivated by the tale of a "Caveman" coming to the rescue of a young woman in distress.

He quickly became the Samurai; my father was going to hate that.

As the notifications rolled in, a deep sense of curiosity flared within me. Maybe it was the adrenaline still coursing through my veins from the events of the night, or maybe it was something else entirely. But one thing was clear—I wanted to know more about Ethan Miller. I continued to look through social media, looking desperately for additional information. I stayed up way too late doing so.

The next day, the mainstream news had caught wind of the story. Reporters were calling, wanting to interview me about the incident at The Rusty Spur. My father was less than pleased with the attention, but even he couldn't deny the impact of Ethan's actions.

Things were getting interesting.

Chapter Five

Victoria

I was lost in thought as Ethan moved around the kitchen, effortlessly preparing breakfast. The man was a marvel to watch. Everything about him, from the way his muscles rippled under his skin to the quiet confidence in his movements, made it hard to focus on anything else. But now that he had put his shirt back on and I couldn't see his biceps, I could at least attempt to think clearly.

Damn kid, I thought, biting back a smile. He had no idea the effect he had on me—or maybe he did, and that was the problem.

I was also tired; I had received the investigation report from Louis last night. It was really comprehensive: Ethan's life, his background, his family, his business, and personal and legal troubles. It was all there. I read late into the night. The girls fell asleep on my bed.

He was absolutely intriguing.

Everything I had seen, read, and witnessed over the past few days made me want to do something reckless, something completely out of character. I imagined taking Ethan by the hand, leading him upstairs, and ripping his clothes off. I could still rock a bikini or lingerie. I'd show him that experience could more than make up for youth. I'd help him see the reason why men had pursued me most of my life and why my husband had not strayed while he was still alive.

Long story short, I am *really* good in bed.

And then, once I had him thoroughly enthralled, I'd whisk him and his amazing daughters off to some secluded island where we could live out our days in blissful isolation. We'd make love constantly, with no one to interrupt or judge us. Hell, I'd even bring Samantha along, I doubted I could handle Ethan on my own. If half of what I read was true, the man was a force of nature, and even with all my experience, I wasn't sure I could keep up with him by myself.

And maybe he wanted more kids. He was still young. I couldn't bear them, but Samantha could for sure. We would have to work that out—

I stopped mid-thought as reality slapped me across the face. My cheeks flushed with embarrassment. I buried my head in my hands.

Victoria Elizabeth Harrington, you scandalous woman! How can you be so crude? I scolded myself internally. I was a lady, after all—a widow with a title and a reputation to uphold. And yet, here I was, fantasizing about a man almost half my age, as if I were some lovesick schoolgirl. Not only that, I was thinking about sharing him with my niece! What the bloody hell was wrong with me?

I shook my head, trying to banish the inappropriate thoughts. But they lingered, stubbornly refusing to leave my mind. It was all too much —the way he looked at me, the way he took care of his daughters, the way he moved with such power and grace.

Okay, fine. I admit it. I have a crush on the boy. Bloody unreal.

But what I couldn't figure out was how to reconcile that desire with the part of me that was still grieving, still tied to the memory of my late husband. It was a conflict I hadn't anticipated, and one I wasn't sure how to navigate. Not to mention it was ridiculous. I barely knew this man. We were from different walks of life. He was an American blue-collar worker. I was an English aristocrat. I was older than him.

What on earth was I thinking?

Oh, if the tabloids could be in my head right now, they would have a field day.

The thoughts made me contemplate. I was not an overly emotional person. I had been trained by some of the best finishing schools in the world. Focused. Controlled. Understand your situation or the problem. Come up with a solution. As the wife of Lord Harrington, I played my role. But our lives had been more than our position. I *loved* my husband. I loved Henry *desperately*. We had such a strong connection despite the way our relationship came together and him being slightly older than me. His death had been very unexpected, and now that he was gone, I admitted I was, and in some ways, still am—lost.

Feelings for someone new had never even crossed my mind.

Did I dare start something with someone that was more than ten years my junior?

Did that sound crazy? It sounded crazy right?

OF COURSE IT WAS CRAZY; IT WAS BLOODY LUNANCY!

I tried to avoid putting my head in my hands. Don't show outward emotion. Do not be impulsive.

For now, all I could do was try to keep my wits about me and find a way to get through breakfast without letting Ethan see just how thoroughly he had unraveled my composure.

Ethan set the plates on the table while I did my best to put on a facade of normalcy. I plastered on a smile and engaged in light conversation with him, all the while fighting the urge to reach out and touch him, to see if he felt as strong as he looked.

As Ethan adjusted the plates of fluffy pancakes and sizzling bacon, I kept my eyes averted, tracing the delicate floral pattern of the China plates rather than the man standing across from me. I felt his gaze, probing, and it took all my willpower not to look up and meet it.

"Breakfast looks amazing," I said, forcing myself to break the charged silence. I looked at him, unable to suppress my upbringing; you look people in the eyes when talking to them, despite my embarrassment.

Ethan's lips curved into a small, enigmatic smile. "Dig in before it gets cold."

Ethan brought his hands to his mouth and cupped them. He yelled for the girls to get their cute butts to the table before he ate all the pancakes.

The girls bounded into the kitchen, looking lively. It was like a breath of fresh air, blowing away the tension that had settled between me and Ethan. The girls chatted animatedly about anything and every-thing. I was having a hard time keeping up with the topic—something about friends from home, Korea, boys, and dancing maybe?

Samantha came in just behind them, looking effortlessly stunning. She gave me and Ethan a grin and sat.

I watched them with a fond smile, grateful for their presence. They were a reminder of what truly mattered: family, connection, love. I listened to their innocent chatter and felt a sense of peace settle over me.

It made me miss Henry. It made me miss my sons.

Everyone dug into the food and thoroughly enjoyed it. Geez, I was going to need to start hitting the gym if Ethan kept feeding me like this. Maybe he liked fat girls?

After breakfast, as the clatter of dishes and the hum of conversation faded into the background, Samantha caught my eye and nodded toward the hallway. It was clear she wanted to talk in private, so I followed her out of the kitchen. We ended up in the sitting room, where the sunlight streamed in softly through the windows, casting a warm, comforting glow over the room.

Samantha turned to me, her expression serious but tinted with a hint of worry. "Alright, My Lady. You have the goods. Spill it. What do you know about Ethan?"

I leaned against the arm of a nearby chair. "Is it too early to have a drink?"

Samantha belly laughed. "It's too early for me, but you go right ahead."

I joined in. "Okay, but before I share, why don't you tell me what happened last night?"

Samantha's expression turned thoughtful. She took a deep breath, hesitating for a moment as if choosing her words carefully. "Last night, everything at the Rusty Spur—it was all over social media this morning. The fight, the dancing... Ethan handled it all so well. Still, there is a wall. He is not an easy person to get close to. Oh, and he kissed me last night. Then thanked me for being his friend."

I froze. She got to kiss him twice already? I hadn't received one yet. How was that fair? I gritted my teeth, then took a deep breath.

When did I become such a jealous bitch?

I put on my quasi-mom hat. I nodded. "So let me guess. You're irritated by the 'friend' comment and confused if Ethan even likes you. You're also worried about the attention he's getting now."

"Uh. Well. Yeah. Pretty much," she replied, her voice quiet but intense. "First, I feel rejected, which is a first for me. But it's more than that, Aunt Victoria. I mean, the way he's so guarded. I'd like to think I am pretty damn enticing. At least most of the time. But he was respectful and didn't get handsy at all. I practically invited him to touch me, but he didn't. Well, not very much or in the way I wanted him to. I know I should be happy about that; he is respectful, and kind, and handsome... ugh, so annoying. We had a crazy night. He rescues ANOTHER girl, is the perfect gentleman, and gives me an amazing kiss, one of the best I've ever had, and then thanks me for being a friend. So, what the actual hell?"

Samantha's southern roots flared at that point. When she started modeling in the big time, she had worked hard to get rid of her southern accent as well as taking my last name. But it came out when she was frustrated or really excited.

I giggled at that. She was probably a bit of both.

Samantha's face flushed with that last comment.

I could see the worry and the hint of frustration in her eyes. Samantha was used to being in control in relationships. She had always been pretty from a young age. People fawned over her from the time she was born. It got worse when she was fourteen, shot up eight inches in a year, and... developed. After that, men literally threw themselves at her feet. Ethan, for whatever reason, simply wasn't like that. She didn't know how to handle it.

Part of me was really amused, I had to admit.

"Samantha," I began, choosing my words carefully, "Ethan doesn't understand what is happening."

Samantha's response came out rushed and irritated. "What does that mean he doesn't know what is happening? What do I have to do, strip down naked and wear a sign that says, 'Hi, dumbass, take me to bed and screw my brains out?'"

Samantha snapped her hand over her mouth. She flushed a deep shade of red in embarrassment. I tried not to laugh. Samantha slowly lowered her hand. "Not that I want to do that. I am a lady, after all. Just reminding you."

I couldn't help it. I laughed hard. "Sammy, my dear, Ethan hasn't been on a first date since he was fifteen and hasn't had a woman in probably the last five years since he got back from his deployment."

Samantha's jaw dropped. "So Ethan has only been with one person? Ever? Wait? Deployment? What deployment?"

I nodded. "If Louis' preliminary report is to be believed, Ethan got Sarah pregnant when he was sixteen and Sarah was eighteen. It was their first time together. He had to grow up quickly. They got married, and he started working immediately. Joined the Marines and got some pretty serious training. He saw a lot of action and was injured. The details are classified, but apparently, it was bad. He got some medals, but I don't know what happened. Sarah started cheating almost immediately when he was overseas. He tried to make it work. She didn't. When Sarah left, he was devastated. I don't think he has ever recovered emotionally, which isn't saying much because he was stunted to begin with. He spends all his time on Maya, Lily, and trying to recover financially, which is a whole other story. He had some sort of run-in with the law because of his brother. We are still getting details on that."

The intensity in Samantha's eyes almost made me take a step back. "So his ex-wife cheated on him while he was hurt and left him?"

Before I could answer, my phone buzzed in my pocket. I pulled it out and glanced at the screen, and my heart sank a little when I saw the notification. It was an update on the investigation on Sarah, Ethan's ex-wife. I ran through the information.

Samantha noticed the change in my expression and stepped closer. "What is it, Victoria?"

I sighed, meeting her concerned gaze. "Sarah cheating most likely started before he left on deployment. This woman is a piece of work. From what it says here I am not sure she has ever been faithful."

Samantha's eye narrowed dangerously.

I put my phone down. "She still treats Ethan like rubbish and isn't much better with the girls. You know she had the gall to get upset with the girls over spending time with us. She sent them a bunch of ridiculous texts over the last twenty-four hours."

Samantha's brow furrowed. "What did she say?"

I shook my head, trying not to get angry. "She's not happy that the girls are here in Silver Ridge. From what I've gathered, she's particularly upset that they're spending time with you and me. I think she feels threatened, and it doesn't help that she's probably seen the pictures from last night."

Samantha looked taken aback. "Threatened? By us? Why? How does that make sense? She left him, right?"

"Because," I replied softly, "Sarah is a deeply insecure and greedy woman. She's always been concerned with appearances, and the fact that Ethan is spending time with women who are—how do I put this— more successful, more independent, and more beautiful than she is, makes it look like he was the better one."

Samantha absorbed my words, a mixture of emotions playing across her face. "So, she's jealous. Not just of us, but at the prospect of Ethan moving on and finding something better than her."

"Exactly," I said. "Even worse, thus far she has not had to worry. Ethan does not pursue women. He has had zero relationships since his ex-wife left him. As far as I can tell, he has been on a handful of dates. He has a childhood friend he goes out with on occasion; her name is Emily. But no real dating. He gets approached a lot, but the kid truly does not recognize that women are attracted to him. It's like he has a block. What happened between him and Sarah left him so wary of letting anyone else get close to him that he literally cannot, and the fact of the matter is that he is intimidating enough that people simply don't push him."

Samantha nodded, though I could see the weight of everything she'd just learned settling on her. "This is more serious than I thought. Even if I wanted to date Ethan, he is so down in the dumps that he probably couldn't handle it. Even if I could convince him that I liked him."

I grinned at this statement.

"Which I'm not saying I do," Samantha said, flushing.

I smiled. "Then I will take him. I bet his hands are magical."

Samantha snorted. Then she looked at me more intensely.

I chuckled. Actually, we both did.

Samantha's expression grew serious. "So now what?"

I shrugged. "I am working on it. I have arranged to have a friend of mine come here to meet him. He needs therapy. They all do, actually. I know that he has mentioned rage issues at the very least. We need to convince them to stay here for the rest of their vacation and then follow up after they leave. He needs friends. He needs dates. He needs to take a woman or two to bed. We are going to help Ethan get his mojo back. You know, smooth out those edges. He will need a lot of work. We can talk about that later."

I gave Samantha another wicked grin. "And then I am going to take him to bed and screw his brains out."

"Aunt Victoria!" she gasped. "I cannot believe you used the word 'screw.'"

I was now fully cackling.

There was a sudden knock on the door that pulled me out of the moment. I glanced toward the entrance, curious, as I hadn't been expecting anyone for at least several hours.

I moved to answer the door, smoothing down my blouse, still laughing as I went.

I looked back and saw Samantha giving me a chipmunk face. It was one that she had done since she was little. It meant she was a combination of flushed, frustrated, and mad. It was adorable. She was processing what I had said and wondering if I was serious. I *wasn't* serious about what I said.

Well, not totally serious.

Alright, maybe I was a bit serious.

"One last thing," I said to Samantha.

She looked but didn't say anything.

"I am taking Ethan to the Manson Ball as my escort."

I opened the door to find Louis standing there, beaming at me with his trademark shit-eating grin. Dressed impeccably in a tailored charcoal suit that hugged his lean, athletic frame, Louis looked every bit the picture of European sophistication. His dark brown hair was slicked back with just a touch of wave, adding an effortless polish to his look, and his hazel eyes sparkled with mischief behind a pair of thin, stylish frames. The neatly groomed goatee added an extra touch of charm, framing his warm smile. His presence was like a burst of sunshine on a cloudy day, and I couldn't help but return his smile.

"Darling!" Louis exclaimed, throwing his arms wide in a dramatic gesture before pulling me into a tight hug. "It's been far too long! Look at you, still as radiant as ever!"

"Louis, I saw you last week. But thank you for coming anyway. I know how you hate the woods," I laughed, returning the hug with equal enthusiasm.

Behind Louis, a small army of stylists, makeup artists, and assistants were already streaming into the house, carrying garment bags, makeup kits, and all manner of luxurious accessories. My eyes widened slightly as I took in the scene.

"I brought the cavalry," Louis said with a wink, releasing me from the hug and stepping inside, his eyes immediately scanning the room. "Where is my project for the day and his lovely daughters?"

As if on cue, Maya and Lily peeked around the corner, clearly intrigued. Lily said in a low voice, "Aunt Victoria..."

I beckoned to them. They came to me and looked at Louis expectantly.

Louis, not missing a beat, instantly dropped to a crouch, opening his arms wide.

"Well, well, well, who do we have here?" Louis said, his voice brimming with excitement. "Two little ladies who are every bit as gorgeous as their Aunt Victoria described them! Come here and give Uncle Louis a hug!"

He gave them a huge grin.

Lily hesitated before she threw caution to the wind. She ran toward Louis and gave him a big hug. Maya, a bit older and a bit more reserved, eyed Louis.

Louis gave her a grin. "Come now, Ms. Maya. We are going to be like family. Might as well just get there now."

I gave her a bit of a push, and Maya followed her sister.

Louis gave a big hug and then stepped back.

"You're confused, I know it! But it's okay. I am pretty much the best friend you've never known you always wanted. Though seriously, look at you two! So beautiful and full of life! I've heard so much about you from Lady Victoria," he said, his eyes sparkling with genuine warmth. "And I'm here to make sure you have the most fabulous day ever!"

Maya and Lily grinned up at him, clearly taken with his exuberant personality.

"This is Louis," I explained, smiling as I watched the interaction. "He's my personal assistant, a dear friend of mine and Samantha's, and he's here to help me and your father get ready for the Manson Ball."

The girls were not surprised. I told them about the Ball last night, though I didn't go into a ton of details.

"And to spoil you rotten, of course," Louis added with a wink. "I've planned a full day of pampering just for you girls. We're talking massages, facials, manicures—the works!"

Maya and Lily's eyes widened in excitement as they looked at each other, then back at Louis.

"Really?" Lily asked, her voice filled with wonder. "What's a facial?"

Louis looked aghast. "Oh, you poor child."

He gave her another hug. He held her at arm's length with a serious expression.

"Facials are a magical experience that makes you even more beautiful than you are now," Louis said, standing up and giving them a conspiratorial wink. "It's how your Aunt and Samantha stay looking so AMAZING. You are going to love it. Silver Ridge has world-class amenities."

Maya snorted, and Lily just looked between the adults.

Louis stood. "And while you are being pampered, I shall work my magic and *Bibbidi-Bobbidi-Boo* the crap out of your father. He shall become something truly magnifique."

This made the girls laugh. Lily added, "You have to be careful,

Louis; daddy is a dork. Are you saying you're going to try to undork him?"

Louis' eyes sparkled with mischief. "Absolutely, my dear child. I am going to undork your father to make him the Belle of the ball!"

The girls thought that was really funny.

Louis clapped his hands together. "But first, I need to meet the hunk of a man. We need to make sure your dad looks as dashing as the photos suggest."

Ethan, who had been standing quietly just past the action, watching the whole scene unfold, raised an eyebrow in amusement. "Me?"

"Yes, you!" Louis said, turning his attention to Ethan, sizing him up with a critical eye. "You, sir, are escorting Lady Harrington, one of the most influential and desired aristocrats of the English court, to the Manson Ball, which is a world-class event. We need to make you measure up to the task. Lucky for you, you have me. I am basically a better-dressed Harry Potter. I am going to magic the crap out of you."

Ethan snorted. "That sounded dirty."

Louis grinned. "Ethan, despite being straight, I have the feeling you and I are going to get along swimmingly."

Ethan looked between Louis, me, and Samantha. He seemed a bit overwhelmed by all the attention, but there was a glimmer of humor in his eyes that made me smile.

"I don't know, Louis," Ethan said. He turned to me, his expression both uncertain and amused. "Vikki, are you sure this is a good idea? I don't know much about your world. I would hate to put you in some sort of tough spot."

Vikki. He just called me Vikki. No one calls me Vikki. Not since Henry. Not even my parents called me Vikki. Oh dear lord, I wanted to kiss his stupid face right here, right now. But Louis saved me the trouble of responding.

"Nonsense!" Louis replied, waving off Ethan's concern with a dramatic flourish. "Lady Harrington chose you. It's an honor, and it will be unlike any experience you've ever had. Plus, you're going to look fantastic. Trust me."

Samantha, clearly enjoying the whole situation, stepped forward to give Louis a quick hug. "Hi, Uncle Louis. I've missed you."

"Dotti!" Louis said, giving Samantha a double kiss to either side of her face. "You look as ravishing as ever."

Samantha turned to Ethan. "You're in for a treat, Ethan. Louis has a way of making everyone feel like royalty."

Louis beamed at the compliment before turning back to the group. "Alright, everyone! We've got a big day ahead. The ladies will be heading to the spa in town for a day of pampering and preparing in the case of Lady Harrington, and I'll be taking Ethan for some serious shopping and man-sculpting. Then lessons on etiquette and dining. We need to make sure he is at his absolute best."

The girls were practically shaking with excitement, and Samantha's smile widened. "That sounds perfect, Louis. We'll meet you boys back at the house later?"

Louis nodded enthusiastically. "Absolutely. By the time we're done, Ethan will be ready to take on the world—or at least the Manson Ball."

Maya and Lily held hands as they followed Louis's assistants, who were already preparing to leave. I watched them go, feeling a warm sense of contentment. Their excitement was palpable, and I was grateful to Louis for arranging this special day.

"Alright, ladies," Louis said, clapping his hands together with enthusiasm. "Time to get ready for our day of indulgence. The spa awaits, and trust me, you're all in for a treat."

We all headed out the door together, a flurry of anticipation filling the air. As Louis guided Ethan towards the car, I caught a glimpse of the way Ethan looked back at us. His expression was exasperated but amused. Oh, I wish I could go with them.

The rest of us made our way to the cars, ready to embrace what promised to be a day of luxury and fun.

Chapter Six

Maya

We are going to the spa. I was going to the spa with Lily, Samantha, and Aunt Victoria.

It felt like going out with my mother. But that was odd because I had never felt this way with my actual mother. Is this what it's like to have a mother who actually cares about you?

That idea didn't seem right. Everything is happening so fast. Just a few days ago, we were heading to the woods to go camping and now, I am heading to a world class spa.

I love camping. I love my dad. But as I get older, it makes me wonder if I love camping or my dad. Though I do love fishing that I do know.

Lily doesn't like it as much. She thinks fish are gross. But she loves sushi. I dare you to figure that one out. I love camping and sushi and Lily and my dad. Things weren't perfect; in fact they were hard but now...

Now, within 72 hours, a whole bunch of stuff had changed.

It felt different.

Currently, Lily and I are going to a world-class spa with two beautiful women who I am pretty sure both like my dad. Even though he is a dork and will never make a move.

I have a phone, a really nice one; so does Lily. Phones that actually connect to the internet and allow us to access more than just emergency text messaging with Mom and Dad. I see my dad smiling a lot. He smiles around us. I think we are some of the only things that make him smile. But now, he smiles around Aunt Victoria. He smiles around Samantha. He blushed several times because of them. He laughed. He got flushed. He had warmth in his eyes when he looked at someone who wasn't Lily or me.

It was all so different.

And Samantha kissed my father. She kissed him into literal acceptance. My father doesn't accept help. He doesn't want charity, he calls it. When Samantha brought up buying jewelry for me and Lily, I knew that it would never fly. My father would not allow it. But then Samantha kissed him. He became tongue-tied. Dazed. And the way he looked at Samantha—seriously, it was the cutest thing I have ever seen.

Three days. That's all it really took for things to change—three days.

I glanced out the car window, watching the trees blur past, and felt my phone buzz in my pocket. It was probably more Instagram notifications. Ever since last night, my feed has been blowing up. Dad might not be big on social media, but I'd been keeping tabs on what people were saying. There were so many pictures and videos from the Rusty Spur—Dad dancing with Samantha, that fight, and of course, a bunch of stuff about Lady Victoria as people connected the dots across the Internet. It was surreal.

I unlocked my phone and scrolled through the latest posts. The most curious development was the post by the girl that Dad saved—Hana Yamamoto. She had posted something new. She'd tagged him as "The Samurai," which was apparently a new nickname people were giving him. I continued to scroll through Hana's account. Her video message to Dad was really, really sweet. If there's anything that life has taught me, it's that you can't always believe what you see on the Internet; maybe she was sincere, maybe she wasn't. Apparently, she was going to have a spa day too.

Is that a rich people thing?

Still, Hana's message was beautiful. It made me smile. I mean, Dad had always been strong and protective, but seeing him get recognized for it was something else.

But then, my smile faded as I noticed a text from Mom sitting in my inbox. I hesitated, not sure if I wanted to open it. I struggled to understand my mother, and it's been getting worse as I've gotten older. I know she loves us—at least, I think she loves us—but she had a way of making everything about herself. And James... ugh, don't even get me started on James. He was the worst. A total creep, and honestly, kind of an idiot.

I am not sure that Mom even likes him. Still trying to process that thought.

With a sigh, I opened the text. It was short, but the tone was unmistakable.

> Mom: "Why aren't you responding? Why are you spending time with those people? I thought you were supposed to be camping, not playing dress-up with that Harrington woman and her model niece. And what about your father? He shouldn't be around women like that. It's not appropriate, Maya. Have your father call me. He is ignoring my texts."

I felt my stomach twist and anger flare. Not appropriate? Not APPROPRIATE. Dad simply hangs out with other women, and you freak out because of it. While you cheat on him and then marry someone else. Okay, Mom, please, make it make sense.

Honestly, it makes me sick. People like to pretend that I am too young to understand. But I know, I know what my mom did to my dad.

And she still had the audacity to send a text like that. It wasn't appropriate indeed. She just didn't get it. I love my mom, I really do, but she is about as clueless as—well, I don't know; I am not feeling particularly clever right now. She is just freaking clueless.

I turned my phone off and slipped it back into my pocket, trying to push her words out of my mind. The last thing I wanted to do was ruin today by thinking about Mom and James. Besides, this trip was about spending time with Dad and Aunt Victoria, and of course, Samantha. I didn't want anything to mess that up.

As we pulled up to the spa, I felt a little better just seeing the aesthetic. The place looked amazing, all sleek lines and warm wood accents, with big windows that let in tons of natural light. I glanced over at Lily, who was sitting next to me in the car. She was staring out the window, a little smile playing on her lips. I could tell she was just as excited as I was. We'd never done anything like this before—Dad wasn't exactly the spa type, and Mom... well, she wasn't really into pampering us unless there was something in it for her.

"I can't believe we're doing this," Lily whispered, her voice filled with wonder.

"Me either," I whispered back, grinning at her. "It's gonna be awesome."

We got out of the car, and Aunt Victoria and Samantha were already heading inside, talking on the phone with Louis, who was on speakerphone.

His accent was funny.

Louis went on and on about last-minute details concerning the ball that Dad was taking Aunt Victoria to. Something about color and shoes, maybe? He was also fussing about making sure we had everything we needed. I have known Louis for about an hour and could tell I was going to like him. He was funny, talkative, and sweet. He clearly loved Aunt Victoria and Samantha. What kind of love? It was hard to describe.

Brother? Friend? Fairy Godmother? Yes, we are going with Fairy Godmother.

We walked into the spa, and the smell of lavender and eucalyptus hit me. I inhaled deeply. Yeah, this was going to be the best day ever.

But even as I tried to focus on the excitement of the day ahead, I couldn't shake the lingering thoughts about Mom and the way she treated Dad. She didn't appreciate him—she never had. And now, seeing how happy he was just being around Aunt Victoria and Samantha, I wondered what it would be like if things were different. If we didn't have to go back to James and his stupid rules, and if Dad could explore something with Victoria or Samantha and just be... happy.

Clearly, not a problem I am going to solve.

The spa was called *Elysian Retreat*, and wonderful aromas were just the beginning. It's hard to describe the place. It wasn't just fancy—it was like stepping into another world. Everything was pristine, from the marble floors that gleamed underfoot to the soft, ambient lighting that made the entire place feel like a peaceful sanctuary. Even the music was amazing—a soft flowering piano.

As soon as we entered, a tall, elegant woman with perfectly coiffed hair and a tailored suit approached us. She had a warm, professional smile that made me feel welcome, but also a little bit in awe.

"Good morning, Lady Harrington," the woman said, inclining her head slightly in a respectful nod. "And Miss Harrington, it's a pleasure to have you with us today. I'm Ellen Laurent, the director of *Elysian Retreat*. We're honored to have you as our guests."

Aunt Victoria returned the smile, her voice as smooth and polished as always. "Thank you, Ellen. We're looking forward to our time here. I've heard wonderful things about your facilities."

Ellen beamed at the compliment, clearly pleased. "We pride ourselves on offering the best service possible. Let me give you a brief tour before we get started."

Ellen led us through the spa. It was a little overwhelming. Everything was so luxurious—there were plush lounge areas with floor-to-ceiling windows overlooking lush gardens, serene treatment rooms with softly glowing candles, and even a private outdoor terrace with an infinity hot tub.

I didn't even know that infinity hot tubs were a thing.

I glanced over at Lily, and I could tell she was just as amazed as I was. This wasn't just a spa; it was like a dream.

Ellen explained all the different services we'd be receiving, and I could hardly believe it. We were getting the full treatment schedule: massages, facials, manicures, pedicures, and even a session in the hydrotherapy pool. It was more than I'd ever imagined, and I felt a mix of excitement and nervousness. I wasn't used to being pampered like this, but it sounded incredible.

After the tour, we were led to a changing room where we were given plush robes and slippers.

The robes and slippers were name brand. I don't even want to know how much they cost.

Once we were ready, we were taken to the treatment rooms. The massage was heavenly—every knot and bit of tension in my body melted away under the therapist's expert hands. The facial left my skin feeling soft and tingling, and by the time we got to the manicures and pedicures, I was completely relaxed.

But the best part came after all the treatments were done. Ellen guided us to the indoor pool area, which was absolutely stunning. The pool was surrounded by tall, white pillars and lush greenery, with sunlight streaming in through large skylights overhead. The water was a shimmering blue, and there were comfortable lounge chairs arranged around the edge.

"This is amazing," Lily whispered as we walked to the pool. I nodded in agreement, feeling a sense of wonder at how perfect everything seemed.

We slipped into the pool, the warm water enveloping us like a gentle embrace. I leaned back against the edge, closing my eyes for a moment, letting the peacefulness of the place wash over me. It was strange being here. A part of me felt like I didn't belong, like I was just playing dress-up in someone else's life. But another part of me—the part that had been craving some kind of escape—was soaking it all in, wanting to hold onto this feeling.

This was not my life. I know it. The Universe knows it. It would all come crashing down, and reality would kick back in. But not today. Not right now.

I let out a breath.

We floated around the pool. But distractions came as I noticed others around us and their conversations. They weren't loud, but in a place like this, whispers seemed to carry. I heard snippets of gossip. I learned a lot just sitting there, even half-listening. They mentioned Aunt Victoria's late husband, Henry, and how society expected her to take on another husband.

I found that odd. They just expected her to have a new husband? How did that work?

There were murmurs about Samantha too—talks of boyfriends, charity, a wild streak, and an ex-husband. The husband talk was a bit weird. Most talked about her beauty and something about being blessed and how unfair it was.

It was amazing how many people were talking about them, especially because they were both in the building. That could have been the reason. I know that Samantha is super famous, but was she so famous that it was surprising when she went somewhere? I didn't take note of anything while we were walking through Silver Ridge.

Or maybe I simply didn't notice.

I glanced over at Aunt Victoria and Samantha, who were chatting quietly at the other end of the pool. They seemed so at ease, so comfortable in this world. It was clear they belonged here, that they were used to this kind of attention. But for me, it was all new, and I wasn't sure how to feel about it.

Lily swam over to me, grinning. "Isn't this the coolest place ever?"

I smiled back, nodding. "Yeah, it really is. I feel like quite the starlet."

We were about to start splashing around when I overheard what seemed like a familiar voice. I looked over and saw a pretty dark-haired girl, who had to be at least half Japanese. I recognized her. It was the girl from last night at the Rusty Spur. The one Dad saved.

What was her name? Hana. Hana was her name. What was she doing here? That couldn't be a coincidence.

She was lounging on the opposite side of the pool with a group of friends. Now, I shouldn't have; I know it's impolite to spy, but my darker nature triumphed over my better senses. I moved close enough to hear them.

My heart skipped a beat as I realized she was talking about the fight at the Rusty Spur.

"...and then he just stepped in like it was natural. Like it was perfectly normal," Hana was saying, her voice filled with admiration. "I've never seen anything like it. He took them all down like it was nothing. I knew what was coming. I knew the story would go viral, which is why I put out my video. It's wild. I can't believe I didn't know who he was before yesterday."

Her friends leaned in, clearly fascinated. One of the girls spoke up, "Wow. So what do we know about him?"

Hana glanced around, lowering her voice slightly. "His name's Ethan Miller, 6'3 and a half, 220 pounds, lives around Newark. He's staying with Lady Harrington."

"I heard," another girl with overly large eyes said, leaning forward, "that he is the personal attendant of Lady Harrington. She brought him on after her husband died. He, uh, takes care of her."

The others giggled at that. Hana didn't. "You know she is like, super old, right? He is a hunk of a man. There is no way he would be with that old lady."

I glowered. How dare they talk about Aunt Victoria like that? Who are they to judge my dad and Aunt Victoria? I mean, they aren't together, but it wouldn't be any of their damn business if they were. I should give them a piece of my mind.

I stopped and thought about Aunt Victoria and even looked across the room at her. She was so proper. So controlled. What would Aunt Victoria do? I think she would pick her battles. I decided not to talk but to continue listening.

"So besides sleeping with the Countess, what else do we know?"

"He fights professionally. Has two children. Married young and has been divorced for a couple of years. Apparently, that did not end well. He is a former Marine and was injured in action and doesn't have a girlfriend. Oh, and his ex is a trophy wife of some middle manager upstate and a total snatch."

I almost sat up at that. How do these people know so much about my dad? It's crazy. And I should probably keep Lily away from them. Especially if they were going to talk about Mom.

I spied the group out of the corner of my eye. Hana asked the question. "So Ethan isn't with Samantha Harrington?"

A girl with red hair shook her head. "Rumor has it; they just met this week."

The girls cooed at that.

"Really?"

"Are you sure?"

"She looked quite smitten."

"I heard it's a ploy to get back at her ex. She was with Roger Pendragon until like two months ago."

The group of girls chattered but quieted down when Hana started to talk. "Enough about Samantha Harrington. How do I get a hold of

Ethan? He has no social media profile. Who has NO social media? Man, I wish he would contact me. My father wants to meet him."

The girls with her eyes bulged.

The reaction made me scratch my head a bit. I don't really understand the big deal, but apparently, Hana's father is important? And Dad has Hana's number.

I felt a strange mix of pride and protectiveness well up inside me. They were talking about my dad—my strong, amazing dad—and it made me feel proud that other people were finally seeing what I'd always known. But at the same time, hearing them talk about him like he was some kind of celebrity felt weird. Dad wasn't just "The Samurai" or some guy who could take down bad guys in a bar fight. He was my dad, the guy who made us pancakes on Saturday mornings and taught us how to build things in the garage.

I looked over at Aunt Victoria, who had noticed my distraction. She raised an eyebrow, silently asking if I was okay. I gave her a small nod, but my mind was still spinning. Everything was changing so fast, and I wasn't sure what it all meant.

But as I floated in the pool, surrounded by the soothing warmth of the water, I decided that change wasn't such a bad thing. It was time for people to see Dad for who he really was—a hero, not just to me and Lily, but to everyone who got to know him.

Then Lily dunked me, and it was on.

Chapter Seven

Ethan

As Louis and I stepped out of the car and onto the bustling city streets of Silver Ridge, I felt more than a little out of place. The high-end boutiques, the tailored suits, and the polished shoes were not in my wheelhouse. I was more comfortable in a pair of work boots and jeans, the kind that could handle dirt, sawdust, and whatever else the day threw at me.

Definitely not my world. But Louis? He was in his element.

"Alright, Ethan, today is all about transformation," Louis said with a broad grin, clapping me on the back. "We're going to sharpen you up, my friend. No offense, but the sexy cowboy look of yours is okay for bars and back alleys. But if you are going to accompany My Lady, you'll have to up your game. Big time."

I cocked an eyebrow. "How much of an upgrade are we talking about here?"

"Think Andy Reid to Patrick Mahomes upgrade."

I stopped. Oh damn. That *is* big time.

I raised an eyebrow.

"What," Louis said innocently. "Ethan Miller, you didn't just assume that because I have alternative tastes that I don't know about football. And don't get it twisted; Tom Brady is the GOAT. Just like Michael Jordan; sorry, LeBron."

It was my turn to stop and stare. "Wait a minute, Louis... Are you telling me you're a football fan?"

He gave a dramatic eye roll. "Please, Ethan, I'm a man of culture. I can discuss the intricacies of Versace's spring collection *and* break down the Cover 2 defense. Now, stop gawking and let's focus—Victoria deserves a partner who looks like he belongs, not someone who just wandered in from a tractor pull."

I laughed. "Man of culture indeed. But not a man of the obvious. I was talking about European football. You shouldn't be so bigoted, Louis."

It was Louis' turn to laugh. "I see; thank you for enlightening me, oh backwater one. Now enough foreplay. Are you ready to do this?"

I chuckled, shaking my head. "I'm all yours, Louis. In the least gay way possible."

Louis waved his hand dismissively. "Oh, just you wait, darling. It's about to get super gay. Let's start here."

We entered a sleek boutique called *Savile & Co.*, a place that reeked of wealth and sophistication. Inside, everything was pristinely arranged, the walls lined with suits that probably cost more than my truck. A tall man with sharp features and a tape measure draped around his neck approached us with a warm, professional smile.

"Mr. Delacroix, welcome back," he greeted Louis before turning his gaze to me. "And you must be Mr. Miller?"

I nodded. "That's me."

"Wonderful. My name's Gareth, and I'll be assisting you today." He gestured toward a series of perfectly tailored suits hanging along the far wall. "Shall we begin?"

Louis immediately dove into a conversation with Gareth about cuts, fabrics, and styles I didn't fully understand. Meanwhile, I stood there feeling like a mannequin, waiting for my turn to be dressed up like one. As they pulled out suits and debated colors—deep navy, charcoal, and even a sharp midnight black, I was ushered into the fitting room.

Gareth measured me while Louis leaned against the door frame. "Ethan, what do you know about the Manson Ball?"

I shrugged as Gareth muttered for me to stay still. "Honestly? Close to nothing, and I'm still not entirely sure why I'm going. Don't get me wrong, I'm happy to help, but taking someone, she barely knows to an event like this feels like a gamble. I mean, just look at me."

Louis waved my concern away. "Trust me, Princess, it's impossible not to look at you. But let's set your rugged charm aside for a second— the Manson Ball is a big deal. Big names, big money, and even bigger expectations."

I gave him a half-smile. "Sounds like a *big* pain in the ass. But it's important to Victoria, and I promised to be there, so I'm not sure it really matters what I feel."

"Small correction: it's important *for* Lady Harrington," Louis mused, adjusting one of the jacket sleeves. "She's always had a taste for the finer things in life, but she's not just about appearances. She chose you for a reason. She appreciates your position—not just what you can bring to her position, but what you bring as a man and outsider."

I looked at Louis, catching the subtle undertone in his voice. "What the hell does that even mean?"

Louis straightened, giving me a knowing smile. "My Lady is going to the Ball because she cannot avoid it when someone directly approaches her. She chose you because she trusts you, and she doesn't trust easily. Victoria doesn't need someone who blends into the background. She needs someone who stands beside her, strong and capable. You're that guy, Ethan."

I shrugged, feeling the weight of those words. "Not sure I see it, Louis. I'm just a guy who fixes things and takes care of his girls."

Louis clapped his hands together. "Exactly! And that's what makes you special. You don't realize what you've got going for you. But trust me—when people see you at that ball, in this suit, with Lady Harrington on your arm—they'll know. Ethan. They will really know."

I cocked an eyebrow. "And what will they know, Louis?"

He grinned. "They will know that Ethan Miller goes balls deep."

He said it with a thick French accent.

And I lost my shit. I mean, really lost it. I laughed so hard I almost peed myself. How undignified. It took me a while to get control again.

Gareth brought out a mirror, and I turned to look at myself. The suit fit ALMOST perfectly—tailored to my broad shoulders and heavy-set frame, with a sleek, modern cut. I barely recognized myself. The man staring back was polished, confident, and... well, damn impressive.

Who the hell is this guy?

"Hmm," I grinned, running a hand over the jacket. I looked at Louis. "Balls deep, huh?"

Louis beamed. "Balls deep, my friend."

After picking out a few more pieces—dress shoes, a classic tie, and cufflinks that Louis swore would add the perfect touch—we left *Savile & Co.* and headed to a food spot called *The Brasserie*. It was a high-end bistro, and Louis suggested we stop for a bite.

They greeted Louis like he owned the place, and for all I knew, he did. We sat down and ordered some drinks. The waiter, a striking redhead whose thick Irish accent held me captive, brought us drinks and left with a wink.

It was then that Louis leaned back in his chair, his tone becoming more serious. "Ethan, I know you've got a lot on your mind with every-thing going on—Victoria, the girls, Samantha. But the way I see it, this is an opportunity for you. You've been out of the game for a while."

I frowned. "What do you mean, out of the game?"

Louis smirked. "The game of life, Ethan. Relationships, opportunities... You're not just some carpenter anymore. Not that there's anything wrong with that. I have fantasized about that myself. But you're walking into a whole new world, and you're will need to be ready for the opportunity that comes with it."

I shook my head. "I'm not sure what you mean. Wait, how did you know I was a carpenter?"

"Ethan, the Lady and Samantha are like my life. You don't think I would let some random, no matter how handsome, around them without following up, did you? Silly man. But set that aside and hear what I am saying about your life," Louis said, leaning forward. "You've already proven you can handle the hard stuff—raising the girls, starting over after your horrible ex-wife, and all of that stuff in the military and brother..."

Louis gave me a softened look. I was flabbergasted. "Louis, how do you know about my brother..."

Louis gave me a gentle smile. "I know everything, Ethan. It's my job. Like I said, Lady Harrington and her niece are my world. I would literally do anything to protect them. Of course, I took the time to look you up. I know more about you than you know about yourself. For example, did you know that you're secretly gay?"

I rolled my eyes.

He grinned. "Worth a shot."

"The point," he continued, "is it's time to start really living again. Grab life by the horns and hump it into submission."

"Did you just quote *DodgeBall?*"

He ignored my question.

Louis continued. "I want you to ask a question. Is that okay?"

I shrugged. "Why not? We are already balls deep."

Louis snorted but reattached his serious face. "Ethan, when was the last time you did something for *you*?"

I didn't have an answer for that. I had no idea.

As if sensing my thoughts, Louis smiled softly. "This isn't about changing who you are, Ethan. It's about letting people see the real you. The man who's been through hell and back and comes out stronger for it. And maybe, just a bit polishing up those rough edges of yours."

Before I could respond, our conversation was interrupted by the arrival of our food—freshly baked bread, seared steak, and a salad that looked way too fancy for my taste. But I had to admit, it smelled incredible.

As we dug in, I glanced over at Louis. "Why are you so invested in all this, Louis? I mean, don't get me wrong, I appreciate it. But why me? Wouldn't it be easier to find someone in Victoria's world? You're starting from scratch here."

Louis paused, a flicker of something unreadable crossing his face before he shrugged. "Two things: One, I like a challenge. And you, my dear Ethan, are certainly a challenge. Second, and more importantly, you saved My Lady, you saved my niece, you asked for nothing in return. I did an investigation on you and invaded your privacy, and that is not okay. So I am taking an interest because of the kindness you've shown and the wrongs that you've experienced."

He paused. "And I think you're cute."

I snorted, but I didn't push him for more. Instead, I nodded, letting the weight of his words settle in as we finished our meal. The fact was, I couldn't live for myself, not with Maya and Lily in the picture. I always had and would live with them. But maybe, I could try a bit harder to find some happiness in and of myself? Was that what he was getting at?

Okay, if that was the case, what made me happy? Did I even know?

As we left the restaurant and headed back to the tailor, I felt a little lighter. The suit wasn't the only thing being tailored today—it felt like I was, too.

Oh dear lord, was that corny.

After our shopping trip, Louis led me down a few blocks to a high-end barbershop called *The Gentleman's Blade*. It had that classic, old-world charm—leather chairs, dark wood, the faint scent of expensive cologne lingering in the air. The kind of place where every detail was polished to perfection.

Louis gestured to one of the barbers, a shorter, older guy with immaculate hair and a perfectly trimmed beard. "This is our next stop, Ethan. We're going to take that rugged look of yours and give it a sharp, clean finish. You'll walk out of here feeling like a new man."

I ran a hand through my hair. It was longer than usual, and I hadn't really done much with it in years, just letting it grow out. My beard? Let's just say it wasn't exactly well-maintained, though I had trimmed it up some for the Rusty Spur. Or at least tried.

Samantha had seemed to like it.

"Alright," I said, still unsure. "But let's not get too crazy."

The barber, whose name was Felix, gave me a nod and smiled, clearly knowing exactly what to do. "Don't worry, young man, we'll keep it sharp but true to who you are. Something that suits you."

I sat down in the big leather chair, feeling a little out of my element. Louis watched from the side, arms crossed with a pleased look on his face, as Felix went to work. First, he combed through my hair, trimming it down sharply. It was a bit strange, if I was being honest. I didn't remember the last time my hair was this short. The beard came next—a sharp line across the jaw, but not too close, still maintaining that edge I was used to.

Felix worked with a precision I didn't even realize was possible. Each stroke of the razor felt methodical, and I could already feel the difference. Lighter, cleaner.

"So, tell me more about this 'Caveman' business," Louis said, his tone light but curious.

I sighed. Louis really did know everything. Not that my Caveman moniker was difficult to find. "It was just a nickname from back when I used to fight a lot of cage matches. People started calling me that because of the way I fought. Apparently, I can be quite brutal. It stuck."

Louis raised an eyebrow. "And now they're calling you 'The Samurai,' thanks to a certain incident involving Miss Hana at the Rusty Spur."

I winced a little. "That was a situation I didn't see coming. I'm not trying to be anyone's hero."

"Well, like it or not, you've become one in the eyes of some. People are noticing you, Ethan, and that's going to change things."

"Yeah," I said, "my fight manager said something earlier. Apparently, people want to sponsor me or something."

Louis considered this information thoughtfully. "And you're against sponsorship?"

I shook my head. "No, it's not like that. But it's strange to get money for just trying to help someone in need. I don't like it."

Louis' expression was affectionate. "You're adorable."

I sighed.

Felix finished the last few touches, wiped away the stray hairs, and handed me a mirror. I stared at my reflection, barely recognizing the man in front of me. The beard was trimmed to perfection, my hair had shape and style, and I looked... sharp.

"Different, to say the least," I admitted, rubbing my chin.

Louis clapped his hands together, grinning like a proud parent. "You, my friend, look damn near perfect."

Felix patted my shoulder. "I think you'll do just fine at that ball, son."

We left *The Gentleman's Blade*, moving slowly but surely through the road. While walking, I caught a glimpse of myself in one of the shop windows. It felt strange to see the clean-cut version of me reflected back, but I had to admit. It was much better than before.

We went to several more stores and got a bunch of new clothes. Louis insisted. Apparently, my clothes were all too baggy for my frame. Afterwards, Louis led me toward a restaurant that looked more like a piece of art than a place to eat. It was called *La Maison de l'Étiquette*, an exclusive spot with a refined elegance that made me immediately self-conscious. The entrance was flanked by tall, golden doors, and everything from the menu to the cutlery was designed with an almost intimidating level of precision.

Louis must have seen the look on my face. "Don't worry, Ethan. This is just the perfect spot to fine-tune your dinner etiquette. After all, the Manson Ball is more than just looking the part; you have to move and act the part, too."

I followed him inside. The maître d', like everywhere else we had been, greeted Louis like an old friend, and within moments, we were seated at a secluded table, away from the hustle and bustle. The dim lighting and soft murmur of conversation gave the place a relaxed, yet undeniably luxurious vibe.

Louis handed me the menu with a flourish. "Now, Ethan, the first thing you need in navigating an event like the Manson Ball is the right look. You got that down. Now comes the next part in the form of dinner, drinks, and conversation. Being who you are, people will be watching your every move."

Louis fanned out his hand like a show model. "Hence the layout. At a tier one event like the Manson's Ball, there will be five courses."

I raised my hand. "Why five?"

"Because four is too little and six is tacky."

I raised an eyebrow. "I've been to fancy dinners before, but this seems a bit... intense."

Louis chuckled. "That's because you've never had to impress the crème de la crème of society. Don't worry, I'm here to guide you. Tonight, we'll work on the basics of formal dining etiquette. It's all about procedure and confidence. Be ready to observe, my friend."

As our first course was served, Louis began to explain the subtleties. "Always start with the outermost fork, work your way in as the courses progress. Here, let me show you how to hold your fork."

A way to hold a fork? Was there more than one way?

Apparently, there was.

Louis adjusted my grip until he was satisfied. "Yes, that is perfect. Food should be enjoyed, not just consumed. We aren't eating for sustenance but for pleasure. So pace yourself in the intake, though as a chef, I assume you have a certain pleasure or joy concerning food."

He wasn't wrong.

"You should enjoy some wine, but keep the intake low as you'll be expected to get a hard liquor drink later in the night. Pick something top shelf. Do you have a favorite classic cocktail you like? Preferably something with whiskey, vodka, or gin?"

I laughed this time. "That would be no. If you've really dove into my past, you know that I don't drink much."

Louis nodded. "Touché."

He considered me. "Go with a Vodka Martini. It's considered a sipping drink, and the amounts are small to begin with. But put it on the rocks so it gets diluted. That way, you shouldn't have any problems with it."

I cocked an eyebrow. "Like the Bond drink."

He grinned like the Cheshire Cat. "You're American; the Brits will love it."

"When it comes to conversation, steer clear of anything too personal at first. Ease into deeper topics, but not too deep. Avoid extensive conversation into religion and politics, especially European royal politics."

I snorted. "Well, if I cannot talk about European royal politics, I am not sure I can even go."

Louis glared at me. "Don't be smart, Ethan."

He kept talking.

I listened intently, following his lead as we navigated through multiple courses, each more intricate than the last. Louis circled back around some of the stuff we already discussed. He pointed out small details, like how to hold the cutlery—not just the forks this time—properly, when to take sips of wine, and even how to signal to the waiter that you were finished with a course. I couldn't help but admire how effortlessly he moved through these social conventions.

Even if it sounded stupid to me.

As we hit the main course, a perfectly cooked filet mignon with a brown butter beurre blanc, Louis leaned back in his chair, his tone more relaxed. "You know, Ethan, this isn't my first time guiding someone through the ins and outs of high society. I've been working with Victoria for years now. I helped her through many events such as this. Her late husband, Henry, was the one who brought me on."

I set down my fork, genuinely curious. "Henry? I haven't heard much about him."

Louis nodded. "You would have loved Henry. His actions are partly why your presence is necessary. You two were alike in some ways but very different in others. Henry was a gentleman in every sense of the word. He came from old money, deeply connected to the English and French aristocracy—"

I interrupted him. "I thought all the French aristocrats were dead. Night of Terror. Head chopping and all that."

Louis gave me a look of surprise.

I shrugged. "I like history."

"Then you should love politics as well. The idea that all the French aristocracy died is a common misnomer. Though it wasn't for lack of trying. European politics have many houses and lines of succession, and while lots of people died in the Reign of Terror, it didn't kill everyone. As I implied, Henry and his family can trace their lines through at least two of the French royal lines and through the main line of the British royal family. Hence their current standing; they are still fabulously wealthy from old money projects. He married the most sought-after courtier in the last 50 years—my Lady, a monetary powerhouse in and of herself, on her father's side. Her family has maintained a position in the House of Lords since its founding. They have held real political power. Though in the last 20 years, there has been something of a back-slide. Most nobles across Europe lost their royal house in the 18th century. Germany and Italy had several royal families, though you don't really hear about them because of their unifications in the late 1870s. That matters because nobles, at least in Europe, have had no real polit-ical power since World War I. Henry's family and Henry himself had power, as did My Lady's paternal grandfather. Henry knew how the idea of hereditary political power could be a problem. That brings us to today's modern political climate. You see, the major European powers are all reestablishing noble courts and making adjustments among their parliaments, trying to bring back some measure of noble rule. The British court spearheaded it, and the Spanish, French, German, and Austrian parliaments have already taken steps. This area of political intrigue is really heating up."

"What's all that got to do with Henry?"

He took his cup and swirled some of the liquid. "I was getting to that when you interrupted me, silly. Henry was a player in every sense of the word. A man of endless desire but also compassion, love, and generosity. Victoria, in her younger years, was largely ignored for her brothers until her family realized how incredibly desirable she was across the courts. All of a sudden, she had power in the connections she could forge. Victoria's family wanted to increase their influence across the political landscape. When she became of marrying age, Henry was the one to win her. He loved Victoria fiercely and was a political power-house because of his money, status, and connections. There were talks of him becoming prime minister of Britain at one point; that's how involved he was."

I could sense the respect in Louis's voice as he spoke about Henry. It was clear the man had left a lasting impression.

"Victoria is now the head of his empire. He left everything, and I mean everything, in her control, which is completely out of the ordinary as most well-to-do families with any significant assets operate out of trusts. But that wasn't good enough for Henry. He loved her too much for something as mundane as that. My Lady became the key to the Kingdom. Everyone is after her because of her wealth and unfettered access. People assume because of her age, Victoria will marry again, but she hasn't really let go of Henry. It doesn't help that there is a bit of controversy surrounding his death."

"Sounds complicated," I said, taking a drink of my water.

Louis nodded. "It is, but at the same time, it is not. Since Henry's death, My Lady has avoided the top-tier events, and it's driving the rumor mill. With you being here, I am hoping this appearance quashes those rumors and hopes of other callers."

I took another sip of water, letting that sink in. Escorting Lady Harrington was more significant than I'd realized. I was about to comment when Louis shifted the conversation. "Louis, if I am understanding you right, you are hoping to deter suitors to Victoria by having her spend time with me, right?"

Louis swirled his wine. "Correct."

"You see the flaw in that plan, right?"

Louis gave me a sharp look. "And what's that?"

"No one would believe that Victoria would actually consider me. That thought is crazy. I couldn't even get my ex-wife to love me, and Victoria is in a completely different class."

Louis rolled his eyes. "People might believe you are an actual contender, and really you don't have to be because as long as you are around, she has the excuse. That's all she really needs."

"Oh," I said. "Well, that's good. I guess."

Louis continued. "And don't worry about your horrible ex. If there is one thing I know, it's that karma is a fickle bitch."

I smiled. "Past love can be hard."

"And speaking of past loves, you're aware of Samantha's ex-husband, right?"

I almost choked on my water. "Ex-husband? What ex-husband?"

Louis gave me a sideways glance, clearly surprised by my reaction. "She's never mentioned him to you?"

I shook my head. "Nope. First time I'm hearing about it."

Louis sighed, setting down his knife. "Well, that's something. His name was Gregory. He was a childhood friend. They were married young—too young, if you ask me. They were passionate, but it was that kind of passion that consumed everything in its path. Gregory wasn't a bad guy, but he couldn't handle Samantha's fame. Eventually, they broke up, and he connected with someone more 'simple.' She has been less serious since then."

I stared at Louis, trying to wrap my head around this new information. Samantha, the strong, independent woman I'd spent so much time with, had an ex-husband? I felt a weird mix of emotions—surprise, curiosity, and something I couldn't quite put my finger on. Protective? Was I feeling protective?

"I never would've guessed," I said slowly, still processing.

Louis smiled knowingly. "She doesn't like to talk about it. Samantha's used to handling things on her own, and she doesn't trust easily."

I paused. "Then should you be telling me about him? I wouldn't want her to think we were talking about her."

Louis shook his head. "I am not telling you anything you couldn't find on Wikipedia. Horrors of the internet."

The waiter approached to clear our plates, and Louis's eyes sparkled with mischief. "Now, enough serious talk. Let's get you ready for the rest of your transformation. It's time to embrace the dashing man you've always been but never believed you could be."

I laughed softly, feeling the weight of all the new information. "Louis, I have no idea what that means."

Louis just giggled.

Time passed, the waiter brought us dessert, and I was left to wonder what else I didn't know about my new friends.

Friends. It had been a while since I had counted someone as a real friend.

Had it really only been 72 hours since I met them?

Louis and I sat back to enjoy dessert, a delicate lemon tart with a crisp crust and a tangy filling. It was then that something strange happened. I felt like someone was watching us. Casually, I glanced around the restaurant, taking in the crowd; well-dressed vacationers, a handful of local professionals, couples sharing quiet conversations, and a bridal group enjoying a day out. It all seemed normal, except for a table across the room that caught my attention.

A group of four men sat together, each impeccably dressed in tailored suits. One of them, in particular, stood out. He was handsome, with sharp, almost predatory features, and his dark hair was neatly combed back. There was an air of smugness about him, the way he leaned back in his chair and seemed to direct the conversation. He wasn't just part of the group—he commanded it.

I noticed him watching us, or rather, watching me. His eyes flicked over to Louis, then back to me, a faint smirk playing on his lips as if he knew something I didn't.

"Who's that?" I muttered under my breath, keeping my gaze steady on the man.

Louis followed my gaze and stiffened. His usual cheerful demeanor faltered for just a second before he straightened up and smiled thinly. "Ah, Roger," he said with a hint of distaste. "The world's biggest tool bag."

I raised an eyebrow, intrigued by Louis' sudden shift in mood. "You know him?"

Louis sighed, his eyes narrowing slightly as he kept his voice low. "Unfortunately. He runs certain... circles. Let's just say he's not the most pleasant company."

Roger caught Louis glancing his way and raised his glass, tipping it toward us in a mocking salute. Louis didn't return the gesture. Something about him rubbed me the wrong way, and it wasn't just the smug expression he wore like armor.

He had a very punchable face.

I kept watching him for a moment, noticing how he interacted with the wait staff. He snapped his fingers to get their attention, barely acknowledging them as they refilled his glass or brought over another dish. It was clear he thought himself above everyone around him.

Louis sipped his wine, still visibly irked. "He's not someone you'd want to cross paths with, Ethan."

"Seems like a real piece of work," I muttered, my eyes lingering on the man as he turned his attention back to his group, laughing loudly at something one of his friends said.

"That's an understatement," Louis said, his voice quiet but firm. "As much as I love to see you pop him like the blemish that he is, he is not worth your time or consideration. Hopefully, you won't run into him."

I turned to Louis. "Why would I run into him?"

"He's rich and well-connected. You are spending time with people that are rich and well-connected. There are only so many of those."

That... made sense in a stupid sort of way.

I didn't press further but sensed there was more to this Roger character than Louis was letting on. I filed the information away. The guy clearly had a presence, and not in a good way.

We finished dessert and started to leave. It was then that I glanced once more in Roger's direction. He wasn't watching us anymore, but I still felt his attention, which was a weird thing to say. There was something unsettling about Roger. I knew if I met the guy, we would not get along.

And yes, his face was definitely punchable.

"Come on," Louis said, righting himself with a sigh of relief. "Let's get out of here before the asshat makes a scene."

I chuckled at Louis' use of the slur. "You know, Louis, "asshat" isn't a very refined word."

Louis snorted. "I will have you know, young Ethan, that anything can be refined if you say it with the right temperance."

I laughed. "I doubt that."

I followed Louis out of the restaurant, through Silver Ridge's main street and to the car. It took us a moment because Louis had bought a bunch of stuff. We rode back to the house in relative silence that was neither awkward nor depressing. It was actually the opposite. Louis had managed to make what could have been a long, grueling day feel like a fun transformation process. As much as I initially resisted, there was something satisfying about looking in the mirror and seeing myself polished in a way I hadn't experienced before.

Once inside the house, Louis guided me up to my room with the shopping bags and garment bags in hand. "Now, Ethan," Louis began in his usual dramatic tone, "the first lesson of maintaining fine clothing is knowing how to properly care for it. No tossing this into some heap on the floor or cramming it in the back of your closet, understood?"

I nodded, watching as Louis carefully removed the jacket from the hanger and hung it properly. "You must hang the jacket like this, let it breathe. The fabric deserves respect, just like the man who wears it," he said, flashing me a look of approval.

"Now, take off the rest, and I'll show you how to hang the trousers and fold the shirts."

I followed his instructions, feeling a bit self-conscious as I removed the very expensive clothing I had just put on a few hours ago. Louis explained every step in detail, from how to hang the pants just right to avoid wrinkles, to which hangers to use for shirts versus jackets.

"Eventually," Louis said with a knowing smile, "I suspect you'll have someone to take care of all of this for you."

I raised an eyebrow at him. "What do you mean by that?"

Louis paused and gave me a look that clearly communicated his thoughts. "Ethan, for a man who's as sharp as you, sometimes you can be really dumb."

I blinked. "What are you talking about?"

Louis sighed dramatically, patting my shoulder. "You'll see. In time."

I shrugged it off for the moment, though the conversation left me wondering if Louis knew something I didn't—or if he was just messing with me again.

After we'd finished with the clothes, Louis led me downstairs to the kitchen, where he began preparing what he called "the perfect cappuccino." He talked me through every step—the grind of the beans, the temperature of the milk, the importance of the froth. Louis had a way of turning even the smallest things into an art form, and as I watched him, I realized how much attention to detail he put into everything.

He handed me the finished product, the cappuccino topped with an elegant swirl of foam. I took a sip, and the rich, smooth taste hit me immediately. "Damn, that's good," I said, genuinely impressed.

Louis smiled, clearly pleased with himself. "You see? It's all in the details, Ethan. Life is big and complex and often gritty and dirty, but we can make it better with a bit of refinement, from the way you dress to how you handle even the most mundane of tasks."

I nodded, realizing that there was more to this than just wearing nice clothes or sitting properly at dinner. It was about presenting myself in a way that reflected who I wanted to be—not just for other people, but for myself.

"Thanks, Louis," I said sincerely. "I appreciate all your help today. I wasn't sure about this whole thing at first, but you've made it a lot easier. It's good to know I've got someone looking out for me."

Louis gave me a whimsical grin. "Anytime, Ethan. I'm here to make sure you shine like the diamond you are. And trust me, this is just the beginning. Next, we head to the ballroom for your dance lessons."

Dance lessons. Oh damn.

Chapter Eight

Samantha

The spa was amazing. I live a privileged life. I am very lucky. One of the reasons I had gotten involved with charity work was that I recognized that fact. My life isn't perfect. I am not perfect. But I have been given a gift. I try not to take my good fortune for granted. I try to give back. I try to be good.

That being said, these luxury spas are really the playground of the rich, and they are one of the things I like most about this world, especially the pools. Maybe I was a mermaid in another life?

I floated in the warm water of the spa's pool, the tension gnawing at my chest from the previous night completely gone. Okay, maybe not gone, but at least subdued. Even as my mind wandered back to Ethan, I was much more relaxed about my contemplation. I thought about his face, his voice, his hands, and his eyes. I tried not to think about his lips.

I was only partially successful.

Part of the problem was that I kept hearing about him. Here I was in one of the exclusive spas, in one of the most exclusive places on earth, and Ethan Miller was a topic of conversation. That was the problem. It was why he invaded my thoughts. It was a surreal feeling—here I was, surrounded by peace and tranquility, while the people around me chattered about him like he was Brad Pitt.

I mean, early 2000s Brad Pitt. The one that dropped panties at a glance.

Yes, I understand that was crass, but you get my point.

And the point was, everyone seemed to be talking about him.

The big idiot.

And yes, I am well aware that Hana Yamamoto is here. It's like she is stalking me. And I know she is glaring. Not sure what her problem is. Whatever.

I let the gentle current carry me for a while, watching Maya and Lily as they splashed and laughed near the pool's edge. The girls looked so carefree, so happy in this moment, and it warmed my heart to see them like that. I had to wonder if this is how mothers feel. I see the girls and just think, how can I make them happy?

Bring it down a notch, Samantha. You are NOT their mother. You are not their stepmother. Hell, you are not even their dad's girlfriend. You're just you, and you've known them less than a week.

Victoria caught my eye from where she sat on the edge of the pool, dipping her legs in the water. I moved closer to her. I voiced my thoughts, "My maternal instinct has hijacked my common sense. I have been sitting here for the last ten minutes watching Maya and Lily and have seriously considered kidnapping them."

"They're good girls," she replied softly, her eyes fond as she watched the two of them play. "They remind me of you when you were their age."

I scoffed, though I couldn't help but smile. "I was never that sweet; just look at them."

"Oh, you were," she said with a wink. "You just hid it better."

Just then, the girls yelled out, "Samantha! Lady Victoria! I think it's time for a game of Marco Polo!"

Before we knew it, half the people in the tranquility pool were playing Marco Polo with us. It was strange; people were naturally drawn to Lily and Maya.

The staff did get mad at us, though, and eventually, we had to stop. What a bunch of killjoys. Aunt Victoria was furious in her very British way. I tried not to laugh when she threatened under her breath to buy the place just to change the rules so Maya and Lily could do what they wanted!

And I thought I needed to bring it down a notch!

After all the commotion in the tranquility pool, we eventually made our way to one of the juice bars. After we spent a good twenty minutes debating the juices and their benefits, Maya, Lily, Aunt Victoria, and I sat down to drink. It was then I thought to ask the girls something that had been on my mind. I wondered about Ethan—specifically, his absence from social media. It seemed odd, considering how people shared every detail of their lives these days.

Curiosity got the best of me. "Hey, girls," I said with a sip of my drink. "Can I ask you something about your dad?"

They exchanged a quick glance before shrugging. "Sure," Maya said, a little cautious. "What about him?"

"I couldn't help but notice... your dad doesn't have *any* social media, does he? I mean, I haven't seen him online anywhere outside, you know, his fight videos. I know he is anti-device, but I think that was mostly to keep you two safe. But when I looked, he had nothing. Not even Facebook. Everyone has Facebook."

Lily shook her head, almost laughing. "Nope. He hates it."

Maya chimed in, her voice more thoughtful. "Yeah, Dad's never been into that stuff. Not like Mom."

At the mention of Sarah, something flickered in their eyes—just for a moment. I raised an eyebrow, sensing there was more to the story. "Your mom's on social media a lot?"

Lily snorted. "All the time. She's, like, everywhere. Mostly on the Gram and TikTok. We think her dream is to be one of those Real Housewives."

Maya reached for her phone, scrolling quickly before handing it to me. "The social media thing has been an argument between our mom and dad forever. We have social media, but Dad doesn't like us to use it a lot. I think that was part of his thing with phones. On the tablets, it is easier to monitor. Though truthfully, I think it had more to do with Mom than us. Here, take a look."

I took the phone and stared at the screen. Sarah's profile was the kind that grabbed attention immediately—beautiful, glamorous, and perfectly curated. Her platinum blonde hair, styled in voluminous waves, framed her sharp features, giving her the look of someone who always knew she was being watched. She had that striking, almost ageless beauty, with flawless skin that practically glowed in every picture.

Photoshop at its best, I assume. No one's skin looks like that naturally.

I scrolled. Each post showcased Sarah in luxurious locations—tropical resorts, five-star restaurants, high-end boutiques—always surrounded by the wannabe rich and famous, always doing rich things with rich people. Her perfectly tailored dresses hugged her curvaceous figure, designed to highlight her status and allure. In every shot, she wore that same polished, confident smile, one that spoke of a woman who had moved on to a different life without a second thought.

The captions were just as meticulously crafted—"Private jet to Cannes," "Dinner at The Ritz," "New season, new wardrobe #luxurylife." It was all designed to flaunt her perfect existence, an existence far removed from the simple, grounded life she'd once shared with Ethan.

Sarah looked every inch the woman who saw herself as God's gift—

entitled, glamorous, and utterly out of touch with anything that wasn't draped in wealth and status.

I had the sudden desire to smack this woman right across the face.

"She posts about her trips," Maya explained, watching me closely. "Fancy dinners, new clothes, yachts. You know... that kind of thing."

"And Dad doesn't want to see that," Lily added, her voice quieter now. "He was never into social media anyway, but after they split... I guess it just got worse. He didn't want to have her new life shoved in his face all the time."

I felt a pang of sympathy. No wonder Ethan stayed away from it. It wasn't just that he didn't care about social media—it was that he didn't want constant reminders of his ex-wife living this glittering, superficial life. The one she left him for.

"That must be tough," I said softly, handing Maya her phone back.

Maya shrugged, trying to play it off. "I think he's just... happier without it. He's got us, and we don't need to be online for that... though there are some practical problems that come with avoiding the technology."

Lily nodded in agreement, but there was something more in her eyes —maybe a bit of sadness, maybe the realization that their family's story was written out for the world to see, but not the whole truth.

The conversation shifted after that, lightening a little, and before I could say more, Victoria appeared, gliding gracefully toward us. "What are you three conspiring about over here?" she teased, her smile warm as she sat down beside me.

"Maya and Lily were just filling me in on why their dad doesn't do social media," I said, glancing over at the girls. "And it got me thinking... maybe we should start one for him. I think it would really help him."

Both girls' faces lit up. "Really?" Maya asked, her excitement palpable. "That would be amazing if you could convince Dad he needed it. He doesn't listen to us."

Lily added, "Yes. You would have to convince him. We've tried to get him to do it before. He tried it for a week, but he kept getting tagged in posts talking about Mom or us. He was not a fan."

Victoria's face turned thoughtful. "We could simply block your mom."

I laughed. "Or even better. Get your mom to block him. What do you think she would do if your dad uploaded a load of pictures with a bunch of pretty girls?"

Maya and Lily exchanged looks again. "She would not like it at all. Mom is weird about things like that. She doesn't like it when Dad gets attention."

Now that was a weird development, but it actually tracks from what I know of Sarah. She was starting to sound like a textbook narcissist. Being a former model, I know a thing or two about that.

I looked at Aunt Victoria. "I was already planning on seeing them, but what do you think of having the Harpies at the house for a couple of days? We could do a little photo shoot."

Victoria raised an eyebrow knowingly, and I didn't need to explain further. She grinned. "Sounds like a party."

I picked up my phone and started texting.

It was actually really easy to set up accounts for Ethan on social media. We kept them private for the moment. We connected them to my account, Maya's, Lily's, and Victoria's, though granted, Victoria's was also semi-private.

"Now," I said to the girls as I took another sip from my drink, "this is obviously going to be an argument with Ethan. What other points can we use to convince him this is a good idea?"

"Honestly," Victoria said, settling deeper into the conversation, "there are some practical applications we haven't discussed. If Ethan's going to keep up with everything he's been doing—whether it's fighting or that restaurant he keeps talking about—he's going to need some kind of online presence. That fact alone should be enough for him to at least give this a try."

Maya nodded. "That is a good point. He always talks about how he wants to open this restaurant, but how's he gonna get people to notice it if he's not online?"

"And, like... if he wants to connect with people, meet new ones," Lily chimed in, glancing at me. "Maybe even, you know... date? He kinda needs to get with the times."

I chuckled, the girls clearly having given this some thought already. They were right, though. Whether Ethan liked it or not, social media was the way the world connected now. If he really wanted to pursue his dreams—whether in business or his personal life—he'd have to at least dip his toes into it.

"That's true," I mused, my mind already racing with ideas. "He can't exactly promote his restaurant by word of mouth alone these days. He'll need something... polished. But it has to be authentic. People love seeing the real person behind the business."

Victoria leaned in, nodding thoughtfully. "And considering his background, that raw, honest side of him could really resonate with people. He's not just another handsome face—they'd connect with his story."

Maya's eyes lit up. "In addition to your idea, Sam, I think we could start with something small! Like pictures of him cooking, working out, spending time with us. Just show his normal life."

"Exactly," I said, smiling at their excitement. "We keep it real. We show the Ethan we all know. Not trying to make him something he's not. Just... Ethan."

Lily grinned, her voice playful. "Oh, and we could post videos of him recipe testing. It's so funny! Dad's food is so good, people would totally follow him for that."

Victoria smiled warmly. "Maya, Lily, I know that you don't like talking about it, but your dad is still fighting professionally. I think it would be easier for him to find sponsorships if he has a following. Because of everything that happened with Ms. Yamamoto and Samantha, it probably wouldn't take that long."

Victoria looked at me. "Heck, if we started the profile and had Samantha follow him, that in and of itself would probably get him a few followers."

My aunt was not wrong.

We all shared a laugh, the lightness of the moment washing over us. It felt like we were all in on something together—something that would help Ethan, even if he didn't realize it yet. I got to work.

"Alright," I said, feeling a surge of excitement. "The account is live but still private; the next step is to post a few pictures and see how he reacts, then talk to him about how the pros outweigh the cons. He might grumble about it, but deep down, I think he'll appreciate the support."

Lily smirked. "Or he'll try to delete it the second he sees it."

"Samantha could always just kiss him," Maya suggested, her grin absolutely wicked.

"Oh, that's a great idea," said Lily. "It worked last time."

Victoria looked amused and a little miffed. "I am not sure that's enough, girls. Maybe I should kiss him this time."

Maya and Lily expressed their surprise. Maya couldn't hide her smile. "I think that would be great, Aunt Victoria. I am sure he would love to kiss you. You're so pretty."

Victoria slid in next to Maya. "Oh, you darling child, what do you want? Can I buy you a pony?"

Maya laughed. "What? Why would you... what type of pony?"

"Hey," Lily said, "I want a pony too. You can kiss Daddy all you want!"

My aunt grinned. "Yes. You too, Lily. Ponies for everyone."

I cut in. This conversation was getting ridiculous. "We'll cross those bridges when we get there. But for now, let's get to work. We'll need some good photos, and we should probably make it look like it was his idea."

Victoria shook her head, smiling at our scheming and trying to hide the fact that her face was turning pink. "Good luck with that. But it's a good plan. Ethan could use something like this in his life—something to help him dream bigger again."

As the ideas for Ethan's social media presence swirled between us, Victoria suddenly sat up straighter, a knowing smile crossing her face. "You know who we need for this? Louis."

Maya and Lily exchanged excited glances. They had met Louis earlier today and were already fond of him. "Your assistant?" Lily asked, her eyes sparkling. "He's helping Dad with the Manson's ball, right?"

Victoria nodded. "Yes, he's getting your father ready for the event, but Louis is the ultimate planner. He's always five steps ahead of me, and if anyone's got content on your dad already, it's him."

Without wasting a moment, Victoria pulled out her phone and quickly tapped out a message to Louis. "I'll just let him know what we're up to. If I know him, he'll have plenty of pictures and ideas for us to work with."

Sure enough, it didn't take long for Louis to respond. Victoria's phone buzzed, and when she opened the message, her eyebrows shot up in amused surprise.

"Well, what do you know?" she said, turning the screen so we could all see. "He's already on it."

The girls leaned in, eyes wide with curiosity. Louis had sent a whole collection of pictures—candid shots of Ethan from their day out.

> Louis: I was already going to talk to this silly man about his lack of online presence. I am so happy you brought this up.

The pictures just kept coming in.

"Oh my gosh," Lily said, scrolling through the images. "These are perfect!"

Maya nodded eagerly. "We could use these for his Instagram and TikTok. We already have so much content, and we haven't even started!"

Victoria smiled, clearly pleased with Louis's efficiency. "Leave it to Louis. We've got more than enough to kick things off now."

I couldn't help but laugh at how easily it was all coming together. "Looks like we don't need to worry about getting photos. Louis has already done half the work for us."

Lily grinned. "Dad's gonna freak out when he finds out we're doing this."

"Yeah, but in a good way," Maya added with a smirk. "He'll thank us later. He just doesn't know it yet."

Maya looked at Victoria. "And Aunt Victoria can just kiss him if he becomes a problem."

"Hey, what about me?" I protested.

"Okay, Samantha, you can kiss him too. We will allow it," Lily said.

Everyone laughed at that point.

Victoria tapped at her phone again, sending a quick thank you to Louis. "Now that we have everything we need, it's just a matter of setting it all up. And once your father's ready for the Manson's ball, we can surprise him with his very own social media accounts. He and your mother won't know what hit them."

Chapter Nine

Ethan

I stood in the middle of what could only be described as a ballroom. Yes, that seemed ridiculous. Rich people really did live differently.

I rolled my shoulders, trying to loosen up before I made an absolute fool of myself. Louis had been unusually quiet since we returned to the Chateau, which meant he was scheming something.

I had only known the guy a day, and still, I knew that thought to be true.

When he'd walked in earlier with a very pretty girl on his arm—a girl who was almost Victoria's exact height, build, and even wore a similar shade of dark lipstick—I realized I had been right. He was definitely scheming.

Louis did not mess around when it came to Lady Harrington.

"Ethan," he said, clapping his hands together, "meet Isabelle Lopez. She is the daughter of a friend from the Dominican Republic. Isabelle is a professional trainer, dancer, and choreographer out in New York. And she is huge on TikTok. She is a gorgeously fantastic person, though her English is terrible."

Isabelle snorted and swore. "Louis, don't make me kick your ass again. You know my mother doesn't like it when I make you cry."

Louis looked indignant. "That was not crying. You brute of a woman. I was merely lamenting your loss of femininity."

Isabelle just laughed. "Loss of femininity? What a silly thing to say. What do you think, Handsome? How's my femininity?"

Isabelle gave me a pointed look and struck a pose that highlighted her figure.

I tried to hide my own smile and the fact that I checked her out. "You are crazy if you think I am getting caught up in this."

Isabelle and Louis apparently couldn't hide their delight, but at what, I was unsure. Louis continued as if not interrupted. "Subpar communications and Isabelle's questionable feminine wiles aside, Isabelle will be your dance partner until we can get my Lady down here. I actually want to assess your base before we have to dance with Victoria." His grin widened as he stepped back, clearly proud of himself. "Remember, the Manson's ball crowd is a judgmental, arrogant, and unforgiving bunch. I am sure you'll have a delightful time."

I sighed. "Louis, I know you think you're funny, but someone should really disabuse you of that notion."

Louis' grin looked slightly manic.

I looked Isabelle up and down, feeling a mix of hesitation and eagerness. Isabelle was striking. I seemed to be spending a lot of time with extremely good looking women these days.

I kept up my observation of Isabelle; she was built like a brick shithouse. Damn.

I paused at my own thought. *I hate that expression. Brick shithouse? What does that even mean? I know what people think it means. Whoever thought that a brick shithouse and beautiful women should be equated is an idiot.*

Isabelle smiled warmly, clearly not the mind reader I knew most women to be. Or maybe I was getting better at hiding my thoughts. Isabelle raised an eyebrow when I didn't say anything, her graceful movements already hinting at her experience in dance. "I'm excited to work with the Samurai," she said, her voice light and confident. "I actually know Hana Yamamoto, and while not exactly a friend, I am glad you helped her."

I chuckled nervously. "I am glad I could help. Hana seems nice. I am happy to dance with you. Though be careful of your feet."

Isabelle offered her hand. "Alright, you handsome man. Let's start with the Waltz. Show me what you got."

I took her hand and started to dance.

Okay... so here is the thing. I haven't been as honest as I probably should have been. The truth is I am not starting from scratch. I had a foundation in dance that most people didn't know about. As a kid, my mother had insisted on lessons, and I picked it up easily. I was also learning martial arts at the same time, and the two activities naturally flowed together. It wasn't until later, when I was with Sarah, that I realized how useful those lessons were. She loved dancing—formal events, weddings, clubs—anywhere she could twirl and sway in a spotlight. So I'd danced with her, time and time again, though that felt like a lifetime ago.

I understand that this is shocking as I told Samantha and Victoria that I don't dance. And that is technically true. The first time I had gone dancing since my divorce was with Samantha last night.

Geez, was that just last night?

That said, I don't dance anymore because it brings back painful memories for me. Or at least I didn't. I guess I am good now. Funny how that works.

I also found that while I was out of practice, I was still pretty good. The muscle memory was there, even if it had been buried for years.

Isabelle positioned me. Her touch was light but firm, and she looked up at me with a soft smile. "Don't worry," she said. "For now—just let me lead."

"I have the feeling you're used to leading," I said absentmindedly.

Isabelle gave me a serious look. "You have no idea. Play your cards right, and I will show you what it means to be led."

I paused. I literally had no idea what to say to that.

Louis, leaning back with his arms crossed, looked positively delighted as he turned on some music—something classical but upbeat enough to keep the energy alive. "Let Isabelle guide you," he said. "I have every confidence you'll be waltzing like a pro by the end of the night."

I took a breath and moved with Isabelle, her movements graceful and smooth. It didn't take more than three or four minutes before my body fell into rhythm. The old patterns, the muscle memory from years ago, started coming back, and I began to glide, as much as a guy my size can, from step to step. Our waltz quickly became more vigorous.

"You've done this before," she said after a few minutes, a teasing smile on her lips.

"Maybe once or twice," I admitted, focusing on keeping my steps fluid.

"More than once or twice," she said, spinning effortlessly under my arm. "And you're quite graceful for someone so large."

I smirked, a little more confident now. "I had a good teacher growing up. And danced quite a bit back when I was married. The martial arts also help."

She raised an eyebrow but didn't push the subject. "Well, aren't you full of surprises? Tell me, Ethan, is there anything else about your body I need to know about?"

She grinned, and it reminded me of The Joker. Is it weird that I found that smile sexy?

Yes. Yes, it was. Something is definitely wrong with me.

Louis, watching from the side and apparently indifferent to the flirting, clapped his hands. "What did I tell you? Isabelle is just what you needed."

I laughed. "I think Isabelle's doing all the work here."

Isabelle shot me a playful look. "You're holding your own. Trust me."

As I worked through the steps with Isabelle, Louis clapped his hands again, signaling for a pause. "Alright, Ethan," he said, stepping closer with his usual air of confidence, "how many dances DON'T you know? Just for reference."

I shrugged. "I have a passing familiarity with most of the formal dances: waltz, mambo, foxtrot, tango."

Louis rolled his eyes. "Silly cowboy. So you have the basics down. Perfect. Let's run through the list of dances."

Isabelle looked at the paper Louis was holding, then handed it to me. Yep. All the majors.

We got back to practicing.

After a couple of hours, Louis handed me a bottle of water. "Well done. But we aren't finished yet. We still need to talk about the formalities—and the not-so-formal parts—of the Manson's ball."

I nodded, wiping the sweat from my brow. Isabelle, patient and poised, stood beside me, clearly waiting for Louis to explain what came next.

"You'll be attending the ball as Lady Victoria's escort AND date," Louis continued, his voice measured. "There is a difference, and if we are going to get through this night without scandalizing the English-speaking world, I need you to pay attention."

I raised an eyebrow. "You know if this was a TV show, I am pretty sure you just set me up for a horrible death or at least a very dramatic scene."

"And in most circumstances, I would be cherishing the drama, but not with the Lady. The smoother, the better. She has suffered enough."

I raised my hand, *like I was in grade school.* "So, almighty Louis, what exactly does that mean?"

He rolled his eyes. "It means all eyes will be on you two. You'll need to be comfortable with the formal dances, but there's also a point in the evening where things become more relaxed, and the press is pushed aside. That's where the informal part comes in. This is where things get tricky."

"Informal?" I repeated, glancing at Isabelle. "What's that supposed to look like?"

Louis smiled, a little too knowingly. "It's about striking the perfect balance."

"Yeah... that is the mother of all non-answers."

"Patience, my young one. The informal portion of the evening dictates the actual nature of your relationship with Lady Harrington. Are you an escort? Are you a date? Somewhere in between? There is a difference, and you, my young roguish friend, will need to keep the masses guessing. You'll need to look close with Victoria—close enough to keep the likes of Robert away—but not so intimate that it creates gossip or people see you as a serious suitor."

Louis stopped talking and looked contemplative. "Okay, we don't want you to look too serious of a suitor."

I frowned. "So we have to look like we're... together, but not *together*? So I shouldn't make out with her in the bathroom. Lame."

"The bathroom is fine, just not the dance floor; if you do engage in bathroom escapades, give her a lovely squeeze of the bum. She will love it," Louis said without missing a beat.

That made me laugh.

Isabelle chuckled softly. "The thing is, Ethan, if you remember our earlier conversation, our Lady is a big freaking deal—rich, gorgeous, even in her later years, with several very powerful titles, access to real political power; and not just one of the wealthiest aristocrats. She is pound for pound THEE wealthiest aristocrat in any of the Royal

Courts. She has more money, land, and holdings than the Royal Family and three Archduchies, and most of the new Courts combined. Don't even get me started on her conglomerate. The point is what she does and who she spends her time with matters. Lord Harrington's death was unexpected; the transfer to her all his personal holdings was unprecedented. She is getting a lot of pressure from her family and the Count's family to remarry, which she has straight-up ignored. What does all that mean for you? It means in three days' time, at the Manson Ball, you and Lady Victoria will be the focus, so you need to project familiarity, even warmth and some affection, without crossing any boundaries."

I shifted my feet, already feeling the weight of what was said. The idea of attending this event as Victoria's date was daunting enough, but now I had to navigate the fine line between looking close and not too close.

Subtly. Me. I am about as subtle as a kick to the face. This was going to be a disaster.

Louis gestured for Isabelle to take her position again. "Isabelle is here to help you practice. She's a stand-in for Victoria, of course, but she'll continue to sharpen you for the formal and informal dances; I will help you with the more casual moments."

Isabelle stepped forward, positioning herself as my partner once again. "Think of this as not just dance practice but date practice," she said, her voice gentle but firm. "When you're with Lady Victoria, you need to be in sync. Everyone will be watching like there is blood in the water."

I am pretty sure the blood-in-the-water thing was based on smell. I decided not to bring that up.

Isabelle smiled as she took my hand, guiding me into a more casual stance. "This is how you'll want to approach the informal dance scene. The informal dances are much less structured. But this isn't a club; the body language needs to send the right message."

She moved us through a few steps, her movements fluid and confident. Her build was similar to Victoria's—tall, curvy, with a striking presence that drew attention. But she was just a stand-in. The real challenge would come when I was dancing with Victoria herself.

"Informal dancing at these events is less performative and more social. Lots of conversation, planning, flirting, and scheming."

"But remember, you've got people who are supposed to act superior; you're not really supposed to have fun, and this isn't a club. So keep the bump and grind for the club or the bedroom."

I raised an eyebrow. "Louis, no one says bump and grind. The 1990s called, and they want their lingo back. So what can I expect, an awkward eighth-grade afternoon social?"

Before Louis could come back with a snarky comment, Isabelle cut in.

"Something more akin to a religious wedding. There will be an undertone of passion but nothing overt," Isabelle interjected. "I know it sounds ridiculous, and it is. But this is really important. You need to make it look like you and Victoria are comfortable with each other. You have to act like you've known each other for a long time, but not in a way that draws the wrong kind of attention. You will need to touch her often. Remember, you're being affectionate."

I nodded, focusing on the rhythm. Isabelle continued. "Her hands and upper arms are a must. Grab her hand when leading her around. Kiss it when retreating or getting her drink or when she returns from a dance. When standing in place, her arm should be wrapped around yours, or your arms should be around her, resting on her hip. No ass grabbing. No matter how great an ass it is."

I laughed. "Welcome to the fine print. No talking about European Royal Family politics. No ass grabbing? World's worst party. What's the point of even going?"

Isabelle's grin turned wicked. "You pull this off, and I will let you grab my ass all night long."

Louis raised his hand. "Mine too."

I gave Louis a sharp look.

He grinned. "You have options, Ethan."

I rolled my eyes.

Isabelle and I started to dance again. But the movements were less formal. She swayed in and out, coming close to me to talk, whisper, and giggle. Her movements were deliberate, and I followed her lead, trying to imagine Victoria in her place. The thought of being this close to Victoria at the ball, with everyone watching, was more nerve-wracking than I cared to admit.

"The key in this situation," Louis said, stepping around us to observe, "is confidence. You need to project that you belong together without looking like a confirmed couple. People should speculate but lack conclusive evidence. Keep the chemistry subtle, but enough to keep the piranhas at bay."

Isabelle guided me through a few more steps, her hand resting lightly on my shoulder. "The informal part of the evening is where people start to let their guard down, but you can't. You need to stay aware of how you're presenting yourself with Victoria."

I focused on the dance, letting the movements guide me. Isabelle was a good teacher, but the reality of dancing with Victoria in front of an entire room of onlookers felt like a different kind of challenge.

"This is how you'll keep people at bay," Isabelle said, her voice soft but sure. "You and Victoria need to look like you're in tune with each other, but not crossing any lines. It's all about subtlety."

I smirked, a little more at ease now. "Subtlety has never been my strong suit."

Isabelle laughed, spinning lightly under my arm. "You'll be great, trust me."

Louis, standing off to the side, nodded approvingly. "By the time we're done, you'll be ready for anything the Ball throws at you. And trust me, it's going to throw a lot."

I let out a breath, relaxing a bit as we finished the routine. This was just practice, but the real test would come when I was standing across from Victoria, trying to balance the formalities of high society with the easy familiarity we'd been building.

Isabelle stepped back, giving me a nod. "You've got this. Just remember, it's all about confidence and trust. You'll need both when you're with Victoria."

Just as I was starting to get comfortable with the practice, Louis cleared his throat, drawing my attention back to him. "Alright, Ethan, now that we've got the basics of the formal and informal dances down, there's something else we need to cover."

I raised an eyebrow. "What's that?"

Louis clasped his hands together, his expression becoming more serious. "You're younger, unmarried, and unconfirmed as a suitor for my Lady. At an event like the Manson's Ball, that means you'll be expected to accept invitations from others to dance. You're going to need to manage that carefully."

I frowned. "Manage it how?"

Isabelle stepped aside, giving Louis the space to explain. He started pacing slightly, as if mentally organizing his thoughts. "You and Victoria will be the focus of attention at the ball. People will want to dance with both of you—some for the attention it brings, others just to socialize, and others still to try to scheme something from either you or Victoria. But there's a delicate balance you'll need to maintain."

I crossed my arms, trying to follow his train of thought. "So... what's the problem?"

Louis stopped and looked directly at me. "The problem is perception. You can't afford to look too available—either of you. If you accept too many dances, it gives the impression that you're there as an escort, not serious about your role as Victoria's date. The same goes for Victoria. If you allow too many people to dance with her, it sends the message that she's more available than we want to show."

I nodded slowly, seeing where he was going with this. "Okay, so... what's the limit?"

"Fifty percent," Louis said matter-of-factly. "You shouldn't accept more than fifty percent of the people who ask you to dance, with specific exceptions depending on who asks and only after your dance card is filled. As for Victoria, it's your job to allow or disallow who gets to dance with her, and the same rule applies—no more than fifty percent. If you let more people dance with her, it creates the impression that she's open to... other invitations."

I grimaced, understanding the subtle implication. The last thing I wanted was for Victoria to look too available, especially with the likes of Robert sniffing around. But Louis wasn't done.

"By limiting the number of dances," he continued, "you're maintaining control. You're showing that Victoria is selective, and so are you. It's about maintaining that aura of exclusivity—like you're both there, but not completely accessible to everyone."

I rubbed the back of my neck, letting the information sink in. "So I have to let some people dance with her, but not too many."

"Exactly." Louis nodded approvingly. "And you have to do the same for yourself. There will be women who ask you to dance because of your age and how you'll stand out at the ball. Politely accept a few invitations from women of Victoria's age or older if you can; there may be a few more women closer to your age there, but it's unlikely they will ask you to dance. It's considered bad form for contemporaries of marriageable age to have a Lady ask for a dance. Anyone younger than 18 is okay, as it's not seen as any sort of courting capacity. Accept every single one of those. Again, young women older than 18 have debuted, and the rules are tighter. Younger than 18 haven't been launched into society and have less structure. Anyone bringing a young lady younger than 18 is slightly out of step with what is current. Only the most powerful, influential, and rich—or if I am honest, dumb—amongst the guests will dare to do that. So absolutely do not refuse them. It would embarrass them and piss off their parents. Keep all this in mind, but don't get caught up in it. You'll be able to dodge a lot of actual dancing by filling up your dance card. I will explain how that works later. The main thing is you're there with Victoria, and that needs to be clear."

I couldn't help but chuckle, despite the weight of the situation. "So it's a balancing act."

Louis smiled. "Exactly. You're there to support Victoria, but also to stand out as her date. People will be watching how you handle it, and your choices will reflect on both of you."

I glanced at Isabelle, who gave me an encouraging smile. "It sounds complicated," I admitted.

"It's not as bad as it seems," Isabelle said, stepping forward. "You just have to stay aware. It's all about reading the room and keeping the right distance."

Louis clapped his hands, signaling the end of the lesson. "You've got this, Ethan. You just need to be selective, and don't let anyone push you into accepting more than you should."

I nodded, feeling the pressure but also a strange sense of excitement.

Chapter Ten

Samantha

What a day. The spa, an evening of music and food. I can honestly say that this was one of the best days I've had in a long time. Probably for Aunt Victoria too. She needed the day out even more than I did. We had so much fun. After the spa, Louis had booked us a table at Sable & Sage, which is an amazing farm-to-table restaurant that is impossible to get into. Things like reservations never did stop Louis. After dinner, we walked through the city center of Silver Ridge, which was surprisingly alive tonight.

The small-town vibe gave way to a more festive energy under the soft, glowing lights of the cafes and live bands. We danced. We took pictures. I got hit on. Victoria got hit on. There were even some younger boys around Maya's age who were checking her out.

She might as well get used to it. She was already a looker at 13. Young, obviously in that transition period from girl to woman, but she had her father's genes, and he was handsome. Sarah was quite attractive as well. We would have to talk about that. Those were confusing years.

I was content, almost reluctant to leave that atmosphere behind as we made our way up the path to the house.

The moment we stepped inside, though, I was snapped back to reality. There, lounging on the couch with a drink in hand, was Louis, looking far too pleased with himself. Next to him was a tall woman with a dancer's grace, her dark hair falling in waves over her shoulders. She was strikingly beautiful, with the kind of curves that drew every eye in the room. I didn't need to glance twice to know who she was—Isabelle Lopez. Of course, Louis would bring in a professional; I should have known better.

She was also something of a frenemy of mine.

That is a whole other story. I can say this: if Isabelle is training Ethan, that doesn't make me happy.

Louis glanced up, his grin widening. "Ladies! Look who's joined us tonight."

Victoria gave Isabelle a dignified smile, then a cheesy grin. Louis's smug expression said it all. "Isabelle, darling, it's been forever! Come over here," she greeted. "You're as stunning as ever. How are you, dear?"

Isabelle flashed a dazzling smile and rose, every movement fluid, almost feline. She just about tackled Victoria. It shocked me a bit. I didn't realize they were that close. "It's a pleasure, Lady Harrington. My mother says hello and that you owe her a shot of whiskey."

Aunt Victoria snorted. "You tell that mother of yours that she knows bloody damn well that it's her turn to buy. I am expecting bottle service, something on the sea this time."

Isabelle didn't try to hide her amusement. "I will make sure to tell her. I will try to say it just like that too. Such a scandal."

"Samantha, it's been too long," she added, turning to me. "Sorry I've been out of touch. When was the last time—yes, Roger's Bahama Bash back in February."

I let out an ironic chuckle. "Has it been that long? Are you still dating Roger's friend? I forgot his name. Adam?"

Isabelle visibly grimaced. "Oh no. It ended just like you said it would. He cheated with some chick from Spain. Told me that we were now in a one-sided open relationship. Such a dick."

I chuckled. She was right; Adam, like Roger, was a dick.

Isabelle and I sized each other up, and I wondered what she was thinking.

Isabelle was taller than I remembered, with skin that seemed to have a natural, sun-kissed glow. Her frame was curvy but toned, a body type that seemed exclusive to Latina women. Her toned arms and legs practically screamed *dancer*. Everything about her—dark eyes, olive skin, confident posture—radiated energy. I could see why Louis had picked her for Ethan's practice. She'd certainly match his intensity and had a similar build to my aunt (which was funny because my aunt was very, very British and white). She was also a hell of a teacher.

I am quite the dancer myself. Maybe not quite as known as Isabelle, as I was more model than dancer, but I can hold my own. But I was nowhere in the same league as Isabelle when it came to teaching. I knew it. Louis knew it.

Still, it didn't stop the fact from being irritating.

Louis cleared his throat, waving a hand as if to redirect attention. "Maya. Lily, my little darlings. How was your afternoon with Samantha and My Lady?"

Maya answered first. "Louis, it was—wow. We—it was so good. Thanks for booking it. I assume it cost a lot of money."

Maya turned to look at Victoria. "Aunt Victoria and Samantha, we know that was a lot of money. Thanks for including us."

Victoria and I exchanged a look. When was the last time that we worried about money? That we simply didn't buy what we wanted? I forget that Maya and Lily have experienced a different world, at least with their dad, and that luxury wasn't exactly something that they indulged in.

Before I realized it, my arms were around Maya, and Aunt Victoria was holding Lily.

"Stick with me, kid," I whispered. "I'm going to show you the world."

Maya buried her face in my chest and just squeezed me.

Louis cleared his throat again. "Uh, what about a hug for the mastermind?"

Maya released me. Lily did the same to Aunt Victoria. They looked at each other, nodded, and then laughed as they ran and jumped on Louis, who anticipated the jump like a boss and was able to set his drink down.

There was giggling from the girls and Louis. It was hilarious to hear him giggle.

After a few moments, the girls and Louis disengaged, and he started talking to them.

"Now, girls, this is Isabelle Lopez. She is the daughter of an old friend of mine. She's helping us ensure your father doesn't embarrass himself at the Manson Ball." He cast a meaningful look at me, as if daring me to question his judgment. Oh, I was definitely going to have a word with him later.

Maya nudged Lily, eyes wide with excitement. "You're THE Dancer, right? I've seen you online! You're amazing!"

Isabelle chuckled, a rich, warm sound, and knelt to their level. "Thank you, little darling. Do you dance too?"

Lily nodded, looking up at Isabelle with admiration. "I try, but I have two left feet or right feet. My feet suck."

"Thank you, sweetheart. I am sure your feet are delightful." Isabelle shot Louis a wink. "Your uncle here was my very first audience. He gave me plenty of 'feedback.'"

"Ah, yes," Louis replied, feigning modesty, "I pioneer in discovering raw talent."

We all rolled our eyes.

The girls reluctantly said their goodnights, their energy finally dipping after our long day. They headed upstairs, Victoria following close behind to make sure they settled in.

As the sound of footsteps faded, I turned back to Louis, unable to keep the question from spilling out. I hesitated briefly as Isabelle was still here, but I couldn't help it. "So, you decided Ethan needed a professional dancer for practice? Was that really necessary?"

I looked at Isabelle. "No offense."

She smiled at me.

Louis only shrugged, his grin unrepentant. "You, my dear, have seemed to forget your experience with the crowd at the Manson Ball. You are gorgeous, a great dancer, and definitely motivated. But you are a lousy teacher. We didn't have time for you to find your groove. Isabelle is here because Ethan's entrance and interactions need to be flawless. He is younger, working class, and has two children. People are going to judge Victoria for naming him as her date. I understand that Robert put her on the spot, but naming Ethan was about as bad a call as my Lady could have made. Second only to going with Robert the Snake. Now, to avoid the worst-case scenario, Ethan needs to clip the haters." He took a sip from his drink, as if he had just solved world peace.

Isabelle arched her brow, looking between us with mild amusement. "Clip the haters? I don't know about that. Ethan certainly and naturally stands out. His looks and demeanor alone do that. But being handsome and noticeable is not enough here. I've been to some of these top-tier events; judgment and prejudice run deep there."

Isabelle had a bit of color come to her face.

Damn it.

Louis continued, oblivious to—or perhaps reveling in—my reaction. "In any case, we'll be running through the routine tomorrow morning. We've gone over formal dining, aristocratic talking points, formal dance etiquette, informal dance etiquette, partnership and affection rules."

Affection rules. Louis. No. He. Didn't. I couldn't believe what I was hearing. "You didn't actually set Affection Rules with Ethan. He isn't a formal suitor, and this isn't the 1850s."

Louis took another sip of his wine. "Samantha, I know you hate the old ways, but the Courts still follow them. Like it or not, Lady Harrington didn't request aid to set a formal escort replacement; she directly stated that Ethan would be her date. There were six or more witnesses. Robert had been clever. Ethan was the only way Lady Harrington could have politely avoided his invitation without involving someone else, and you know we cannot do that as all others would have an ulterior motive. Allowing any pretender even the preview of courtship is a bad idea. Like it or not, My Lady set Ethan up as a potential suitor. From where I am standing, she didn't really have a choice."

Victoria cut in at this point, having just returned, her cheeks turning a warm shade of red. "Affection rules, Louis. You cannot be serious. First of all, those are for the freshly debuted, not widows. Ethan does not possess a title, so the rule wouldn't apply to him anyway. Finally, Ethan is already going out of his way to assist me. Ethan is not required to process so much formality. This is too much of an expectation for him. It doesn't matter if he doesn't follow all the rules; it's not like he is actually a suitor, and I just need to get away from Robert."

Louis gave Victoria a side glance. "Everyone here knows that your position is tenuous with the death of Henry. You have both your in-laws and parents making plans, and all the major duchovny are just looking for an excuse for one of the Elders to step in and formally mediate a new relationship."

Louis adjusted his body. Then, his countenance shifted, and he stared at Victoria in a very serious way. "You know as well as I do that it's all over if one of the Elders decides to formally pull rank. You've got enough clout to ignore them. But I know that would isolate you, and that is the last thing you want, especially with what is going on with your sons."

Victoria sighed, her face still red. Her expression was tough to read. Sadness? Weariness? Constipation? It was hard to tell.

I turned to Louis. "Wait. What is going on with Harry and John? What aren't you telling me?"

Louis and Victoria exchanged glances like someone caught in the act. My aunt answered. "School drama. Later."

I didn't like the sound of that. But I would set it aside. "Okay, Louis, what are the set affection rules?"

Louis shrugged. "The basic preliminary courtship stipulations. Polite kisses. Hand holding. Touching at the hips, waist, and upper arm. Absolutely no ass grabbing; no matter how delightful that ass may be."

Victoria's face went a deeper shade of red.

Louis kept talking. "Ethan did say that the event was pointless if there couldn't be ass grabbing."

I didn't think it could happen, but my aunt's face got even redder.

Isabelle snorted this time and looked back over her shoulder. I wasn't sure why.

"Anyway," Louis said, "Ethan needs to keep the wolves away, and a bit of affection will do just that ESPECIALLY if Ethan maintains the affection rules. Ethan is the key to making it all work and allowing the others to see him as a potential threat. He has to blend into My Lady's world. Your world."

That gave me pause. My world. Ethan blending into my world sounded good to me. Real good.

I fought the urge to facepalm.

Louis continued. "As such, he will need at least a couple of hours of practice with My Lady. But she cannot be the one to lay the foundation. She needs to spend most of her tomorrow at La Belle Couture. Then Victoria and Ethan will be dancing tomorrow most of the afternoon, and then we have a dinner."

Victoria looked surprised. "Is Genevieve back in town? I thought she was on sabbatical in...where was it? Florence?"

Louis smiled. "Milan. I called her the moment I found you'd be going to the ball and you'd be taking Ethan. She was all too pleased to come back and make you look your best."

"Louis, that wasn't necessary. I have so many dresses; I could have just worn something old. I've lost a bit of weight, but I could have had one of the other tailors adjust it."

Louis shook his head, his tone firm but with a hint of fondness. "All those dresses have history, Victoria. They were worn when you stood beside Henry. This is a new chapter. You're attending the Manson Ball with Ethan. The symbolism of your appearance can't be overstated, and Genevieve understands that better than anyone. Besides, you aren't really going to deprive Genevieve of the opportunity to create, now are you?"

Victoria sighed, rubbing her temple. "Louis, have I ever told you that you have a flair for the dramatic?"

"I prefer to call it foresight," he replied with a grin, raising his glass in mock salute. "We both know what's at stake. Your initial reluctance was the right call, but when Robert cornered you, you took the only path you could without blowing everything up. This ball is no longer just a social event; it's a battlefield. Every glance, every whisper, every dance—it all matters."

I watched Victoria as she processed his words. Her usual poise faltered slightly, her fingernails tapping against one another. Aunt Victoria is one of the most unflappable people that I know. She was always so composed, so in control. But it was the crease at the edge of her mouth that gave her away. She resigned, but she was not happy about it.

"I understand," she said finally, her voice softer than usual. "I'll go to La Belle Couture tomorrow and meet with Genevieve and leave Ethan in Isabelle's very capable hands."

"Excellent," Louis said, his grin widening. "I'll accompany you, of course. We'll have the whole morning to perfect your look, and then the afternoon is for Ethan's training. Everything is falling into place."

Victoria cast him a dry look. "Falling into place or into chaos?"

"Chaos is where I thrive, my Lady," Louis replied with a wink, earning a small laugh from Isabelle. "And remember it was you that invited him."

Louis' voice was so sweet that if I didn't know him better, I would have thought that he was actually sincere.

"I am sure that Ethan will enjoy your company. Just remember, according to the affection rules: no ass grabbing."

I glared at him, and Isabelle and Victoria didn't even try to hide their laughter. Assholes.

After a chuckle, Victoria stood, smoothing the fabric of her dress as she straightened her posture. "We've all had a long day, and tomorrow sounds like it will be even longer. I think it's time to call it a night."

She turned to Louis, her tone softening. "Thank you, Louis. For everything. You, relentless, slave driver of a man."

Louis pressed a hand to his chest in mock humility. "Always, my Lady."

Victoria rolled her eyes but smiled, and with a graceful nod to Isabelle and me...

I couldn't help but interject, crossing my arms. "So tomorrow, Victoria and Louis will be with Ms. Genevieve while Isabelle and Ethan are going to be dancing. Who is going to be supervising them exactly?"

Isabelle snorted.

Louis gave me a wry look, and Victoria seemed to be doing her best to control her face.

She was failing miserably.

"What?" I said defensively. "I just meant that Ethan needs all the help that he can get. I can help with Affection Rules and another dance partner."

I sounded too defensive even to my ears.

Chapter Eleven

Victoria

I had a hard time sleeping that night.

I was nervous. Why was I so nervous? Needless to say, I was happy to meet with Louis early in the morning and head to Silver Ridge.

La Belle Couture was as much a sanctuary as it was a workshop, nestled in an unassuming corner of Silver Ridge's high street. The building itself was a fusion of timeless elegance and modern flair, with polished glass windows that gave passersby a tantalizing glimpse of the magic happening inside. Genevieve, the genius behind the boutique, never missed a chance to put on a show, even in her storefront displays. Draped fabrics shimmered under soft lighting, and sketches of haute couture designs hung like artwork on the walls.

When I entered, Genevieve herself was waiting, her keen eyes already assessing me before I'd even set down my handbag.

"Countess," she said, sweeping forward with arms outstretched. Her voice was velvet smooth with the faintest trace of her Parisian roots.

"You look radiant as always. But mon dieu, you've lost weight since I last saw you. This simply won't do. We'll have to start from scratch!"

Genevieve Delacroix—no relation to Louis, or so they claimed—was a force of reckoning. Tall and willowy with jet-black hair always swept into an effortlessly messy bun, she dressed in flowing black ensembles that gave her the air of a 1940s film star. Her presence filled the room as though she were the one draped in couture.

"Genevieve," I replied, allowing her to kiss each of my cheeks, "it's good to see you. I've missed your theatrics."

She laughed, a sound as rich as her fabric selection. "And I've missed working with someone worth dressing. Come, sit. We have much to discuss, and the Manson Ball waits for no one, not even you."

As I settled into one of the plush chairs in her fitting area, Genevieve clapped her hands, summoning her assistants. They moved with military precision, bringing out sketches, fabric swatches, and even a silver tray with tea and delicate pastries.

"What are we thinking?" she asked, her sharp gaze fixed on me. "You must dazzle, Countess. The ball shall be your stage. And this dress will be your opening act."

I sighed, sipping my tea as I glanced at the array of options before me. "Something elegant, Genevieve, but also modern and maybe a bit more sexy. I don't want to look like I'm clinging to the past."

I thought of Ethan. Yes. Something modern. Sexy even.

Genevieve tilted her head, studying me like one of her mannequins. "Elegant, sexy, and modern... I have just the thing."

With a dramatic flourish, she unveiled a sketch that took my breath away. The dress was a masterpiece: a sky blue silk that would flow like water, with a plunging neckline and an intricate, gold-threaded lattice design along the bodice. The sleeves were sheer, ending in delicate cuffs, and the skirt had just enough of a slit to hint at daring without being inappropriate.

"Do you trust me?" Genevieve asked, her voice soft but commanding.

"Always," I replied.

Her team moved quickly, taking measurements and fitting the base of the dress around me. As they worked, Genevieve continued her running commentary. "You'll turn heads, my dear. That shade of blue with your complexion and eyes—it's perfection. And the gold? It's a nod to your heritage, to power, to everything you are."

Her words were reassuring, but I couldn't shake the tension building in my chest. I wasn't sure I was ready. I knew that I did not have a choice. I knew that Robert designed his invitation to trap me into saying yes. Yet, I had been lucky. If the Duchess had come with him... well, I wasn't sure I could have gotten away with the rejection, even with Ethan there. Still, Ethan... poor Ethan getting dragged into my mess. Perhaps I should have simply gone with Robert.

"Genevieve, your ears are always to the ground. Have you heard who will be attending?" I asked, in a vain attempt to distract myself.

Genevieve didn't look up from adjusting the fabric at my waist. "The regulars from the Courts, I imagine. Robert, of course. I heard what you did to him. It made me laugh. But whispers in the wind told me that his mother might even make an appearance, which would be... interesting."

My stomach tightened at the mention of Robert's mother, Eleanor Haverford, the Duchess of Westfall. She was known for her sharp tongue and sharper ambitions. She'd been a force to reckon with even before Henry's death, and her presence tonight would mean one thing: maneuvering.

"And the Blackmoors?" I asked, my voice carefully neutral.

Genevieve paused, her eyes flicking to mine. "Alexander, certainly. He wouldn't miss an opportunity like this. Don't be surprised if their son is in attendance. You know the Blackmoors are almost as desperate as the Haverfords to make a connection with you. Whether Lady Evelyn joins him remains to be seen."

I nodded, my thoughts racing. Alexander Blackmoor was always a wildcard—charismatic, cunning, and dangerous in ways that weren't immediately obvious. Henry and he, though cousins, were constantly at odds. "Who else?"

Genevieve resumed her work, smoothing the fabric over my hips. "Lord Sebastian Fairfax is back from his estates. Which is surprising, as I recall he was a close friend of Henry's."

That was true. Fairfax was charming in a way that made you forget he was dangerous. He had been one of Henry's staunchest allies, but his loyalty had its limits.

"And Lady Cassandra Wentworth," Genevieve continued, her tone lighter now. "Though if she's coming, it's probably just for the gossip. That woman would attend her own funeral just to hear what people say about her."

Despite myself, I smiled. Cassandra was sharp-tongued and not exactly intelligent, a woman who thrived on drama and intrigue.

Genevieve stood back momentarily, watching how the dress clung to my frame. "The unconfirmed names are more interesting. I've heard Lady Margaret Astor-Blythe may be showing up."

I lifted an eyebrow. The Duchess of Belhaven almost never attended the Tier 1 events. She hated them. Actually, I was pretty sure she hated most things except her granddaughter, Anna.

"That is interesting," I simply said. "Surprising."

The mention of these names brought my situation sharply back into focus. It was fine. Totally fine.

Genevieve finished her adjustments and stepped back, admiring her work. "Perfect," she said, her voice soft with satisfaction. "Victoria, you will be the queen of that ballroom."

I looked at myself in the mirror, the blue silk catching the light in a way that made it shimmer. For a moment, I almost believed her.

"Let them look," I murmured to myself. "Let them see."

I moved in the dress. I was pleased. This ball might be an absolute disaster, but at least I would look good.

Chapter Twelve

Samantha

Lunch was set on the long oak table under the pergola, sunlight filtering through the vines above. The view of the Smoky Mountains stretched in the distance, serene and endless. But I wasn't paying attention to any of it. My focus was locked on Ethan and Isabelle as they ate their salads like they hadn't spent the last two hours showing off.

Correction—dancing. But to my increasingly irritable mind, it felt like showing off.

So I had to acknowledge the elephant in the room. Ethan cut his hair, and hot damn, did he look incredible. He was wearing clothes that were formed and fitted to his frame. He looked freaking amazing. I literally dropped the coffee I had been brewing when he walked into the room.

We held awkward conversation, but the atmosphere was good until Isabelle came to the kitchen and ruined the moment. Then we all went outside to dance, and it only got worse from there.

Ethan and Isabelle started to dance.

Ethan was good. Infuriatingly good. He moved like someone who'd been trained in dance—not someone who casually claimed to avoid it. When he first twirled Isabelle across the floor, I'd expected an awkward, lurching attempt. Instead, what I saw was smooth and controlled, each step deliberate yet natural. He'd matched her pace as if they'd been partners for years.

And Isabelle. Of course, she was flawless. She spun and dipped with her usual effortless grace, her movements fluid like water. Together, they made it look easy—too easy.

I stabbed a piece of tomato with unnecessary force, feeling ridiculous for the knot twisting in my stomach. It wasn't jealousy. That would be petty. I wasn't jealous.

I was annoyed.

Annoyed that Ethan had lied—okay, maybe "lied" was too strong—about his abilities. He had deliberately downplayed his experience, and for what? To surprise us? To make me look like a fool for doubting him? When we were at the Rusty Spur, I had the passing thought that for someone who claimed "not to dance," we moved awfully well together.

Maybe that fact was something I should have thought about prior to this.

"Please, pass the bread," Ethan said, pulling me out of my thoughts.

I slid the basket across the table, trying to meet his gaze. "Nice moves out there," I said, keeping my tone casual.

He glanced up, his expression unreadable. "Thanks."

That was it. No explanation, no acknowledgment of how much better he was than he'd let on.

"Where'd you learn to dance like that?" I asked, leaning back in my chair.

He paused mid-bite, setting his fork down. "Here and there."

Here and there? Seriously?

Isabelle, ever the opportunist, jumped in. "He's underselling it. My cowboy here has more rhythm than most men I've taught. He's a natural."

Her cowboy? Her cowboy? What did she mean, *her* cowboy? I felt my eyebrow twitch.

Ethan gave her a sideways glance, the corner of his mouth lifting in a faint smile. "I'm just following your lead."

"And doing it well," Isabelle purred, leaning slightly toward him.

I took a long sip of my iced tea, letting the chill cool my rising irritation. They weren't flirting, not really. But there was an ease between them—a connection born of hours spent moving together in perfect sync.

"What happened to 'I don't dance'?" I pressed, hoping to get a better answer.

Ethan shrugged, his shoulders broad under the fitted dress shirt he was wearing. Damn, it was distracting. "Yeah. I should have been a bit more forthcoming. I said I don't dance. Not that I couldn't dance. I learned to dance young. My mom made me take lessons; said it would help with coordination and my martial arts."

Isabelle chuckled. "It shows. And let me guess—someone convinced you to pick it up again later in life? A girlfriend, maybe?"

He hesitated for just a moment before nodding. "Yeah. My ex-wife loved to dance."

Ethan's face went somber, like he remembered something painful.

The table fell quiet for a beat. Even Isabelle seemed to sense she'd stepped into sensitive territory.

"Well, whoever taught you," I said, breaking the silence, "they did a good job. You've clearly had more practice than you let on."

Ethan met my gaze then, something unreadable in his expression. "Guess I underestimated myself."

There it was again—that maddeningly vague deflection. But I had a pretty good idea where this was coming from. Sarah liked to dance.

Ethan had danced with Sarah, and he probably stopped dancing when Sarah left him.

I swear, if given the chance, I am going to strangle that woman.

I didn't press further, but as the conversation shifted to lighter topics, I couldn't shake the unease. Watching Ethan and Isabelle dance together had stirred something in me, and it wasn't just irritation. It was the way they'd moved so effortlessly, the way their chemistry had seemed... natural.

And then there was the way Ethan had looked at her, focused, with intent, but not distracted. Like he was present, but not completely caught up.

The knot in my stomach tightened as I forced myself to finish my lunch. It wasn't jealousy. I. Don't. Get. Jealous.

I was just... annoyed.

Definitely annoyed.

Lucky for me, I had things to keep me distracted; namely Ethan's budding social media presence. We had not gone totally public yet, but his name was out there, and people were asking for connection.

I looked over the pictures I took of Ethan and Isabelle dancing. They looked way too good together. Maybe I should erase these. I was suddenly pissed I didn't take more pictures at the Rusty Spur.

Ethan shifted in his chair, clearly uncomfortable with the idea of being a centerpiece. "Can you two offer any advice, like practical advice, to, you know, avoid attention? I have a bad feeling that I am going to mess this whole thing up for Vikki."

Isabelle leaned over, her dark eyes sparkling. "Sorry, handsome. You're the mystery. The rugged cowboy out of place among the aristocracy attending to the single most coveted widow in the English Court. You cannot avoid the attention, my friend."

"Great," he muttered. "This is going to be a disaster."

"Ethan," Isabelle said, "can I be real with you?"

Both Ethan and I looked at Isabelle, and it was strange how serious she was. Ethan gave her a soft smile. "Are you saying you haven't been real with me up until this moment?"

She laughed. "Shut up and listen."

Ethan waved his hand as if to say "go ahead."

Isabelle's expression softened, but there was a sharpness in her tone that made both Ethan and me sit a little straighter. She leaned forward, her dark eyes locking on Ethan with an intensity that felt almost conspiratorial.

"Ethan, I need you to picture the most ridiculous period drama you've ever seen—*Bridgerton, Downton Abbey, Pride and Prejudice,* something with elaborate gowns, endless tea parties, and people scheming over who dances with whom, and what land they are going to take from which colony. Now, take all of that, strip away any real power those people might have had, and transport it into a modern world where they are constantly fighting to *pretend* they're still relevant on a very public international stage."

Ethan blinked, processing. Isabelle didn't give him time to respond. I just listened. Not exactly how I would have put it, but she isn't wrong.

"Then," she continued, her voice gaining momentum, "put someone like *you* in the mix. A straightforward guy who doesn't care about their games, has no title, no connection, and very little in the way of manipulable assets. Sorry to put it bluntly. But you are someone that people in that world look down upon. Even the ones with good intentions."

Isabelle gave me a look.

"Hey!" I said.

She continued blatantly, ignoring me. "Add the fact that you're escorting one of the most sought-after women in the English Court— someone they all either envy, hate, lust after, or wish they could control —and you've just thrown a stick of dynamite into their cozy little powder keg."

Ethan raised an eyebrow, leaning back in his chair. "That's supposed to make me feel better?"

"No," Isabelle shot back with a small grin. "It's supposed to make you understand. The way people look at you, the way they interpret every move you make—it's all part of this world. You're a wild card, Ethan, and nothing makes these people more nervous than something— or someone—they can't control or at least—predict."

Ethan let out a slow breath, his fingers drumming on the table. "Great. So, I'm basically a live-action plot twist."

Isabelle smiled slyly. "Exactly. And that's your strength. They'll be curious; they'll whisper; they'll watch. Let them. You don't need to win their approval. You just need to show up, be the man Victoria trusts you to be."

Ethan shook his head with a laugh. "You make it sound so easy."

"It's not," Isabelle said with a shrug. "But you've got one thing they can't fake—authenticity. That alone makes you ten times more interesting than half the people in that ballroom. Let them wonder. Keep your answers short, stay grounded, and whatever you do, don't let them see you sweat."

He nodded slowly, his fingers relaxing. I watched as the tension in his shoulders eased slightly. Isabelle had a way of cutting through the noise, of making even the most overwhelming situations feel manageable.

"And if all else fails," Isabelle added, a mischievous glint in her eye, "do something bold."

Ethan laughed. "Bold. I thought I was trying to avoid attention."

I jumped in. "You're not listening, Ethan. Attention isn't something you are going to be able to avoid. So do the opposite. What do they call it? Steer into the skid."

Ethan gave me a wicked grin. "Coming from someone that doesn't drive."

I snorted. "It's not like I *can't* drive; I just choose not to—and okay, I am not that great at it."

Isabelle stood and twisted her body around her normal ritual to loosen up. "Now that I have successfully lifted your spirit and stored up your confidence, let's see if you can handle a Viennese waltz."

Ethan stood and said to me, "Samantha, baby girl, why don't you observe? You might learn something."

I bristled at his tone, but before I could respond, Ethan was already following.

"Let's go, cowboy," she said, her grin playful but determined.

As they moved back to the practice area, I folded my arms and leaned against one of the pergola's main wooden beams, watching them fall into step.

Isabelle took Ethan's hand, guiding him into the starting position. He followed her lead, his movements smooth and deliberate. Isabelle's eyes were smoldering, and Ethan's smile was genuine.

They moved through the steps, slowly at first, and then faster, smoother, with more precision. Their chemistry was undeniable. They glided across the floor like they'd been dancing together for years, their movements perfectly synchronized.

I hated it.

Not because they looked good together—though they did—but because it reminded me of how easily Ethan seemed to adapt. He was supposed to be the outsider, the rugged, down-to-earth guy who didn't belong in Victoria's, or mine, or even Isabelle's world. But here he was, proving he could fit in just fine.

Too fine.

I clenched my jaw, forcing myself to stay quiet as Isabelle praised his progress. This was all for the ball, I reminded myself. Just a performance.

Chapter Thirteen

Ethan

The sun peeked over the Smoky Mountains, casting a warm golden hue across the lawn. I stood in the backyard, the grass cool beneath my bare feet. I focused on my breathing, steadying myself as the birds chirped a morning serenade. This moment of calm before everything shifted into high gear was precious.

It had been a rough 36 hours. Honestly, I didn't even feel like myself. Louis and Isabelle were slave drivers. Maya and Lily were caught up in everything, researching Modern English Courting Rules like I was a princess coming of age. They really got a kick out of this. They watched my practice, making sure that their commentary wasn't ignored. My girls were understanding. Louis was happy, always happy. Isabelle loved teasing me, and Samantha—Samantha was acting weird.

Everyone was relentless, not that it was all bad. I finally danced with Victoria yesterday, and the way she blushed when I pulled her close made me chuckle. Actually, it made me smile just thinking about it. I pulled her close and dipped her, moving her with precision, if not elegance.

We moved through several of the formal dances that were on the list for the "Formal Arrangement," as they called it. I can only assume this is the period where—actually, I have no idea. It could be the time they beat us with sticks for all I know. I ASSUME these are the dances that we are going to be performing, but who knows.

Still, we ran through a bunch of dances, and I thought we did a pretty good job.

"You're way better at this than you have any right to be," she said as I spun her out. She twirled back towards me before I answered.

"Well, what you don't know is that I'm secretly a spy sent here to seduce you and whisk you off to worlds unknown."

Victoria's eyes narrowed as her cheeks flushed. It was freaking adorable. "Oh, is that right? Well, Mr. International Man of Mystery, where exactly will you be whisking me off to? I will need to figure out what to pack."

I leaned in close, my lips next to her ear as I dropped my hands to her hips. I whispered, "Kansas."

And then I stood back and gave her the goofiest of grins. She stepped back from me but not before swatting my arm and saying something about me being cheeky.

Victoria. She was fun. We continued to practice and dance and touch and connect. It was strange how at ease I felt around Victoria. Maybe I just dug the matronly vibe. Oddly enough, I found myself getting nervous, but not for myself. For Victoria. I found the prospect of embarrassing her weighed heavy on my mind.

I didn't know much about this world. But Lady Harrington was not going to experience additional hardship because of me. No way in hell.

I fell back into the present. I dropped into my fighting stance, grounding myself in the familiar flow of my fight practice. This had long been a refuge for me. Each movement felt fluid, a reminder of the discipline I'd embraced. I stretched, pivoting with precision, letting my muscles remember their strength. The rhythm of my body—each punch, each block—helped me flesh out the vague thoughts that clung to my mind like cobwebs.

I was pretty sure I was as ready as I was going to be for this thing. I had worked hard, traveled down this path toward refinement, and polished my conversational skills. Every word I'd traded with Isabelle, Louis, and Samantha; every lesson concerning politics, fashion, and current events; it all began to swell in my mind. I had tried to prepare, to make it all fit, only to feel the absurdity of it all pressing in like a thick fog.

The ball, an elaborate performance masked as a social event, struck me as entirely ridiculous. Underneath the glitz were sharks in designer suits, only looking for a chance to take a bite. Each smile was another transaction. Each dance spun into elaborate schemes—a chaotic ballet with high stakes.

I landed a roundhouse kick, the air moving sharply against my leg. What did it mean to be a part of that world? To walk into a ballroom with the veneer of sophistication while the undercurrents twisted like an unpredictable river? I was an outsider, trying on someone else's clothes for the evening—and it felt laughable.

The anticipation bubbled around me, loud and gaudy. The ball would begin, and I would be an unexpected guest among the glimmering elite. They would whisper, exchange glances, and I'd wear it like a badge of honor. I had braced myself against that uncomfortable truth, each breath carrying a quiet rebellion. I wasn't playing their game, not really.

"Ethan?" A voice broke through my thoughts, soft and curious.

I halted mid-motion, turning to find Samantha emerging from the house, her hair catching in the morning light. She was dressed in the gym attire she seemed to prefer.

I bowed to her. "My Lady."

She rolled her eyes. "Oh, I am no lady."

I raised an eyebrow. "You're quite the lady to me."

Again, she rolled her eyes but didn't hide her smile. "Anyway, someone named Toni called your phone like fifty times. Sorry, I didn't mean to intrude, but with that many calls, I figured he was a stalker or someone important."

"Ahh, Toni. He is my fight manager," I replied, my fists still clenched, my feet shoulder-width apart. "Probably wants to talk about... actually, I have no idea what he wants to talk about. He has a tendency to ramble."

She nodded. "I hope it's okay. I answered and told him you were unavailable."

I chuckled. "I am sure he loved that."

"He said that as soon as I saw you, and I quote, 'his money-making mug,' to give him a call back. It's urgent."

I sighed. "Got it. That guy. He is always working an angle. I will call him after this thing tonight. Thanks, Samantha. Maybe I should hire you to be my secretary."

I laughed. "No, that wouldn't work. No way I could afford you."

Samantha's face turned contemplative while I fell back into my fighting stance.

A smirk tugged at her lips. "Practicing for the ball, or for when the snooty aristocrats launch themselves at you?"

"Maybe both." I relaxed my stance, shaking my head. "Honestly, I just needed to clear my head."

She studied me longer than necessary, her smile fading as she considered my words. "This is going to be intense, huh?"

"Intense is one way to put it. Stupid is another." I stepped forward, the grass still dewy beneath my feet.

"What do you mean?" she pressed, folding her arms.

I let out a breath, running a hand through my hair. "Your aunt...she is special. You probably know that. Actually, you both are. Maybe I simply don't understand your world; no, it's clear that I don't understand, but honestly, it seems really dumb that she is forced to do something like take someone she barely knows to a classy social event just to avoid some jackass who cannot take 'no' for an answer. Like I said, the whole thing is just dumb. I am thinking that I should just find Robert and beat him until he gets the point that Vicki just isn't that into him."

Her brow furrowed deeper, but I pushed on through my hesitation. I really did need to unburden myself.

"It's not like I hate dancing or spending time with beautiful women. It's just something that Vicki shouldn't have to do, you know? As for me, I go from being a regular guy to shimmying around in a tuxedo with people who think a twirl on the dance floor grants them power over another person. I can't help but feel like it's a big joke; that I'm the punchline, and if I don't play my part right, it's going to hurt your aunt. I really don't want your aunt to get hurt."

She paused for a moment, considering my words, before walking next to me and taking up a yoga pose that made her butt look amazing.

And I was pretty sure she caught me looking.

"Ethan, who do you think Victoria Harrington is?"

I frowned, caught off guard by the question. Samantha held her pose, her gaze steady, waiting for an answer. I exhaled, wiping a hand across the back of my neck.

"She's... your aunt, obviously, a lady of the court—I know she has an impressive title or two of some kind, though I don't know exactly what it is," I said cautiously, unsure where Samantha was going with this. "She is a woman. A damn impressive one at that. Strong, classy, beautiful, knows what she wants. But if you're asking me for something more insightful, then I'm stumped."

Samantha tilted her head, a small smirk tugging at the corner of her lips. "You're not wrong, but you're not exactly right either. My aunt's full title is Lady Victoria Elizabeth Harrington, Duchess of Harrington, Countess of Ashbourne, Marchioness of Somerwynd, and Baroness of

Thistlewood. She's not just my aunt, a Countess, Duchess, Marchioness and Baroness. She is a real-world player. She is the CEO of a large multinational corporation, though she is mostly retired now. She has land and holdings across the world. She's a woman who moves mountains without anyone noticing the quake."

I crossed my arms, intrigued. "Yeah...I am not getting the point, Sam."

Samantha dropped the pose and stood, dusting off her hands before stepping closer. "Ethan, my aunt's position is precarious because she *allows* it to be. She respects her mother and father and former in-laws and matching traditions because that is what they expect of her. But they don't have any power over her—no real power anyway. Sure, her political life can get complicated if the Elders get involved, but they cannot really force her to do anything. So, we come to you. You're not just her plus-one, Ethan. She chose you. People have been pursuing Aunt Victoria for most of her life. She could have lied to Robert and called someone who would have been happy to escort her. She would have gotten some backlash because she didn't go through the right channels, but most of that would have been noise. She didn't do that. Out of everyone who could've escorted her to that ball, she picked *you*. Not because she had to, not because it was convenient, but because she trusts you to stand beside her."

I blinked, momentarily stunned. *"She trusts me? Why?* I barely know what fork to use, and if you think about it, it's hardly been a week since we met."

Samantha laughed softly, the sound warming the cool morning air. "Ethan, you saved our lives. You put yourself in danger. You didn't ask or even expect anything in return. Victoria sees that you're real. You are what you are, you say what you mean, and you don't pretend to be something that you're not."

Apparently, the irony of the statement wasn't lost on Samantha. "At least most of the time."

I chuckled.

Samantha continued. "The point is that someone like you is rare in her world—hell, it's rare in my world. So, yeah, the ball is ridiculous, and the stakes are high, but you're not the punchline, Ethan. You're part of her armor."

I swallowed hard, her words settling uncomfortably in my chest. I looked out over the mountains, my jaw tightening. "So, I'm her shield against the sharks?"

Samantha shook her head, her voice softer now. "No, you're the leviathan in the deep, Ethan. Not a shield. You're her partner in this. And if anyone can make those snobs think twice before underestimating her—or you—it's Ethan Miller."

The air grew quiet between us, charged with unspoken thoughts. I finally met Samantha's gaze, a flicker of determination sparking in my eyes.

"Well, when you put it like that," I said, a small, crooked grin breaking through, "I guess I'd better make damn sure I don't let her down."

Samantha smiled back, her expression filled with something I couldn't quite place—admiration, maybe, or understanding. "You won't. And remember, they're kind of predictable. Louis has trained you, and he is the best. The others are all pomp and circumstance. You will be noticed. Just take advantage of it."

"I feel like a broken record, but are you sure? I'm not interested in being noticed."

A flash of amusement flickered in her eyes. "Like Isabelle said yesterday. No, you won't be able to avoid the attention. I would remind you, it's not like you're the first, I don't even know how to say this, non-elite, to attend one of these first-tier events."

I laughed. "You should have just said commoner."

She grimaced. "I hate that word."

I shrugged. "It's accurate, though. So I am not the first commoner to come to one of these. You're going to have to hand-feed me what you're trying to say, Sam."

She smiled when I called her Sam.

She continued. "The point that I was making... People are people. People find love with people outside the elite circles. There are plenty of titled individuals who have absolutely no means or prospect beyond their titles. And plenty of people with means that have nothing to do with royalty or nobility. 'Commoners,' as you call them, have been to these events before; even events like the Manson Ball. It's not about you per se; it's about Aunt Victoria. You coming as *her* escort is a novelty because of how privileged, titled, and desired she is."

I got it then. It took me a while, but I think I understood. "So if it was you and me going, people would care a lot less, but because it's your aunt, they are scandalized. I am getting that right?"

She nodded. "Which is why you won't be able to avoid attention. Who you are becomes important because of who you're with."

Damn. Yeah, I got it.

She touched my arm. "You're going to be fine, but if you get into a situation where you absolutely don't know how to navigate, just remember, fortune favors the bold."

She gave me a lopsided grin.

"Bold?" I echoed, an eyebrow raised.

"Why not?" she shrugged, the laughter still lingering. "Forget about the rest of them. Be you. They can't control that."

I went back to practice, and Samantha continued her yoga.

I kept sneaking glances at her. She remained, her presence solid and unwavering, as if she was trying to anchor me in this madness. For some reason, I felt really close to her.

I was just beginning to solidify those thoughts when her laughter rang out, light and airy. I turned, catching her delighting in something else altogether.

"What?" I asked, feeling my frown widen.

"You're cute when you're frustrated," she grinned, winking, that teasing spark flaring back into her eyes.

I rolled mine, trying not to smile but failing. It felt absurd to find solace in her words at a moment like this.

"Come on," she said, nudging me playfully. "It's time for you to complete your Cinderella transformation."

"Sure, but couldn't it be Fred Astaire?"

"You'd have to consider talking with cute animals less."

I snorted. "Well, in that case, Cinderella it is."

We made our way to the house.

Samantha

The house buzzed with energy as the final preparations for the ball came together. Louis's voice echoed from somewhere upstairs, issuing commands like a general preparing for war. Maya and Lily darted through the halls, giggling as they documented the entire transformative process with their new phones. Isabelle stood by the living room, looking effortlessly chic and far too amused by the chaos.

And then there was me, waiting at the base of the grand staircase, trying to act like I wasn't holding my breath.

The sound of footsteps drew my attention, and when Ethan emerged, it felt like time slowed. He wore a tailored dark suit, perfectly cut to highlight his broad shoulders and trim waist. The crisp white shirt contrasted sharply against his sun-kissed skin, and the black tie added a touch of classic elegance. His hair was styled—short, clean, and sharp—but still retained that effortless charm, like he'd just rolled out of bed looking that good.

My mouth went dry. Damn it, he cleaned up well. Too well. He had looked good at the Rusty Spur, his effort on his own showing that he cared what he looked like for our little outing. But someone had prepared him to look his best, and they did an amazing job. I briefly considered walking up to him, ripping off his shirt, and leading him to my room. I resisted. But my goodness, was it tempting.

"Wow," Maya said from somewhere behind me, her voice filled with awe. "Dad, you look... fancy."

"Fancy?" Ethan chuckled, adjusting his cuffs awkwardly. "I'll take that as a compliment."

Isabelle let out a low whistle, her gaze appraising. "Ethan, if you walk into that ballroom like this, half the aristocracy is going to faint. The other half? They'll be lining up to take you home."

I bit back a groan. Of course, Isabelle would say something like that. And of course, Ethan had the nerve to look modest about it, like he didn't know he looked good enough to be on the cover of GQ.

"Don't inflate his ego too much," I said, crossing my arms to mask my irritation. "It's already big enough."

Ethan's gaze flicked to mine, and his crooked grin made my stomach flip. "You think I've got an ego, huh?"

"You? Never," I replied with a smirk, but I quickly turned my attention to the stairs as another sound drew everyone's gaze.

Victoria descended like royalty, her hand lightly grazing the banister. The gown Genevieve had created was a masterpiece—a shimmering blue silk that clung to her figure in all the right ways before flowing into a soft train. The neckline was daring but tasteful, adorned with intricate beading that caught the light with every step. Her hair was swept into an elegant chignon, with a few loose strands framing her face, and her makeup was understated but flawless. She didn't just look stunning— she looked untouchable.

The room fell silent. Even Louis, also dressed to the nines, who always had something to say, looked momentarily speechless. His hand came up to wipe at the corner of his eye, and when he spoke, his voice was uncharacteristically soft. "My Lady... you are a vision."

Victoria reached the bottom of the stairs, her poise unshaken despite the scrutiny. "Thank you, Louis," she said, a faint smile gracing her lips. "I hope this will suffice."

"Suffice?" Isabelle echoed, her voice laced with disbelief. "Victoria, you're going to shut down the whole damned thing. No one else stands a chance."

I didn't disagree, but I couldn't bring myself to voice it. Instead, I busied myself by taking a few pictures with Maya and Lily, who were snapping away like paparazzi.

"Hold still, Aunt Victoria!" Maya called, her phone poised. "This lighting is perfect!"

Victoria indulged them with a small laugh, posing gracefully while the girls squealed over their shots. Ethan, meanwhile, stood slightly off to the side, his hands in his pockets and a faint smile on his face as he watched the scene unfold.

"Alright, everyone," Louis clapped his hands, regaining his usual exuberance. "Group photo! We need to capture this moment for posterity."

Victoria and Ethan moved to the center, with the girls flanking them like tiny attendants. Isabelle and I hovered at the edges, reluctantly pulled in by Louis, who insisted that no one was exempt.

Maria, one of the maids, took the picture.

When the pictures were done, the atmosphere shifted. It was time to leave.

The limo waited at the front, sleek and shining, a physical reminder of the evening ahead. Maya and Lily scrambled into the back with their usual enthusiasm, and Isabelle followed, leaving Victoria, Ethan, and me standing on the porch.

Victoria turned to Ethan, her gaze steady. "Are you ready?"

Ethan hesitated for a fraction of a second before nodding. "As ready as I'll ever be."

She smiled then, a rare and genuine expression that softened the sharp edges of her beauty. "Then let's go."

Ethan offered her his arm, and she took it with practiced ease. They descended the steps together, looking every bit like they belonged in this world of glittering decadence. And as I followed behind, I couldn't help but feel a pang of something I couldn't quite name.

Jealousy? Pride? Maybe both.

Whatever it was, it didn't matter. Tonight wasn't about me. Tonight was about Victoria—and Ethan—and the storm they were about to walk into.

Chapter Fifteen

Victoria

The cool evening air brushed against my skin as I stepped onto the porch, my hand lightly resting on Ethan's arm. For a moment, I allowed myself to savor the tranquility of the experience—the soft hum of the limo waiting at the end of the drive, the faint murmur of the girls' excited chatter from inside, and the steady warmth of Ethan beside me.

He looked... devastating.

I hadn't been prepared for it. When I saw him standing in the foyer earlier, dressed in that perfectly tailored suit, I had been struck speechless. It was no secret that Ethan was attractive. I knew it. Samantha knew it. Hell, most of the Internet knew it. But up until now, he had been attractive in that rugged, grungy, everyday way—broad shoulders, strong jawline, and those sharp, intelligent eyes. He was a man. A real man. But now... it was different. He was different. He was polished, refined, and utterly commanding. The way the suit clung to him spoke volumes about Louis's efforts. He hadn't just dressed him; Louis had transformed him into someone who could stand tall among the aristocracy and stand out. Stand out in a big way.

The boy was utterly striking. I had no other way to describe it.

He reached out to take my hand, his touch grazing my lower back, which was bare to just above my butt. His touch made me shiver, the fingertips brushing my skin. I felt a burn. A fire in my heart? Or my loins? I wasn't sure. It was a feeling I hadn't felt in a long time. It was going to be a long night.

I looked into his blue-gray eyes but quickly turned away. I felt my face warm.

"Thank you," I said softly as we walked toward the limo.

"For what?" He tilted his head, the faintest hint of a smile playing at his lips.

"For doing this. For everything. You saved our lives. You cooked us meals. You have shared your family time. And now you are escorting me to this silly ball. Thank you for putting up with all of it—the endless lessons, the scrutiny, the absurdity of it all. It's hard to believe it's been less than a week since meeting you and your girls. It feels much longer than that."

I grinned. "Yeah, I have that effect on people."

I punched him lightly with my unheld hand. "You know what I mean. I am very happy to have met you and your girls, Ethan."

"Me too, Vicki. Me too."

"Also, you look incredible."

"Well, thank you, my lady." He said with a shrug, a gesture so casual it almost made me laugh. "You are quite striking yourself. I'm just trying not to embarrass you."

I stopped then, turning to face him. The driveway stretched long and quiet behind us, the night alive with the faint rustle of trees and distant chirps of crickets. His words hung in the air, simple yet disarming.

"Do you really think you could embarrass me?" I asked, my voice quieter now, though the weight of the question was anything but.

His brow furrowed as he considered me, his gaze searching. "Yes. Of course. I am, what do the girls call it, basic? I know how important this is for you, and while I don't understand all the implications or how it might actually affect you, I don't want to be the reason it goes sideways."

I wanted to laugh at his honesty, his earnestness. Instead, I moved closer to him. I reached out and touched his face.

Also, I liked how he instinctively reached for my hips.

I touched him with my fingertips—his cheek, the line of his jaw, his lips. I touched him and looked into his eyes. "Ethan, you're not a liability. You're my strength tonight. You belong to me—with me, yes, with me. With me for the Ball. Yes. Please don't ever doubt that."

His jaw tightened, and for a moment, I thought he might say something. But he didn't. Instead, he gave a small nod, his eyes softening as he offered me a faint smile.

The limo door opened, Louis's head popping out with an impatient grin. "Are we having a heartfelt moment, or are we going to make this a fashionably late entrance, my Lady?"

Ethan rolled his eyes, and I felt a reluctant laugh bubble up. "We're coming, Louis," I called back, and Ethan guided me forward again.

Louis leaned into Ethan, grinning. I didn't hear what they said, damn it. But it made Ethan smile. He looked at me. I pretended not to notice. I saw him mouth something to Louis: *don't worry, only in the bathroom.*

Don't worry, only in the bathroom?

What did that mean?

The drive to the venue was quiet but charged. I sat next to Ethan, my heart beating fast and hoping he didn't hear it. Louis alternated between scrolling through his phone and issuing last-minute reminders.

Ethan, however, sat beside me, silent but not withdrawn. He stared out the window as the township of Silver Ridge gave way to the sprawling estates on its outskirts. I wondered what he was thinking. The quiet intensity in his expression was something I had come to recognize—part focus, part reflection.

I surprised even myself when I reached for his hand. Ethan's hand—large, weathered, like a piece of leather. I held his hand in both of mine. It was so warm. He didn't say anything; he didn't resist. The only indication that he even noticed was the trace of a smile at his lips.

When the venue came into view, I heard Ethan's breath catch.

I understood why. The Manson Estate isn't just a mansion. It was an estate in every sense of the word—complete with a castle, grounds, and guest cottages. Towering turrets framed the expansive property, the stone façade glowing in the warm light of hundreds of lanterns. A wide driveway curved toward a grand staircase, where guests in glittering gowns and tailored suits ascended with practiced elegance. The hum of classical music floated through the air, faint but tantalizing.

The scene was pandemonium. Tier 1 events were always crazy, but this one seemed like even more than usual.

Ethan leaned closer to the window, his eyes narrowing slightly as he took in the scene. "This... is something else."

Louis chuckled from across the car. "Welcome to the lion's den, my friend. Every international power broker, politician, magnet, and moron worth knowing will be inside those walls tonight. Smile, charm, and if all else fails, dance. You've got this."

Ethan's gaze flicked to me, his brow lifting in question. "That sound about right to you?"

I smiled, placing my hand lightly over his. "It sounds like a plan. But remember, Ethan, you're not here to impress anyone. You're here because I trust you. That's all that matters."

His expression softened, a quiet confidence settling over him.

The scene outside the Manson Estate was pure chaos—a glamorous, electric chaos. The driveway was lined with sleek black cars that gleamed under the cascading lights, while the walkway was a red-carpet spectacle alive with movement. Photographers jostled for position, their cameras clicking at a rapid-fire pace as guests ascended the grand staircase. The hum of voices, the flash of bulbs, and the muted strains of an orchestra from within created a symphony of opulence and anticipation.

When our limo pulled up, the energy seemed to shift. All eyes turned toward the car, the crowd's buzz amplifying as murmurs rippled through the onlookers. The car slowed to a stop, and the driver stepped out to open the door. I adjusted the skirt of my dress, smoothing the silk against my legs. Ethan stepped out first, his hand extended to me.

For a moment, I hesitated. Not because I doubted him, but because I knew the second I stepped out of this car, the night would begin, and there would be no turning back.

I placed my hand in his, and he helped me out with a steadiness that bolstered my own. Together, we turned toward the castle, the grandeur of it all reflected in the soft glow of the lights.

"Ready?" Ethan asked, his voice low and steady.

I glanced at him, the corner of my lips tugging into a small, resolute smile. "Always."

And with that, we ascended the steps together.

"That's Lady Harrington!"

"Who's her date? Is it true she's bringing someone new?"

"Get the shot! Don't miss it!"

Ethan and I stood momentarily as the public turned their attention to us. The world seemed to hold its breath.

Ethan commanded his space, his broad frame and confident stance immediately demanding attention. The lights caught the sharp line of his jaw, and his piercing gaze scanned the crowd with a mix of unease and curiosity. He adjusted his cuffs with casual ease, oblivious to the hysteria he'd just sparked.

The cameras exploded in a frenzy of flashes.

I stepped up next to him and grabbed his arm. The air became electric. A collective gasp rippled through the crowd as I squared up to my date, and a gust of wind caught the drape of my gown and the silt in my dress exposed a bit more leg than was otherwise proper. Heads turned, whispers ignited, and the paparazzi surged forward, their voices overlapping as they called my name.

"Lady Harrington! Over here!"

"Your Grace, Your Grace! Please, over here! Who's your escort tonight?"

"Young man. Countess, can you look this way?"

I was already holding Ethan's arm, but he turned and covered my hand with his, his calm demeanor anchoring me amid the chaos. His steady presence made me feel invincible, like we were the only two people in the world, and the angle of Ethan's body made me feel like a presidential candidate and he was my trusty bodyguard. Ethan smiled politely. He nodded and acknowledged, but his gaze seemed to scan constantly, like he thought I was in danger. Oddly enough, it didn't seem out of place—like he was simply acknowledging the crowd around us while keeping himself between me and the mob.

It made me think of Henry.

Together, we began our ascent up the grand staircase, stopping periodically for pictures.

Ethan did not blend in. It felt like every eye was on us, every ear listening for our moderated conversation. I was used to attention, but this was strange even for me.

Reporters lined the walkway, their questions firing off like bullets.

"Lady Harrington, who designed your dress?"

"Young man, how does it feel to attend such a prestigious event?"

"Countess, is this a formal debut for you and your date?"

Ethan kept his composure, his lips twitching into a polite smile as we passed by. He exuded an unassuming charm that only seemed to intrigue the crowd further.

Halfway up the stairs, an attractive reporter managed to edge closer. She was young, with sharp cheekbones, amazing chocolate hair, and a confident air that suggested she was used to getting what she wanted. Her microphone was poised like a weapon.

"Mr. Miller," she called, her tone honeyed but insistent. "It's Mr. Miller, right? Please, a quick word? The world is dying to know—how did you meet Lady Harrington?"

Ethan paused, realizing someone actually asked his name. I watched as Ethan's eyes found the reporter. He watched her briefly, his expression contemplative. Her face went a bit pink. Ethan then turned, glancing at me before stepping slightly forward, again shielding me from the prying cameras. His smile was warm but guarded as he addressed her.

"Lady Harrington and I met under rather unique circumstances," he said, his deep voice cutting through the clamor. "Let's just say she has a knack for making an impression."

The reporter's eyes lit up, sensing a story. "Unique? Care to elaborate?"

Ethan chuckled, shaking his head. "I think you'll find the Lady herself far more interesting than anything I have to say. I will simply say that I met the Countess through one of her charitable efforts."

His charm was disarming, his tone polite but firm. Before the reporter could press further, he shifted slightly, his gaze steady but kind. "If you'll excuse me, my Lady has heels on, and I need to get her inside. Enjoy the ball," he added, moving forward and effectively ending the exchange.

As we continued up the stairs, I leaned closer, my voice low enough for only him to hear. "Are you are secretly some sort of politico? How—when—did you—how are you already so good at this? You handled that well."

He glanced down at me, his grin lopsided but genuine. "You don't get to be a cowboy without knowing how to sidestep a charging bull."

I snorted. "Ethan, you aren't a real cowboy."

He grinned. "I know, but wasn't that a great line?"

I laughed, in a rather unladylike way I might add, the sound light and genuine amid the whirlwind around us.

The doors of the Manson Estate loomed ahead.

Chapter Sixteen

Victoria

Ethan and I crossed the threshold of the Manson Estate, and even I, who had been here before, had to let out a bit of a whistle. The entry was absolutely breathtaking. The foyer was expansive, with soaring ceilings adorned with intricate frescoes that depicted mythological tales in painstaking detail. The polished marble floors gleamed under the light of crystal chandeliers, their refracted glow giving the space an ethereal quality. Reporters, staff, security, and caterers moved around continuously as the elites mingled.

The hum of voices grew louder, layered with accents from around the world. I knew the event was going to be well attended. It was one of the reasons I had initially planned to avoid it and had made an appearance at Samantha's Gala last week. The Manson's Ball, as a Tier 1 or World Class event, wasn't just for the elite of Silver Ridge or even the state. An event like this one was a convergence of the powerful from Eastern Europe, Britain, and the United States. Men in sharp tuxedos and women in dazzling gowns, dripping in diamonds, rubies, and emeralds, moved through the space with the kind of practiced elegance that could only come from generations of privilege. Titles and whispered legacies hung in the air like an invisible fog.

A group of European nobles swept past us, their conversation in rapid French. One man in particular stood out—a distinguished figure in a navy tuxedo with a regal bearing that could only mean one thing: old money. Ethan's eyes narrowed slightly as he studied them.

"Who's that?" he murmured, leaning closer to me. His warmth was grounding, a reminder that I wasn't navigating this alone.

"That's the Duc de Clermont," I whispered back. "One of the wealthiest landowners in France. His family's vineyards supply most of the champagne served at events like this."

"Of course they do," Ethan muttered under his breath, his lips quivering into a faint smile.

To our left, a cluster of American elites made their entrance. A woman in a shimmering gold dress was at the center of their group, her laughter loud and unapologetic. Beside her, a man with dirty brown hair shook hands with almost everyone he passed, his movements smooth and calculated.

"That's Rebecca Rockwell," I said, gesturing discreetly. "Her family owns half the media outlets in the U.S. The man with her is Senator Brian Clayton; he has been pursuing Ms. Rockwell for almost a year. He's... persistent, but her father hates him."

Ethan seemed to consider my words. "How could you possibly know that? The father thing, I mean?"

I gave him a wink. "What can I say? I am well informed."

Ethan nodded, his expression unreadable as he observed the crowd. But when we were guided toward the grand entryway, his focus sharpened.

The entry to the ballroom was breathtaking. Twin marble staircases curved downward in perfect symmetry, framing the space like something out of a fairy tale. The banisters were gilded, the railings adorned with intricate designs that seemed almost alive in their detail. Above, a massive stained-glass dome cast kaleidoscopic colors over the room. And at the base of the stairs, an enormous set of oak double doors stood open, revealing the ballroom beyond—a glittering expanse of polished floors, gilded mirrors, and tiered chandeliers.

Ethan paused, his gaze sweeping over the architecture with a newfound appreciation. "This place..." he murmured, shaking his head.

I tilted my head, intrigued. "What is it?"

"It's modeled after Château de Chantilly," he said, his tone almost reverent. "I read about it once. The staircases, the symmetry, even the stained-glass dome—it's all inspired by the château."

I blinked, startled. "Ethan, how on earth did you know that?"

Ethan shrugged. "When you spend a lot of time reading to two little girls who love castles and princesses, you pick up a thing or two. I also love the Bond films. Though Roger Moore was my least favorite."

Louis, who was suddenly by our side like a freaking magician, stopped abruptly and turned, his expression one of genuine surprise. "Ethan, my friend, you continue to impress. Most wouldn't recognize the inspiration here, let alone call it by name."

Ethan met his gaze, his confidence unshaken. "Really, I would think that anyone who has as much taste and culture as I do would recognize it instantly."

I snorted in a very unladylike way.

Louis's grin widened, clearly delighted. "Ethan, you're being super gay again."

He put a finger to his lips and winked. It was Ethan's turn to snort. I just shook my head. Ethan's casual knowledge had drawn both Louis's admiration and my own. As we descended the staircase, I caught the glances of other attendees—curious, calculating, intrigued by Ethan's appearance.

And I couldn't have been more pleased.

Louis searched through the crowd. "You two make your way in. I have something to attend to."

I cocked an eyebrow at this. "Something wrong?"

Louis looked at his phone. "Wrong? No, I don't think so. But let me see first."

With that, he was gone.

We reached the ballroom, where the full spectacle of the evening unfolded before us. The orchestra played softly in the background, their music weaving through the conversations and laughter. Attendants circulated with trays of champagne and hors d'oeuvres, their movements practiced and seamless. The room itself seemed alive, a pulsating hub of influence and ambition.

As we entered, the whispers began again, the weight of a hundred gazes falling on us. Ethan didn't seem to notice or care; he kept looking around the space, clearly intrigued by the layout and architecture.

A young man, probably in his twenties, approached us. A waiter, but he sure looked fancy. The waiter was polite, his bow practiced and discreet, as he took our drink orders. He returned moments later with our drinks. I sipped my champagne, the cool bubbles barely soothing the simmering nerves that coiled in my chest. The room hummed with conversation, laughter, and the faint strains of the orchestra—a flawless symphony of aristocratic indulgence.

But all I could see were the stares.

Everywhere we moved, women turned to look at him. Ethan, in his impeccably tailored suit, stood out. He radiated something raw, something real, in a room full of polished pretenses. And they noticed.

The younger ones stole shy glances, some giggling behind lace fans or whispering comments. The bolder ones, both unmarried and married —my contemporaries—didn't bother with subtlety. They stared openly, their expressions a mixture of intrigue and hunger. Lady Evelyn Blackmoor, draped in an emerald gown that clung too tightly for good taste, exchanged a smirk with her friend, Lady Anneliese Fairmont. I knew that look.

"Do they not have better things to do?" I muttered under my breath, my tone sharper than I intended. I had really hoped that the Blackmoors weren't going to be here tonight.

Ethan didn't seem to notice—or perhaps he chose not to give it his attention. He moved beside me with calm confidence, his touch consistent and affectionate. He touched my hand, my hips, and my upper arm. He guided me, stepping between others as he ventured deeper into the room. His presence grounded me, yet he remained infuriatingly unaware of the stir he was causing. I doubted he realized the effect he had on these women—or me.

We continued into the ballroom, and I caught glimpses of familiar faces. The French ambassador was holding court near the orchestra, his laugh too loud and his glass perpetually half-full. A cluster of Americans —oil and tech moguls with their surgically enhanced wives—lingered near the bar. And, of course, the European nobility, lords and ladies from centuries-old houses, cloaked in traditions as heavy as their jewels, glided through the crowd like sharks circling prey.

This was my world. And tonight, Ethan Miller, with his working-class roots and disarming charm, had somehow become its unexpected focal point.

I caught movement ahead of us. A little girl, no older than four, ran across the polished marble floor, her tiny feet slipping in her excitement. Before I could warn her, she tripped, landing hard on her hands and knees. Her cries pierced the air, drawing the attention of those nearby.

Without hesitation, Ethan knelt beside her, his movements quick but gentle. The murmurs around us swelled, curious eyes turning toward the scene he'd created.

"Hey there," Ethan said softly, his deep voice soothing even from where I stood. "That was a rough fall. Are you alright?"

The girl's tears slowed as she looked up at him, her wide eyes still glistening. She sniffled, her tiny fists wiping at her cheeks. "I—I fell," she said, her voice trembling.

"I saw that," he replied with a small smile. "But you know what? You got back up. That's what brave girls do, isn't it?"

Her sniffles stopped entirely, her gaze locking on his face with sudden wonder. "Are... are you a prince?"

I stifled a laugh, but Ethan's response was as smooth as it was endearing. "Me? Nah, but I can see that you're a princess, and if you'll let me, I'd be honored to be your knight for the evening."

The girl's face lit up with a smile, her earlier tears forgotten. She said in a small voice, "What is thy name, sir knight?"

She said this like she was quoting Chaucer. Coming from a four-year-old, it was the most adorable thing I had ever seen in my life. Ethan grinned, putting his hand over his heart and giving the child a slight bow. The position was awkward, but Ethan made it look graceful. "You can call me Ethan, my Lady, and what shall I call you?"

The child gave Ethan the brightest smile I had ever seen and said, "I am Anna."

"Then you shall be Princess Anna."

The two just smiled at each other.

"Now," Ethan said, still smiling at Anna, "Princess, can you point me to your mom, so I can escort you back to her?"

Anna's face suddenly went sad. It literally broke my heart. "Mommy isn't here—but GramGram is!"

"Then we shall find GramGram," Ethan said.

Around us, the whispers grew louder. I could see the women watching—Lady Evelyn, Lady Anneliese, even the oil baroness with her diamond-encrusted clutches—all melting into expressions that bordered on adoration.

Ethan stood, carefully helping the little girl to her feet as a woman, probably her nanny, hurried over, gratitude etched into every line of her face. I waved her off, already knowing what Ethan would do.

Then, without speaking a word, Ethan leaned down and scooped the little girl into his arms, her small frame cradled effortlessly against his chest. She let out a high-pitched giggle and laugh, then blinked up at him with wide, tender eyes, her earlier tears replaced by an almost dreamlike trust. Her tiny arms wrapped around his neck as she nestled her head against his shoulder, the motion so natural it made my chest tighten.

"Alright, Princess Anna," Ethan said softly, his voice carrying a warmth that seemed to melt the air around us. "Let's get you back to your court."

I couldn't suppress the small smile tugging at my lips. Trust Ethan to charm a child into forgetting she'd been crying just moments ago.

"There," pointed Anna, her head still cuddled up to Ethan. (I really wished I had my camera at that moment). "There's GramGram."

Ethan turned, his eyes scanning the crowd until they landed on a figure seated near the grand staircase—a woman whose commanding presence could have silenced an entire room. The Duchess of Belhaven, Lady Margaret Astor-Blythe.

Lady Astor-Blythe watched Ethan with amusement. I paused momentarily. Lady Astor was actually here. Genevieve had been right.

Lady Margaret Astor-Blythe had earned her reputation as a formidable force within the aristocracy. Widowed young, she'd never remarried and had taken the reins of her late husband's extensive shipping empire, transforming it into a global powerhouse. Known for her sharp tongue and sharper mind, she was equal parts respected and feared. Yet, her presence was odd. She rarely came to events. People were uncomfortable around her, and she rarely played politics. But she was here with Anna. Interesting. As Ethan approached, her stern features softened, her steel-gray eyes warming as she watched the little girl in his arms.

"GramGram!" Anna giggled. She tightened her grip on Ethan's neck, her tiny fingers clutching the lapel of his jacket.

Ethan reached the Duchess and gave her a polite nod, his usual ease tempered by the weight of the moment. "Your Grace, I believe this young lady belongs to you."

The Duchess rose gracefully, her movements belying her years. She reached out, her hands steady as she brushed a strand of blonde hair from Anna's face. "Thank you, young man," she said, her voice rich and resonant, every syllable carrying the authority of a lifetime of command. "Anna has a knack for making new friends."

"She's a princess," Ethan replied, a crooked smile tugging at his lips. "Knights always look out for princesses."

Anna giggled at that.

The Duchess's gaze lingered on Ethan for a moment, her keen eyes assessing him. Whatever she saw must have met her high standards because a small, genuine smile touched her lips. "Indeed. And she's lucky to have found such a gallant knight."

Anna squeezed and was fully resting her head on Ethan's shoulder. She had also closed her eyes. Those same eyelids fluttered as she snuggled into Ethan, pulling him closer. The sight was unexpectedly tender, a stark contrast to the Duchess's formidable reputation. She hesitated for a moment, then gestured for Ethan to follow her to a nearby settee.

"I apologize for any trouble she caused," the Duchess said as she settled onto the settee. "Her parents are abroad, and I'm afraid I indulge her more than I should."

"No trouble at all," Ethan said, his voice warm and genuine. "She's a bright little girl. Sweet. Reminds me of my daughters when they were little."

The Duchess's lips twitched into a faint smile, reaching out and brushing a hand over her granddaughter's hair. "She reminds me of her mother at that age—spirited, headstrong, and utterly exhausting."

I stepped forward then, her expression poised but curious. "Lady Astor-Blythe," I said, my voice smooth and practiced. "It's lovely to see you this evening."

The Duchess looked up, her sharp gaze flicking to me. "Lady Harrington," she said, inclining her head in acknowledgment. "It's been some time; you are as ravishing as ever."

"It has, and thank you," I replied, my tone warm but measured. "Anna's grown so much since I last saw her."

"She has," the Duchess said, her gaze returning to Ethan. "And it seems she's taken quite the liking to your escort."

Ethan shifted slightly. "She's a charmer," he said simply, his grin easy but respectful.

The Duchess's eyes narrowed slightly, not in suspicion but in consideration. She looked from Ethan to me, a spark of intrigue flickering in her gaze. "Lady Harrington, would you be so kind as to formally introduce me to your companion?"

There was a bit of a gasp, indicating two realities: one, people were listening to their exchange, and two, the people listening recognized the fact that Lady Astor-Blythe was asking for a formal introduction to the young man.

This young man had no ties, titles, or connections. Lady Astor-Blythe wanted to connect. Lady Astor-Blythe never wanted to connect.

I smiled, my chin lifting just a fraction. "Lady Astor-Blythe, may I introduce you to Mr. Ethan Miller? Ethan is a former military man, professional fighter, and a father of two young girls. He agreed to escort me as a favor. Ethan, please say hello to the Duchess of Belhaven, Lady Margaret Astor-Blythe. She is the wife of the late William Astor-Blythe and the head of the Tudors Shipping Conglomerate."

Ethan gave her a slight bow as Anna was still in his arms.

The Duchess nodded slowly, her expression inscrutable. "Victoria. You and I will have a chat. Please bring Mr. Miller. I would love to get to know him."

The Duchess then turned to Ethan. "Young man, if it's not too much trouble, please save a dance for this old lady."

Ethan gave her another slight bow. "I would be honored, Duchess."

Lady Astor-Blythe did something unexpected. She winked at me and spoke in a whisper. "I'll look forward to seeing how he manages tonight."

With that, the Duchess turned her full attention back to Anna. The nanny removed her from Ethan's arms. Ethan and I stepped back into the crowd, the weight of her gaze lingering long after we'd left her side.

As we moved through the throng of glittering guests, I cast a glance at Ethan, who seemed more at ease than he had any right to be. He caught my eye and raised a brow. "What?"

"Nothing," I said, a small smile playing on my lips. "I swear you are a lucky charm or something."

Chapter Seventeen

Louis

Ah, the Manson Ball. A shimmering, glittering behemoth of an event that never failed to dazzle and drain me simultaneously. If Silver Ridge had its version of Versailles and Woodstock, this was it, and I was here for every ridiculous, over-the-top moment. The chandeliers dripping with crystals, the perfectly symmetrical flower arrangements, the couture gowns that probably cost more than some small countries' GDP—it was a spectacle designed to impress and intimidate in equal measure.

I perched by the bar, sipping a martini (dirty, of course) as I surveyed the scene. The crowd tonight was textbook upper-crust drama —European nobles who still thought their titles meant something, American tycoons whose money made them pushy and demanding, Hollywood starlets looking for the princess treatment, and everyone in between. It was a delicious cocktail of egos, ambition, and more insecurities than a middle school dance.

Ahhh...my people.

But tonight, the real star of the show wasn't a prince or a CEO or even Victoria Harrington herself. No, the unexpected centerpiece of this gilded circus was Ethan Miller.

The kid cleaned up well. I mean, I knew he'd be a hit, but even I had underestimated the effect he'd have on this crowd. He wasn't just handsome—he had that raw, grounded presence that made him stand out in a room full of polished artifice. The way he carried himself, the way he spoke to people, with genuine warmth and interest—it was refreshing, almost disarming. He didn't belong here, and yet, somehow, he was the most magnetic person in the room.

I watched as he moved through the crowd with Victoria on his arm. He wasn't trying to impress anyone, which, ironically, made him all the more impressive. While the other men in the room were puffing up their chests and throwing around their titles, Ethan was... just Ethan. He greeted every person with the same level of respect, whether they were a duchess or a server. It was maddeningly endearing.

The scene with little Anna was straight out of a Hallmark movie, and I loved every second of it.

And Victoria. My darling Victoria. She looked radiant tonight, of course. Genevieve had outdone herself with that gown, and Victoria wore it like the queen she was. But that description didn't quite capture it. My lady laughed more easily, her smiles coming quicker. It was like her grace, beauty, and aura just turned up to eleven. It was almost magical. And I'd bet my best pair of Louboutins that Ethan had something to do with it.

I turned my attention back to the crowd, my trained eye picking out the key players of the night.

I saw Lord Alexander Blackmoor enter the room to less fanfare than he was used to. He was ever the wolf in his impeccably tailored charcoal suit, standing surrounded by his usual cadre of sycophants. His smile, all charm and teeth, was perfectly calculated—too perfect, in my opinion.

It wasn't genuine; it was a mask, a weapon honed over years of manipulation.

I bristled at the sight of him. I'd never liked Blackmoor, not when Henry was alive and certainly not now. There was a slickness to him, a constant undercurrent of ambition that felt more like a snake slithering through tall grass. He moved through the aristocracy with the grace of a dancer but the cunning of a predator, always two steps ahead and playing a game no one else seemed to fully understand—or perhaps cared to.

Henry, on the other hand... Henry had been a man of substance. A true noble, not just in title but in character. Where Blackmoor schemed, Henry strategized; where Blackmoor manipulated, Henry inspired. Watching Alexander now, his laughter too loud and his charm too practiced, I couldn't help but think how much better the world had been when Henry was still in it. Blackmoor had always been a thorn in Henry's side, a rival whose lack of scruples made him dangerous. And now, without Henry to temper his influence, Blackmoor was flourishing in ways that made my stomach turn.

"Slippery as an eel in oil," I muttered to myself, my tone dripping with disdain. I had no doubt he'd slither his way over to Victoria at some point tonight, like a spider weaving a web. He always did. And it was up to me to ensure that this time, he didn't get the chance.

I searched halfheartedly for Robert Haverford, my least favorite of Victoria's suitors. Robert was the worst. A childhood friend who had spent time with my lady in her youth, Robert had long held an almost obsessive desire for her. Everyone knew it. He had stepped back when Henry married my lady, too much of a coward to provoke Henry directly, but he had slithered out of the cesspool he was spawned from since Henry's death and in the last several months been getting more aggressive.

I would have to try to find a way to neutralize him. I wondered how much it would be to hire a hitman?

I was joking; mostly.

When he finally arrived, Robert entered the ballroom like he owned the place, his sharp suit tailored to perfection, his smile just shy of smug. His date, a stunning but vapid Spanish actress, clung to his arm like an accessory. What was her name again? Lucia? Lola? Something that ended in "a." She was all legs, hair, and air; pretty, sure, but utterly devoid of substance.

I couldn't suppress the smirk that crept onto my face as I saw him glance in Victoria's direction. He'd brought his little showpiece here tonight for one reason and one reason only: to make Victoria jealous. How predictable. How utterly boring.

And completely ineffective, I thought with a gleeful flick of my wrist as I sipped my drink. Because Victoria wasn't looking at Robert. She wasn't even aware of his existence at that moment. Her focus was entirely on Ethan.

And so was everyone else's.

The orchestra shifted then, the music swelling as the evening's first formal dance was announced. A ripple of movement spread through the room as couples began to pair off, some gliding toward the dance floor with the kind of confidence that came from years of lessons, others hesitating at the edges, unsure of their steps.

I leaned forward, my martini forgotten as I watched Ethan extend his hand to Victoria. He didn't make a grand gesture of it—no bow, no flourish—just a simple, steady offer. She hesitated for only a moment before placing her hand in his, her lips curving into a soft smile that spoke volumes.

They moved toward the dance floor, drawing attention as they went. Even the boldest women who had been ogling Ethan all night seemed to falter, their gazes shifting between him and Victoria with a mixture of curiosity and envy.

The music began, a waltz that was as intricate as it was elegant. Ethan led Victoria with a confidence that shouldn't have surprised me at this point but still did. His movements were fluid, precise, almost instinctive. And Victoria... she was glowing. They moved together like they'd been doing this for years, their connection so seamless it was almost unfair to the rest of us mere mortals.

Across the room, Robert's jaw tightened, his hand clenching around his glass of scotch. He leaned in to whisper something to his date, who giggled and flipped her hair in response. It was a pathetic attempt to reclaim attention, and it failed spectacularly.

"Well done, kid," I murmured to myself, a rare moment of genuine affection sneaking past my usually sardonic exterior. Ethan wasn't just holding his own—he was thriving. I laughed softly, delighted by the turn of events. Tonight was already proving to be far more entertaining than I'd anticipated.

And as Ethan spun Victoria effortlessly across the dance floor, the thought struck me with a clarity that sent a thrill down my spine. I needed to keep Ethan as part of Victoria's world. I didn't know what that looked like or how. But Ethan was making Victoria happy, borderline joyful. I would have to figure that out later.

As I leaned casually against the bar, savoring my martini and the increasingly entertaining dynamics of the evening, a cluster of younger guests caught my eye. They were like a flock of fledgling socialites, their excitement bubbling just below the surface despite their best efforts to maintain poise.

Ah, but what's a glittering evening of old-money power plays without the exuberance of youth to shake things up?

Leading the group was a girl I recognized instantly—Lady Penelope Hastings. Her long, chestnut-brown hair cascaded down her back in soft waves, framing a face alive with curiosity and youthful determination. Her warm brown eyes sparkled with an enthusiasm that was uniquely hers, a blend of innocence and ambition that only a 17-year-old standing on the edge of adulthood could embody. She was vibrant, a beacon of energy that seemed to illuminate the space around her.

The Hastings name had garnered much attention recently. Penelope's older brother, Lord William Hastings, had only just inherited the title after the tragic death of their parents in a plane crash two years ago. At twenty-five, he was now the head of their household—one of the smaller noble families but with substantial influence and wealth thanks to their deep connections to British banking. Despite his youth, William had quickly made a name for himself as both savvy and shrewd, though the circumstances of his rise were undeniably bittersweet. Penelope, still growing into her role within the aristocracy, carried herself with an eagerness and passion even if she was lacking in common sense.

Last year's Spring Fashion show comes to mind. Young ladies who are attractive, impulsive, and have trust funds can get into A LOT of trouble.

Behind her, two other young women trailed closely, whispering animatedly. I heard snippets of Italian and Spanish as the three conversed. I knew them, by sight if not personally. One was the petite Contessa Sofia della Torre from Italy, her honey-blonde hair twisted into an elegant chignon, her green eyes bright with mischief. The other was Doña Adriana Navarro, a striking girl with jet-black hair and sharp, intelligent eyes, representing one of Spain's oldest if not influential families. All three were dressed impeccably, their gowns age-appropriate but still dripping with the kind of designer flair that would make even the most seasoned fashionista take notice.

Lady Penelope approached me with purpose, her heels clicking confidently against the marble floor. I watched her with amusement, knowing full well she had something brewing. She'd been a standout at a youth fashion show in Milan last year, and her vibrant personality had left an impression on me. The girl was a hurricane of ambition, charm, and a touch of innocent naivety, and I adored her for it.

"Monsieur Delacroix!" she exclaimed, her voice carrying just enough excitement to make her companions giggle. "It *is* you. I thought I saw you earlier."

"Lady Hastings," I greeted warmly, setting my glass down and spreading my arms for an air-kiss on each cheek. "You look fabulous, as always. And who are these charming young ladies you've brought along?"

Sofia and Adriana blushed slightly but introduced themselves with polite curtsies. I gave them an approving nod. "A contessa and a doña. Penelope, your circle is as impressive as your fashion sense."

Penelope laughed, waving off the compliment. "Oh, stop. You'll make my head too big." Then her tone shifted, her excitement bubbling over. "So, who *is* he?"

Ahhh, I should have known this was coming. I blinked innocently. "Who?"

She rolled her eyes dramatically. "Don't play coy, Louis. Everyone's talking about him. The tall, handsome man who walked in with Lady Harrington. Ethan Miller. He's... *everywhere* on social media. My feeds are flooded with pictures of him, Samantha Harrington, and Hana Yamamoto, and he doesn't even have an account!"

Ah, social media. The great equalizer. I resisted the urge to laugh at her unbridled enthusiasm. I also decided to hold back the information that Ethan did have an account. Even if he didn't know it. "So, you already know who he is; that is quite disingenuous of you, Lady Penelope," I teased.

Penelope snorted, her cheeks pinkening slightly. "Well. I know some things. I want to know *everything*."

"You and Twitter have something in common," I said with a chuckle, leaning in conspiratorially. "Ethan Miller, 29 years old. Former military, single father, professional fighter. He has two beautiful girls, Maya and Lilly; you're actually only four years older than Maya."

Penelope considered this. "So that means he had a baby at—"

"Sixteen," I nodded. Ethan was young and had a baby with his horrible ex. I don't really think I need to go into that, though.

"Yeah, but four years is enough, right?" Penelope said this more to herself than to me. I couldn't help but giggle, internally though I didn't show it.

Sofia leaned forward, her green eyes wide. "Is he really dating Lady Harrington? They look... close."

"They are close," I said, choosing my words carefully. "But don't let your imaginations run too wild, ladies. Ethan's here as a favor to my lady. They are connected but not formally at this point. Ethan escorted my lady because he's grounded, loyal, and entirely too good for the likes of some of the vultures circling tonight."

Penelope's eyes narrowed slightly, a gleam of mischief sparking. "He seems genuine. That's rare."

"Very rare," I agreed, crossing my arms and regarding the girls with a knowing look. "But don't get any ideas, Penelope. You're far too young for someone like Ethan."

Penelope's eyes narrowed further, the gleam of mischief in her gaze only growing brighter. "Far too young?" she repeated, her tone laced with slight offense. "Louis, you're acting like I'm a child. I'm seventeen, and I will be eighteen in three weeks, practically an adult."

"Practically an adult," I echoed dryly, raising an eyebrow. "You're barely out of a youth fashion show in Milan. Ethan, on the other hand, is a grown man with responsibilities—two daughters, to be specific—and enough harrowing life experiences to fill a thriller novel."

She tilted her head, a playful smirk tugging at her lips. "You're making him sound like he's ancient. Twenty-nine isn't that old, and I would point out that I am closer to his age than he is to Lady Harrington, Louis."

"Age isn't just about the number, my dear Penelope; it's also about experience," I said with a pointed look. "And besides, you've got your whole debut ahead of you. You'll have plenty of young, eligible suitors vying for your attention soon enough."

Penelope waved a hand dismissively. "Eligible suitors? Please. Most of them are just prepackaged princes, pop stars, or posers with titles and trust funds. Ethan? I think he is different. I don't even know him and can already tell he's... real."

"Real and entirely out of your league," I countered, though I couldn't help but smile at her persistence. "I'm not saying you don't have charm, Penelope. But your stages of life are as far apart as the Spring and Winter Solstice. Ethan's seen loss; he's seen war. He's seen injury. He's seen failure and betrayal. He's seen violence and the results of rage. He may seem like a prince, and in a certain sense, he is, but he's also tortured."

Adriana, who had been listening quietly, leaned in with a thoughtful expression. "Is he dangerous, Louis?" she asked, her Spanish accent lending a lyrical quality to her words. "He wouldn't like to hurt us, would he?"

All three girls looked at me like I was about to serve them a massive helping of chocolate cake.

I wanted to facepalm. The princess type loves a bad boy.

I chose my words carefully. "Oh, he is dangerous. Just not in the way that you think. Trust me, ladies. Ethan isn't one to pursue. I wouldn't even fantasize about it."

Penelope's smirk deepened. "You are not helping my interest, Louis. You can't blame a girl for being curious, especially when the man looks like that."

"Yes, the beauty conundrum," I agreed, wagging a finger at her. "But curiosity and mischief are a dangerous combination, my dear. Stick to observation; besides, you don't want to deal with Samantha."

Penelope's eyes grew large, as did her companions. "Samantha... you mean Samantha... she likes him? Wait. No. I don't want to know; alright, alright. I promise I won't cause trouble."

"For once," I muttered under my breath, earning a playful shove from her.

It was typical Penelope—bold, spirited, and just a touch rebellious. As much as she enjoyed testing boundaries, I knew she respected them too. Still, I made a mental note to keep an eye on her. Mischief was her middle name, after all.

Adriana's face filled with wonder. "He does have an air about him. I have never seen someone who seems to care so little about the important people around them. He hasn't taken his eye off of Lady Harrington."

Sofia nodded in agreement. "Focused. Attentive. Wow. He—just—everyone else is trying so hard..."

I smiled, my affection for Ethan growing even more. "That's Ethan for you. Genuine to a fault."

Penelope sighed dreamily, clearly smitten despite my warnings. "Well, Lady Harrington is lucky to have him."

"Indeed she is," I said, glancing across the room to where Ethan and Victoria were now mingling with the crowd. "Trust me, darlings, the ball has only just begun."

As Penelope and her young entourage drifted away, their bubbling laughter still echoing faintly, I allowed myself a sip of martini and a moment to savor the delightful chaos of the evening. That serenity lasted approximately five seconds before I was ambushed by the unmistakable figures of Lord Algernon Whitley and Lady Francesca Montague.

Algernon's perpetually furrowed brow practically screamed trouble, while Francesca's sharp gaze locked onto me like a hawk spotting its next meal. This was going to be good—or catastrophic. Either way, I was intrigued.

"Louis," Francesca began, her tone both honeyed and urgent, "oh thank goodness you're here. I heard you weren't coming. We are in desperate need of your help."

"Oh Francesca, flattery will get you everywhere," I replied, spreading my arms theatrically. "But unless this is about champagne, scandal, or some salacious secret, I may need to feign a fainting spell."

"Be serious for once," Algernon grumbled, his tone as dry as a neglected martini. "It's about the charity auction."

"Ah, the pièce de résistance of the evening!" I exclaimed, delighted. "Do tell me, what's gone awry? Surely the jewel in this glittering crown of elitism is untarnishable."

Francesca leaned in closer, her voice dropping to a conspiratorial whisper. "We've had two last-minute dropouts from the date auction. One man, one woman. And we need replacements. High-profile replacements."

I raised an eyebrow, feigning shock. "Scandalous. Who dropped out?"

"Lord Ashcroft and Lady Marchand. It is a disaster. They were the headliners. We are scrambling. We need someone of prominence to fill the gaps or we won't get anywhere near the donations we need, and that would be terribly embarrassing."

"And you've come to me," I said, drawing out the words, "because...?"

Francesca offered a tight smile. "Because you know everyone who matters."

I tilted my head, considering her words. "And by prominence, I assume you mean someone who will draw attention. A star. A headliner. A... spectacle?"

"Yes," Algernon said curtly. "Exactly that."

I let my gaze sweep across the room, assessing the options. But I had a feeling I knew where this was going.

Then Francesca leaned in, her sharp eyes narrowing. "What about Lady Harrington?"

I froze mid-sip, blinking at her as if she'd suggested auctioning off the Crown Jewels. "Lady Harrington? *Victoria*? You cannot be serious."

"Why not?" Francesca countered, crossing her arms. "She's single, she's stunning, and she's the most talked-about woman in the room. The donations would be unprecedented."

"Yes, and she's also a widow," I replied, my tone sharp enough to slice through glass. "Do you have any idea how gauche it would be to parade her onstage like some gilded peacock? Absolutely not."

"Louis—"

"Not. Happening," I said firmly, cutting Algernon off before he could even begin to argue. "Victoria is upper crust and sought after; the bidding war would be ridiculous, but it would cause too much of a ruckus, which is the last thing that my lady would want, and certain individuals would use it as a chance to open courting discussions. That is unacceptable. I will not allow anyone that kind of access to Lady Harrington. She is still in her mourning period. It would be tacky."

Francesca frowned, but before she could press further, my gaze landed on Ethan. He was standing near the edge of the dance floor, looking rugged and magnetic. He had just finished twirling Victoria with surprising grace, his easy charm drawing smiles from everyone around him. And that's when the idea hit me.

"What about him?" I asked, gesturing toward Ethan.

Francesca followed my gaze, her brows lifting in surprise. "Him? But he's..."

"Perfect," I said, cutting her off before she could finish. "Handsome, mysterious, and completely unexpected. He's the cowboy in the castle, the rogue among the royals. The bourgeois and the proletariat alike will love it. Trust me, he'll be the highlight of the auction."

Algernon frowned. "But he's not—"

"Exactly," I said, interrupting him again. "He's not one of *us*. That's the whole point. The women will go wild for him."

Francesca hesitated, her gaze darting back to Ethan. "Do you think he'll agree?"

I smiled slyly. "Leave that to me."

I paused. "And I actually might have an answer for your other participant as well. Let me make a phone call."

Chapter Eighteen

Sarah

I swirled the wine in my glass, but the rich red liquid did nothing to soothe my nerves. The hushed conversations around me—the laughter, the clinking of glasses, the soft glow of candlelight illuminating Le Jardin's pristine white tablecloths—none of it mattered. My mind was elsewhere.

I had been annoyed prior. My girls and Ethan were totally ignoring me. Usually, I would be okay with them not checking in; they were supposed to be camping in the woods, fishing, cooking on stovetops, doing normal boring mundane things. But now that I knew they were in Silver Ridge hanging out with that Harrington woman and her model niece, it was all I could think about.

I still had no answers as to how they met, why they were spending so much time together, and what any of it meant. It was driving me nuts.

Because neither my daughters nor Ethan were responding (at least with anything helpful), I had been left to stalk Maya, Samantha's, and Lady Harrington's social media. It didn't take long, but I caught wind that something was going on from Maya's Instagram as pictures of a luxury spa day came across her feed. Something about helping the Countess get ready for the ball.

Lady Harrington was getting ready for some sort of event.

The next clue came in the form of Maya taking pictures of an amazing blue dress and a dark-colored suit.

Her caption was simple: "What do you think? How will they look in it?"

She didn't elaborate further.

The comments section buzzed with excitement:

"That dress is stunning! Who's going to wear it?"

"The suit looks sharp! Can't wait to see them on someone."

"Is there a special occasion coming up? What aren't you telling us???"

"They'll look amazing in these outfits!"

While the commenters speculated about the outfits and potential events, none seemed to have concrete information. This only deepened my curiosity. What event were they preparing for? And who exactly were "they"? I needed to find out more.

It was then that I decided to take a break. I got away from it for a while, but eventually came back. I couldn't help myself. I needed answers.

I shouldn't have looked.

I knew it would only piss me off.

But the moment I opened Instagram and saw the latest post from Lady Victoria Harrington, I felt my stomach drop.

It was a picture of them.

Ethan, standing beside her at the Manson Ball, looking every inch the perfect gentleman. He was in an amazing dark-colored suit, a perfectly tailored ensemble that accentuated his broad shoulders, burly arms, and tapered torso. He cut his hair. He cleaned up his face. His blue-gray eyes popped. I'd never seen him so made up. He had always been strong, handsome, but it was like someone latched on to his greatest features and turned it up to 11.

Even worse, Ethan looked like he belonged there, his stance easy, his expression effortlessly self-assured.

Lady Victoria Harrington was right beside him, dressed in the stunning ocean blue gown, poised and elegant, her hand lightly resting on his arm. The caption beneath it was maddeningly simple:

A wonderful evening at the Manson Ball with someone important.

Someone important?

As if he was part of her world.

I clenched my teeth as I scrolled through the comments.

"Power couple energy! 🤍 🔥"

"I don't know who he is, but I need to know immediately."

"Lady Harrington is always ahead of the curve. Look at this man. LOOK AT HIM."

"Ethan Miller? Just found his account. Thank me later."

I nearly dropped my phone.

His account? Since when did Ethan have an account? He hated social media. I made sure he hated it.

I clicked the tagged name, and my stomach twisted as @ethan-millerofficial loaded onto my screen.

100K followers. Verified. In a day.

The account was active; full of newly posted photos. From just that week alone, there were dozens of pictures; Ethan eating dinner, Ethan shopping, Ethan practicing martial forms out in the yard, Ethan cooking with Maya, Lily, and the Harringtons, Ethan dancing with a stunning Latina woman. The account was getting updated as I watched in real time. Candid shots of Ethan speaking with nobles, standing beside Victoria. A video of Samantha Harrington adjusting Ethan's tie, laughing at something off-camera.

I exhaled sharply, my irritation simmering, but before I could shove my phone away, another notification popped up.

Maya Miller posted a new story.

I hesitated for half a second before clicking on it.

First, a photo.

It was of Ethan and Victoria standing together, captured mid-conversation, his hands on her hips, her hands touching his face. There was a limo in the background.

I stared at the picture. It wasn't like the staged photos from earlier; this was intimate, almost casual, like they were completely at ease with each other. She was in the middle of saying something, like she was trying to comfort him. Lady Harrington was looking deep into his eyes, a clear expression of adoration on her face. She looked serious.

Too serious, like nothing else in the world mattered but him.

Maya's caption was simple but effective:

Question? Is it good to be lovey-dovey with friends? 👀

The blood in my veins turned ice-cold.

I clicked to the next story before I could even process the full weight of that comment.

This time, it was a video. Taken in the biggest living room I have ever seen; there was a massive fireplace in the background and art every-where. I even recognized some of the pieces.

Ethan was in the center of the frame, laughing as he lifted Samantha Harrington into the air, spinning her around effortlessly while she shrieked in mock protest. Victoria was in the background off to the side, shaking her head, clearly amused. Lily was clapping in the corner, giggling madly. Samantha's voice rang out as she clung to Ethan's shoulders, breathless from laughing.

The caption was just as simple:

It's always fun watching my dad play with one of his girl friends. 🩶

I froze.

I felt sick.

I don't know Samantha Harrington, but I know her reputation. Samantha is known for her cool personality; the cool, guarded, unattainable Samantha Harrington. This persona was so much a part of her image it's basically her brand. But here she was, laughing, playing, and teasing him the way a girlfriend, not a girl FRIEND, would tease her man.

My grip on my phone tightened, my pulse hammering in my ears.

First, Maya's posts were really popular, with a ton of likes, comments, and follows. I know how handsome and charming my ex-husband is, but seeing it confirmed in real time isn't something I want to see.

But that isn't the worst. The worst of it was watching Samantha Harrington act like a schoolgirl in love.

Like he was into her and like she was into him.

I gritted my teeth, setting my phone face down on my lap.

No. That was unacceptable. She doesn't have my permission to be with Ethan. The thought was ridiculous.

I needed to end this.

He couldn't remain with these women, and the girls couldn't remain with him. I would have to enact my plan sooner rather than later.

I had been generous with custody—more than generous—but this? This was a problem.

My phone buzzed again.

Louis Delacroix posted a new story.

I exhaled sharply, forcing myself to relax. Louis wasn't directly involved in any of this, despite being Lady Harrington's secretary. Delacroix was a socialite, not a threat, because there was no way that a man like that would let Ethan close to the Harringtons without good reason. Delacroix was known for his good taste. He wouldn't let this slide. But when I clicked on his story, any sense of control I had left shattered.

The video was short, taken from across the ballroom. Ethan was standing near the stage with a group of men, looking slightly annoyed as he adjusted his cuffs.

Louis's voice could be heard laughing over the footage.

"Okay, friends, you're some of the first in the know. Ethan Miller is going up for grabs! As many of you know, the Dating Auction is a long-term tradition at the Manson's Ball. I just got a request for Ethan to be part of it. Ladies, prepare your wallets; this could get interesting."

No.

No, no, no.

I watched the video again, my brain scrambling to make sense of what I was seeing.

Ethan was being auctioned off?

A charity auction. That's what this was. A date auction at one of the most obnoxiously high-profile events of the season. Women would bid on him for a chance to spend time with him, to claim him for the night.

That thought made me really angry.

Vanessa took a slow sip of her wine, eyes flicking toward my untouched plate. "You've barely touched your food, Sarah. Is everything okay?"

Nicole smirked, leaning in with a conspiratorial whisper. "Are you looking at your kid's Instagram again? You should have gone with them, and then you could hang out with them and stop obsessing over your ex."

James groaned. "Excuse me? Did you really just say that in front of me?"

"Oh, relax, James," Vanessa said, waving a dismissive hand. "It's an expression. It's like saying you have a crush on Brad Pitt. It's not real, and really, it's not our fault that Ethan Miller is the most interesting man on the internet right now."

Nicole sighed dramatically, glancing at me. "It is impressive, Sarah. You managed to marry and leave a man who went from complete nobody to mystery heartthrob overnight. Do you have a talent for picking future celebrities, or are you just really bad at holding onto them?"

My nails dug into my palm beneath the table. "Oh, please. He's not some overnight sensation."

Vanessa smirked. "Really? He is everywhere."

Nicole giggled. "Even I followed his Instagram. Have you seen it? He looks so good; it's really amazing."

I forced a smile. "How nice for him."

James scoffed. "He's not special. The only reason anyone cares is because Victoria Harrington paraded him around like a peacock. Sad, really."

Vanessa rested her chin in her hand, amused. "And yet, none of us are the ones standing next to Lady Harrington at a royal-adjacent ball. That's Ethan." She turned to me. "Tell me, Sarah, how does it feel watching another woman turn your old handyman into the internet's most eligible bachelor?"

I clenched my jaw. "I couldn't care less."

Vanessa grinned. "Mm-hmm."

Nicole sighed wistfully. "Honestly, I'd kill to be at that ball. All those men in suits, all that money—"

"You'd bankrupt yourself in the first hour," Vanessa teased.

"Worth it," Nicole said, unbothered. "And speaking of money, did you see the update from Mr. Delacroix?"

That caught my attention. My fingers twitched toward my phone, but I forced them to stay still.

Vanessa smirked. "YES! Ethan's going to be the highlight."

Nicole practically purred. "Can you imagine? Women fighting over him, bidding obscene amounts just for the chance to take him out."

I couldn't listen to this anymore.

I shot up from my seat, ignoring the confused looks from the table.

"Sarah?" James said, his tone sharp.

I barely heard him. I grabbed my clutch, smoothing my expression into something calm and collected. "Excuse me," I said lightly. "I need to make a call."

Before anyone could respond, I turned on my heel and walked—no, marched—toward the exit.

I didn't care about the restaurant, or the dinner, or the prying eyes of Vanessa and Nicole as they whispered about me the moment I left.

I needed to fix this.

The second I stepped outside, the cool night air hitting my flushed skin, I dialed my lawyer.

It rang twice before he picked up. "Sarah?"

"What we talked about. Do it," I said immediately, my voice sharp and unwavering. "I don't care what it takes—just get started. Tonight."

There was a beat of silence. "Sarah, these things take time. You can't just—"

"I don't want excuses," I snapped. "I want action. Get it done. Do it now, or I will tell your wife I have been blowing you in your office."

A slow inhale on the other end of the line. "Don't be hasty. What has got you so worked up? Is this about Ethan?"

"It's about my daughters," I said coldly. "And making sure they aren't raised by a man who has no business pretending he is something he is not and acting like he can move on like I am nothing."

Another pause. "You understand what you're asking, don't you? This isn't a simple request, and this is likely going to get ugly."

"I understand perfectly," I said, my grip tightening on my phone.

The image of Ethan in that suit, standing beside Victoria, standing on that stage, flashed in my mind.

No.

I wasn't going to let this happen.

I wasn't going to let him win.

"I'll expect an update in the morning," I said firmly before hanging up.

I took a deep breath, smoothing down the front of my dress. My heart was still racing, but I felt steady now. Focused.

This wasn't over.

Not by a long shot.

Chapter Nineteen

Victoria

Dinner proceeded without a hitch. For an evening filled with potential landmines of social faux pas, it was a surprising relief. The meal was, of course, exquisite—filet mignon cooked to perfection, soufflés that melted on the tongue, and wine that tasted like liquid gold. It was all perfect. Ethan even held his fork correctly.

That thought made me chuckle.

Seated beside me, Ethan navigated the evening's conversational currents with an ease that belied his working-class roots. Lords of the English Court and elites from across America had joined our table, their conversations peppered with talks of stocks, land acquisitions, and political clout. Ethan didn't speak out of turn, didn't fumble or misstep. He listened intently, asked thoughtful questions, and somehow managed to charm even the most jaded of them.

There was, however, one who was giving him a bit more notice, and I was not a fan.

She introduced herself as Miss Madison Caldwell, a Texas oil heiress and the fiancée of some tech mogul whose name I barely registered. She was beautiful in an artificial, Barbie doll way, with platinum blonde hair, lips full enough to make her surgeon proud, and a gown so tight it left little to the imagination. She could have been anywhere from 30 to 50 and was mostly plastic. Her laugh was too loud, her perfume too strong, and her cup size was, as Louis would put it, "impressively engineered."

And she was utterly relentless.

"Oh, Mr. Miller," she purred, leaning far too close for propriety. "You have the most fascinating background. Military, you say? And now a fighter? You must tell me everything. Your life must be so... thrilling."

I tightened my grip on my champagne flute, struggling to maintain my composure. Her hand lingered on his arm for a fraction too long as she spoke, her giggles punctuating her every sentence. Ethan, ever the gentleman, smiled politely but kept his responses short.

She leaned over the table, giving Ethan a full blast of her cleavage.

I have rarely been in situations where I wanted to enact violence upon someone. I guess there is a first time for everything.

"It's not that thrilling," he said with a shrug, gently withdrawing his arm. He also sat up a bit straighter and kept his eyes on hers. "Mostly hard work and discipline. Nothing too glamorous."

"Oh, but I bet you've got some stories," she pressed, her perfectly manicured fingers brushing his sleeve again.

"Not as many as you might think," he replied, glancing at me briefly.

It was a small thing, just a flick of his eyes in my direction, but it felt like a lifeline. I returned his gaze with a subtle smile, silently willing my irritation to stay hidden.

Madison wasn't dissuaded, though. "Well, I'd love to hear all about it sometime. Maybe over a drink? Or—"

"I'm sure Mr. Miller's time is quite spoken for this evening," I cut in, my tone cool but civil.

Madison blinked at me, her painted-on smile faltering with clear irritation for just a moment before she recovered. "Of course, Lady Harrington. You're so lucky to have such a fascinating companion tonight."

"Indeed," I said smoothly, turning my attention back to Ethan, who was biting back a grin.

The moment passed, and the conversation shifted to safer, if duller, topics—until it didn't.

It was Lord Alistair Weymouth, one of the more irritating fixtures of the European aristocracy, who had been trying to get Madison's attention for most of the evening, blatantly ignoring his wife. A man of middling intelligence and excessive pomposity, I should have known he would try to stir the pot to make himself look good in front of the vapid blonde.

"So, Mr. Miller," he drawled, his voice dripping with condescension, "what's your take on the recent debate surrounding nobility's role in modern governance? Surely, as an outsider and yankee, I suspect you find the whole thing repugnant."

I bristled, ready to intervene, but Ethan surprised me.

He didn't flinch.

Instead, he met Weymouth's gaze with steady confidence. "I don't know if I would go that far," Ethan said, his voice measured. "Complicated is a better word. Nobility's reestablished involvement in everyday governance seems like a backslide. I think back to things like the Magna Carta and how hard the people worked for self-governance, and I wonder if it's wise to dig up old wounds, so to speak. Let's look at England, for example. They've had some amazing rulers, but that much power in the hands of a single person has the ability to really shape a country. Look at Henry VIII. Six wives, the establishment of the Anglican Church, the sacking of monasteries—all because he wanted to wed Anne Boleyn, who he executed not three years later. I understand that some people want to use their influence and stability for the greater good, but that type of power structure is dangerous. Ask the French about endless revolution; it's not a pleasant topic."

Weymouth raised an eyebrow, clearly not expecting such a composed response. "Well. I would expect no less from an American. Down with the monarchy and all that. Far from what I would call a nuisance position."

Ethan's lips curved into a faint smile. "Clearly, the concept of nobility, or at least the social elite, has its place in society. I think it is enviable to a certain point. We don't have traditional nobles, but we have similar social elites. Have you heard of the Kardashians? They have something like titles with money, fame, and the ability to affect people. Dealing with that type of power is difficult enough. Hereditary power is even worse and a lot easier to avoid. I think history has shown that it is not a good thing. The idea that an accident of birth gives you the ability to govern others is crazy to me."

The table fell silent for a moment, the weight of Ethan's words hanging in the air. Even Weymouth seemed at a loss, his attempt to trip Ethan up having failed spectacularly.

Louis, seated a few tables away, caught my eye and raised his glass in a silent toast. How on earth did he hear Ethan talking?

"Fascinating," Lord Hastings interjected, breaking the tension with a smile. "Lord Harrington, may he rest in peace, argued as much. The will of the people should be just that, the will of the people, not those who by accident of birth subvert it. Well said, Mr. Miller."

I nodded politely, his expression calm, but I could see the flicker of pride in his eyes. He'd navigated the discussion flawlessly, and I couldn't help but admire him for it.

Admiration, however, quickly gave way to something else.

Something more heated.

There was something undeniably sexy about the way he'd handled himself—confident but not arrogant, composed but not detached. The conversation had been polite, intellectual, and utterly captivating.

I needed a moment.

"Excuse me," I said, standing abruptly. "I need some air."

Ethan glanced at me with concern, flickering across his face. "You okay?"

"Fine," I said, offering a small smile. "Just a little warm in here."

As I stepped onto the balcony, the cool night air was a welcome reprieve from the stifling atmosphere inside. The stars twinkled above, and the distant hum of music from the ballroom softened into a faint melody. I leaned against the balustrade, taking slow, deep breaths to calm the flurry of emotions stirred by Ethan's performance at dinner.

How had he done that? Ethan had just intellectually outmaneuvered one of the most condescending lords of the aristocracy. It wasn't just his words that struck me; it was the way he'd said them—confident, grounded, and utterly unshakable. It had been... infuriatingly attractive.

It reminded me of my Henry.

Damn kid.

Before I could dwell too much on that thought, the sound of footsteps behind me drew my attention. I turned, half-expecting Ethan, but instead found Louis sauntering onto the balcony, martini in hand and a mischievous glint in his eye.

"My Lady," he drawled, his voice carrying that familiar note of theatricality. "I just witnessed a miracle. Is it Christmas already? Because Lord Weymouth may be a blowhard, but he is no fool. If I didn't know any better, I would have thought Ethan was a seasoned diplomat."

I rolled my eyes, though I couldn't suppress a small smile. "That was your doing, wasn't it?"

"On the contrary, I told him to avoid the topic. The cowboy must have looked it up on his own. It paid off," Louis teased, leaning against the balustrade beside me. "Victoria, my love, this man is an absolute gem. We should keep him. I say we adopt!"

I scoffed, though the warmth in my cheeks betrayed me. "Ethan isn't a dog, Louis. We cannot just say we want to keep him."

Louis' grin was borderline malicious. "Your mouth says one thing, my Lady, but your eyes and body language say another."

I glared at him, though there was no real heat behind it. "Did you come out here to spout nonsense, or do you actually have a reason?"

Louis grinned, setting his martini down on the balustrade. "As a matter of fact, I do. I need to speak with Ethan. It's about the charity auction, and I wanted to give you a heads-up before I did."

I raised an eyebrow. "What about it?"

"Well," Louis began, drawing the word out with dramatic flair, "we had a couple of participants drop out last minute. Tragic, really. But I've managed to secure replacements. And one of them is our dear Mr. Miller."

I blinked. "You're putting Ethan in the auction?"

"I plan to ask him to participate, yes," Louis said, as if it were the most obvious thing in the world. "He's the perfect candidate. Handsome, mysterious, a literal knight in shining armor. The women will go wild for him. And the resulting ordeal will be hilarious."

I crossed my arms, my gaze narrowing. "And what about the female replacement?"

Louis's grin widened. "Ah. Interesting question."

I paused and considered. I watched Louis, and he just continued to grin. "You didn't."

"I did," Louis said. "She's doing it for the cause, bless her heart. And between her and Ethan, I guarantee the auction will be the highlight of the evening."

Before I could respond, the sound of the balcony doors opening again drew both our attention. Ethan stepped out, his expression one of mild curiosity as he took in the sight of us.

"Am I interrupting something?" he asked, his tone easy.

"Not at all," Louis said, straightening with a delighted smile. "In fact, you're just the man I was looking for."

Ethan raised an eyebrow. "Louis, you were just inside; I am pretty sure you heard the whole conversation with Lord Windbag."

"Stop remembering random things, Ethan," Louis assured him, though his grin said otherwise. "Moving on, I need a favor."

Ethan glanced at me, and I gave him a small shrug.

Ethan nodded at Louis.

Louis wasted no time launching into his pitch, complete with dramatic gestures and just the right amount of flattery. To his credit, Ethan listened patiently, though I could see the moment he realized what Louis was asking.

"You want me to be part of the auction?" Ethan said, his tone skeptical.

"Yes," Louis said, clasping his hands together as if in prayer. "Think of it as your contribution to the evening's success. And it's for charity, Ethan. You're not going to say no to charity, are you?"

Ethan sighed, running a hand through his hair. "You're relentless, you know that?"

Louis beamed. "It's one of my many charms."

After a moment of hesitation, Ethan nodded. "Fine. I'll do it. But only because it's for charity."

Louis clapped his hands together, his smile triumphant. "Marvelous! I knew I could count on you. Now, if you'll excuse me, I have to make some final arrangements. Oh, and Ethan? Do try to enjoy yourself. You've already conquered the aristocracy tonight; the auction will be a breeze."

With that, Louis swept back into the ballroom, leaving Ethan and me alone on the balcony. He turned to me, his expression somewhere between amused and exasperated.

"When speaking with him, have you ever had thoughts like, I don't know, quicksand?" he asked.

I laughed. "Yes. I know exactly what you mean."

Ethan

So now I am going to be part of an audition, like a charity dating auction? Who does that? How is that a thing? Especially in these circles. Rich, powerful, influential people are auctioning off dates to each other?

Unbelievable.

Okay, so I am going to be brought by someone for a date. Why did I have a bad feeling about this? I couldn't help but think back to movies like *White Chicks* or *Date Movie*.

Those were done for comedic effect (I love Terry Crews). But in real life, people don't actually do crap like that. It's just crazy.

I could this going one way. Total and utter disaster. A date? Me? With someone I didn't know? How awkward. When was the last time I was on a date?

Oh wait, never; not since taking Sarah out when I was 15, and I'm pretty sure I did that on a dare.

Unless I counted the Rusty Spur with Samantha.

Was that a date? Did that count? I didn't really know.

Maybe I should just run away.

I didn't run away. Instead, Louis, Victoria, and I returned to our table just as dinner was finishing. People started to sip on hard drinks and finish up plates of dessert.

Before we knew it, the formalities of the evening dissolved into something much more relaxed, and I wasn't sure whether to feel relieved or overwhelmed. Gone were the carefully choreographed waltzes and rigid social rules, replaced by an atmosphere that felt... well, chaotic.

People were everywhere, mingling in clusters, laughing, and—most unexpectedly—dancing with an almost reckless abandon. The grand ballroom no longer felt like an intimidating castle of privilege but more like a middle school gym during a sock hop. If middle schoolers wore diamonds the size of my knuckles and couture dresses, that is.

I'd been prepared for a lot tonight and developed a certain amount of expectation toward this upper-class event. But this? I was not expecting this. This was something else entirely.

I'd barely stepped off the sidelines when the requests began. Women of all ages—some bold, some shy, others demanding and downright annoying—approached me for a dance. I obliged as best I could, mentally cataloging the dos and don'ts Louis had drilled into me. Be careful who you say "no" to and who to place on my dance card. Remember, don't hold them too close. Don't step on their toes. Pleasant conversation. Avoid deeper conversation. Kiss their hand if they are over 18. Make sure you don't accept too many or seem too available. Always accept invitations from the elderly. Easy, right?

Not so much.

One moment I was spinning an elderly French Countess who insisted I call her "Mimi," and whose husband looked like he wanted to punch me. Next, I was partnered—through the valiant efforts of what I could assume was her sister—with a young doe-eyed Southern belle, who blushed so furiously I wondered if she might faint. Then there were the parents—mothers and fathers alike—subtly (or not-so-subtly) trying to suss me out on behalf of their daughters. I assumed these were on behalf of the women closer to my age who had made their debut.

Man, this world was fascinating. Louis was by my side as my attendant. He kept track of my dance card on Victoria's behalf. A change from the original plan of having me run interference, but a welcome one. I would have to ask Louis why the change later.

By the time I finished my third dance in a row, my head was spinning almost as much as my feet.

I was just about to sit down when little Anna appeared.

"Sir Knight!" she squealed, her blonde curls bouncing as she ran toward me.

I crouched just in time to catch her. "Princess Anna! What are you doing? It's late!"

"Dancing!" she declared, her little hands tugging at mine. "Come please!"

Who could say no to that?

For the next two songs, I picked Anna up and went through a series of spins, twirls, and hops that left her giggling uncontrollably. Her laughter was infectious, and soon, a small circle of onlookers had formed, watching with amused smiles as we commandeered the dance floor. When the second song ended, I set Anna down, but not before she gave me a big squeeze. Then, in perfect little princess fashion, she curtsied dramatically before running back to the Duchess, who nodded at me with a rare, approving smile.

A tap on my shoulder brought me back to the dance floor. The girl gave me a graceful curtsy and then looked me dead in the eye.

"Mr. Miller," the girl said with an exaggerated air of formality, extending her hand. "May I have this dance?"

I chuckled. Penelope Hastings has made her moved. I caught the eye of her older brother William, watching us in amusement not ten feet away. I raised an eyebrow, and he simply smirked. Apparently, I wasn't going to get any help from him.

I turned to face Penelope. I dipped my head. "Lady Hastings."

She gave me a puzzled and slightly shocked look, which she quickly hid. "You know me? Well, isn't that a pleasant surprise?"

Her tone was breathy and hopeful.

"I met your brother a bit earlier when he came to see Lady Harrington. He told me a lot about you."

Her eyes narrowed. "You met William, and he talked about... Wait, what did he say?"

Her expression shifted from delight to horror before she was able to mask it.

I smiled and tried not to chuckle. This was an impressionable young lady, and I would not insult her determination by laughing at her. "Lord Hastings was very complimentary. Something about being the jewel of your family and a paragon of virtue."

Penelope smiled but came off more as a grimace. "That does sound like him."

My eyes narrowed playfully. "Lady Hastings, I am curious. I thought young ladies of a certain age were not supposed to ask old men like me to dance. You should be careful; you may ruin your reputation spending time with such unsavory characters."

Penelope's eyes glittered. "Savory. Yes, that is more than an adequate description. As for my request, you should know, Master Miller, that I am almost 18. I can ask whoever I want to dance. As for the effect upon reputations, I assure you your virtue is safe with me. So what do you say? Will you dance with me?"

I studied her briefly. "Okay, but you cannot cause trouble."

"No promises," she said, grinning as I led her to the floor.

Penelope was a chatterbox, her words coming in a rapid-fire stream as we danced. She peppered me with questions about everything—my daughters, my time in the military, my favorite color. It was exhausting and endearing in equal measure. She wasn't shy about sharing her own opinions, either, and by the time the song ended, I felt like I'd just survived a pop quiz.

"You're everything and nothing like I expected," she said as I escorted her back to her group.

"I am not sure what that means," I replied.

She gave me a sly smile. "You will."

I didn't have much time to dwell on that cryptic comment because Victoria appeared next.

"Lady Hastings," she said, "I hate to butt in, but Ethan..."

She gave me a heated look.

"Dance with me?"

"Always," I said, taking her hand.

The energy in the room shifted when we danced. It wasn't the same as the formal waltzes from earlier. This was slower, more intimate. Her arms rested comfortably around my neck, and my hands settled lightly on her hips. We swayed to the music, the rest of the room fading into the background.

"Are you surviving the chaos?" she asked, her tone teasing.

"Barely," I said with a chuckle. "What about you? Any great prospects for the future Mr. Harrington?"

"Just one," she said, her smile tinged with something bittersweet. Then she stopped and adjusted her gaze.

The silence stretched before us.

After a moment, I said, "I don't know how you do it."

Her gaze softened, and she tilted her head slightly, studying me. "And what is that, Mr. Miller?"

"How you maintain such amazing composure in the light of the stacked odds. You inspire, my lady."

The compliment seemed to catch her off guard, and for a moment, she didn't appear to know what to say. The song shifted, blending seamlessly into the next, but neither of us moved to leave the floor. We stayed close, talking quietly, our voices lost in the murmur of the crowd.

Another song came on. And then another. And then another. We danced four songs together. Then others approached and were swept away with new partners. We came back three songs later.

Time seemed to melt away as we danced. It wasn't about impressing anyone or keeping up appearances anymore. It was just us—two people sharing a moment that felt completely separate from the chaos around us.

I didn't want it to end.

And judging by the way Victoria's arms tightened slightly around my neck, neither did she.

The end of the song came, and I reluctantly let go of Victoria, but not before I kissed her hand.

I looked across the room. "Excuse me, my lady. I believe I have a duty to fulfill."

Victoria followed my gaze as it wandered over to the Duchess of Belhaven.

Victoria tried to hide how pleased she was. "Enjoy. I should check my card."

I took a deep breath, straightening my jacket as I approached the Duchess of Belhaven, where she was sitting next to a very tired-looking Anna.

Lady Astor-Bylthe was whispering softly to her nanny, who was trying to gently remove the child. Lady Astor-Bylthe's commanding presence was undeniable, even as she carried herself with a grace that softened her sharper edges. She eyed me as I neared.

"Your Grace," I said, bowing slightly as I reached her. "I believe you requested a dance?"

The Duchess arched a brow, a smirk tugging at the corners of her lips. "Indeed, Mr. Miller. I am pleased you remember this old lady." Her tone was light, but her words carried the authority of someone used to having their requests met.

I offered my hand, and the Duchess took it with surprising warmth. I led her out to the dance floor and formally bowed. Not to be outdone, Lady Astor-Bylthe's curtsy was every bit as feminine and graceful as Victoria's.

I bet this woman was unstoppable in her early years. Probably a lot like Victoria herself. No wonder she was respected.

The music began, and I gently swayed with Lady Astor-Bylthe as she asked me almost as many questions as Lady Hastings. It amused me to no end.

Her tone shifted after a bit, becoming more serious.

"I have to ask you a favor, Ethan," she said in a voice that had zero brevity.

I nodded, indicating my willingness to listen.

"Anna turns 5 next month and has been talking about her birthday party for what seems like years now," the Duchess began, her voice steady as we moved in sync. "I know she just met you, but you left quite the impression on her. Maybe you remind her of her uncle. She made me swear I'd invite you personally. So, Mr. Miller, consider this your formal invite."

I chuckled, my grip firm but gentle. "It would be an honor, Your Grace. I'm not sure what I did to earn Anna's favor."

"So gallant, Sir Knight," the Duchess said, her sharp gray eyes meeting mine. "People in this world quickly develop a bollocks meter, and Anna has more experience with that sort of situation than most children should."

Lady Astor-Bylthe looked sad.

"Bollocks is like bullshit, right?" I said with a grin.

The Lady laughed. "Yes. Child. Bollocks is like bullshit."

My grin widened but then faltered. "What sort of bullshit has Anna had to deal with?"

The thought of the little girl having to deal with anything more serious than a basic scolding pissed me off to no end.

She looked me right in the eye. "A story for another time, I'm afraid, and I must say I am pleased to see how well you've done with Lady Harrington. Tell me, how did you get so well-versed with all our 'bull-shit' traditions?"

I shrugged. "Louis."

The Duchess let out another laugh. "I should have known. That man. Seriously, he is the best. And, for you, how have things been with Lady Harrington? Just from your perspective."

I considered it. How had tonight been? Honestly, for the most part, it had been fun. Victoria was incredible, and the experience was unique. I couldn't say that I would be rip-roaring to do this again anytime soon, but for the most part, I had very little to complain about. I got to spend time with a beautiful woman, and who could complain about that?

I settled on, "Victoria's an incredible woman. Being here with her tonight feels like stepping into a different world, but she's made it feel... natural."

The Duchess smiled faintly, though her gaze held a hint of concern. "Just be careful, Mr. Miller. This world has its own rules, and not everyone plays fair."

I raised an eyebrow. "Something I should know?"

The Duchess's lips thinned slightly, her tone growing sharper. "The Duchess of Haverford, Robert's mother, is here tonight. Eleanor Haverford doesn't leave her estate unless she's plotting something. And believe me, her son's interest in Lady Harrington is not without motive."

"Oddly enough, you're not the first to mention Robert," I said carefully, my jaw tightening. "Lord Hastings gave me a similar warning."

The Duchess gave a low, mirthless chuckle. "Of course he did. William is such a sweet boy. Horrible what happened to his parents. But Robert is a peacock—flashy, vain, and ultimately harmless, without someone pulling his strings. Eleanor, on the other hand, is a viper in pearls. Subtle, calculating, and utterly relentless. If she's circling Lady Harrington, it's for a reason."

My brows furrowed as I processed her warning. "I appreciate the heads-up, Your Grace."

The Duchess's smile returned, this time with a sharper edge. "Think nothing of it. And if Eleanor tries to corner you, don't let her old English charm fool you. That woman could make Satan blush with her manipulations."

The song drew to a close, and I escorted the Duchess back to her seat. As we reached her table, she paused, her expression shifting to one of sly amusement.

"One last thing, Mr. Miller," she said, her voice dropping to a conspiratorial whisper. "Eleanor Haverford has spent decades trying to outdo me in every way—charity work, social influence, even grandparenting. But tonight, you've managed to make her seethe simply by existing! Well done."

I couldn't help but laugh. "Glad I could be of service, Your Grace."

The Duchess inclined her head, a glimmer of genuine warmth in her eyes. "Do take care of Lady Harrington, Mr. Miller. And don't forget Anna's birthday party. She'd never forgive me if you missed it. It's next month in Mayfair. I will send the jet for you, and feel free to bring your lovely daughters."

I paused. Mayfair? Like Mayfair, England? I turned to look at Lady Astor-Bylthe.

Apparently, she knew exactly what I was thinking. "You heard me, child. I will send the private jet for you and your children. I would also like to introduce you to my sister's youngest daughter."

She winked. I laughed again. *Such a lovely woman.*

I made my way back to Victoria. The soft hum of conversation in the ballroom was interrupted by the clear chime of a bell. A voice rang out, rich and commanding, silencing the crowd.

"Ladies and gentlemen," the announcer began, "the charity auction will begin shortly. Please make your way to the auction hall."

I turned to Victoria, who was now standing beside Louis, her expression calm but her eyes sparkling with anticipation. Louis caught my eye and gave me a wink.

"Ready for round two, Mr. Miller?" Victoria teased, her lips curving into a playful smile.

I grinned. "As ready as I'll ever be."

The trio moved with the rest of the crowd, the buzz of anticipation growing louder as they approached the auction hall. Whatever came next, I knew one thing for certain—this night was far from over.

Chapter Twenty-One

Victoria

Thus far, the evening had been almost magical, a sharp contrast to my experience at any event since my dear Henry's passing. I had been so reluctant, afraid to place myself in the situation I was currently in, that I realized I had been hiding.

It's amazing how quickly things change.

Well, no more of that nonsense. I suddenly felt brave and in control. It was a delightful feeling, and I was ready to face what came next. With much fanfare, the focus of the event began.

The charity auction commenced, and Lord Alfred Montgomery commanded the stage with his usual flair. A seasoned and charismatic figure within the aristocracy, Lord Alfred was known for his charm, eloquence, and ability to command a room with ease. In his mid-50s, he exuded an air of refinement and confidence, balanced with a genuine warmth that made him widely respected, even by those who might not fully trust him. I didn't personally know him very well, as he and Henry didn't really run in the same circles. I did know his son, who had a thing for Samantha when she first came on the scene and adopted my last name.

The press set up for the auction with haste, having been ushered away from the ballroom during the informal portion of the evening—a common tactic for tier 1 events. But they had to be let back in as Manson Ball had reached its most anticipated event, and in just a few hours, the whole ordeal would be done.

I turned to look at Ethan, his profile handsome in the lights. I admit I was going to be sad when we finished. It had been an evening to remember.

The room hummed with excitement as Lord Montgomery introduced the cause—the Windsor Foundation's Education Initiative, a program aimed at funding scholarships and improving access to education for underprivileged children.

As he detailed the night's goals, I found myself half-listening, my mind already preoccupied with what was to come. The auction always held its surprises, but tonight's promised to be particularly unpredictable. Two participants had dropped out, Lord Ashcroft and Lady Marchand, but their replacements, Samantha Harrington and, shockingly, Ethan, had stirred up considerable interest.

I was really surprised to see that Lord Johnathan Ashcroft and Lady Viviane Marchand had dropped out. Lord Ashcroft, the quintessential playboy, rarely missed an opportunity to bask in the attention of society's elite—especially the debutantes, who clung to his every word. His absence was nothing short of suspicious, though not entirely shocking. He was probably at some exclusive afterparty in Monaco or Dubai, likely indulging in champagne and chasing a different sort of spotlight. The fact that Ethan was replacing him was somewhat amusing to me, as Ethan had taken the scene by storm. When Lord Ashcroft got around to checking on the night's events, as he certainly would, Ethan taking the spotlight would undoubtedly irk him. Lord Ashcroft thrived on being the center of attention, and seeing someone else, particularly an outsider, claim that position was sure to ruffle his feathers.

Lady Marchand's withdrawal, however, was laced with more intrigue. A fashion icon with an almost compulsive need to remain in the limelight, she had spent years crafting her image as the queen of style and sophistication. Samantha knew her well, and Lady Marchand had something of a rivalry with my niece. Lady Marchand wasn't exactly secretive about the whole ordeal either, but it was a one-sided competition; Samantha, ever confident, barely acknowledged Lady Marchand's existence, especially because Samantha's modeling jobs were fewer and farther between these days.

According to Louis, their sudden exits had initially caused a ripple of concern among the organizers, but with Samantha and Ethan stepping in, the roster had been reinvigorated in a way no one expected.

Not that anyone else knew Samantha and Ethan would be the highlight.

If anything, their replacements promised to make the evening far more memorable than if Ashcroft and Marchand had stayed. And judging by the buzz already spreading through the ballroom, everyone else knew something was going on too.

Ethan, seated beside me, looked calm, though his hand tightened around his glass. I reached over, brushing his arm lightly. "You'll be fine."

"This is stupid. I am stupid. Why am I doing this again?" he muttered. I probably wasn't supposed to hear that last part.

Lord Montgomery's voice rang out, pulling everyone's attention back to the stage. "Ladies and gentlemen, thank you for your generosity and enthusiasm. Tonight, we have a truly exceptional lineup, beginning with the lovely Miss Caroline Duvall."

And so it began.

Caroline's introduction was met with cheers. A classic debutante with impeccable manners and a dazzling smile, she strode onto the stage, radiating confidence. The bidding began modestly at £1,000 and climbed to £35,000, where it was won by a European nobleman seated with his equally delighted wife. I was pretty sure that she was related to Caroline in some way but couldn't remember. The room buzzed with approval.

The following participants varied widely in age, profession, and charm. An American actress. A Mexican oil heiress. Korean K-pop models, one male and one female. Some bids soared, reaching as high as £75,000, while others closed at more modest sums. Each new participant brought a wave of laughter and good-natured competition among the bidders.

Some might consider the whole affair tacky, but in fact, the charity auction was one of the long-time traditions of the Manson Ball. More than one relationship among the social elites had started at this very event.

The auction proceeded; more names were called, and the crowd grew increasingly lively. The hum of conversation, the excited bidding wars, and the occasional bursts of laughter created a dizzying backdrop.

It was then that I saw him.

I knew it would happen eventually. Robert Haverford had been circling all night, paying little attention to the beautiful Spanish actress he brought to accompany him. I am not dumb. I know why he did. Still, I was hoping that it would be a bit later. I had braced myself for this moment. He was, after all, the very reason I had dragged Ethan into this chaotic evening in the first place. I knew at some point he would approach me; that didn't mean I had to like it.

He approached with that calculated smile of his, a masterful blend of charm and arrogance. His polished demeanor, tailored to perfection, immediately set my nerves on edge. It had always irritated me, even when we were kids.

Out of the corner of my eye, I noticed Louis stiffen, his jaw tightening imperceptibly as Robert drew closer.

"Lady Harrington," Robert greeted me smoothly, his tone steeped in faux warmth as his eyes locked onto mine. "Might I have a moment?"

I forced a polite smile, though it barely touched my eyes. "Robert, I'd love to give you a moment, but as you can see, we're in the middle of—"

He cut me off, his voice low but firm, exuding a confidence that bordered on entitlement. "I apologize, Victoria, but it's important."

I glanced at Louis, who was already bristling, then turned back to Robert. "I see," I said, my tone carefully even. "Okay, Robert. Sit, please."

He lowered himself into the chair beside me, far too comfortably for my liking. The audacity of his intrusion was typical, but it still grated on me.

"Thank you," he said smoothly, folding his hands on the table. He didn't waste time. "Your companion for the evening is causing quite a stir." His gaze flicked briefly to where Ethan was seated a few tables away. "You used him masterfully to avoid my invitation. I thought I had you cornered. His use was unexpected, but effective."

I kept my expression neutral, though his words made me bristle. Before I could respond, he leaned in slightly, his tone growing heavier with meaning. "Victoria, it's time to stop pretending. You know why I'm here."

I arched a brow, feigning ignorance. "Do I?"

Robert's smile turned sharper, his mask of civility slipping ever so slightly. "You're a widow of remarkable status, with the ability to influence matters far beyond what most could ever imagine. Your place in society, your legacy—both are tied to decisions you make now. You need someone to guide you. Mold your potential. Henry was fine. I understand why you did it. But he is gone now. And I think it's time you started taking my interest seriously."

The audacity left me momentarily speechless. He didn't come here to ask; he came to dictate.

Before I could formulate a response, another voice cut through the tension, soft yet commanding. "Robert, darling," said Eleanor Haverford as she approached, her words honeyed but carrying the weight of undeniable authority. "Men of status do not speak to their women in that manner. At least not in public."

I turned, meeting her sharp gaze. She was a picture of poise, her icy elegance a stark contrast to her son's more overt confidence.

"Duchess Haverford," I said smoothly, inclining my head in acknowledgment. "How lovely to see you."

Eleanor's lips curved into a small, enigmatic smile. "Victoria," she replied, her tone laced with the kind of politeness that felt more like a warning than a greeting. "It's been far too long. You're as radiant as you were at your first wedding. You haven't aged a day. I was just speaking with your mother about the subject."

My stomach tightened. My mother?

"Were you now?" I said lightly, though my voice felt distant even to my own ears. "I didn't realize you were in contact."

Eleanor's smile deepened, her satisfaction barely concealed. "Oh yes. We have reconnected in the last year. She's been most helpful. We've had a fascinating conversation about the importance of preserving certain alliances, especially in times like these."

The subtle implication hung in the air, and I knew exactly what she was doing. Eleanor Haverford was many things—subtle wasn't always one of them, but tonight she had come armed. Whatever game she was playing, it was bigger than just Robert's usual advances.

I forced a smile, though my heart was racing. "It's always a pleasure to catch up with family and friends."

Her eyes glinted. "Indeed. And Victoria, do keep in mind—some opportunities only knock once."

With that, she turned to Robert. "Come along, Robert. Let's not keep Lady Harrington from her guests."

Robert hesitated for a moment, his expression unreadable, before standing. He gave me a curt nod, his mask firmly back in place. "Victoria, I'll see you again soon."

I didn't respond, merely offering a tight smile as they departed.

As they moved away, Louis leaned in, his voice low and sharp. "What the hell was that?"

I exhaled slowly, my grip on my champagne glass tightening. "Nothing good," I murmured, my mind already racing to piece together Eleanor's intentions—and why on earth my mother would be involved.

I nodded stiffly and watched the retreating backs of Robert and the Duchess. The Haverfords had been pushing for an "alliance" for years, but they only wanted the family connection with me—not my two brothers or sister. I think it was a pride thing. They didn't like that my family had agreed to the marriage proposal of Henry. Now it was different. If Eleanor was involved with my mother...

I shook off the thought as Lord Montgomery's voice rang out again. "And now, the moment many of you have been waiting for—Mr. Ethan Miller!"

The applause was thunderous. Ethan stood, adjusting his jacket, and strode to the stage with surprising grace. Under the bright lights, he looked devastatingly handsome, his broad shoulders and calm confidence commanding attention. My breath caught, and I found myself gripping the edge of the table.

I suddenly didn't want this to happen.

Lord Montgomery's introduction was enthusiastic. "A decorated veteran, an Mixed Martial Arts fighter, and a philanthropist in his own right, Mr. Miller is a unique addition to tonight's lineup. Ladies, gentlemen, prepare your paddles."

The bidding began instantly, Madison Caldwell leading with an audacious £50,000. Her confident smirk was met with a ripple of laughter, but the numbers climbed quickly.

"£75,000," called a woman from across the room—one of Ethan's earlier dance partners.

Madison countered without hesitation. "£100,000."

The room buzzed as the bids soared. Penelope Hastings entered the fray, her hand shooting up. "£200,000!"

There was a pause. No one had ever paid more than £100,000 for any one person in the history of this auction.

I looked for Lord Hastings. I found him shaking his head and laughing.

Ethan shifted onstage, clearly uncomfortable, but Lord Montgomery milked the drama. "Ladies and gentlemen, we're at £200,000. Do I hear £250,000?"

"£300,000!" Madison declared, glaring at Penelope.

The brunette from earlier joined in. "£350,000!"

Penelope's voice rang out again. "£500,000!"

The crowd erupted in murmurs. Madison hesitated, then raised her paddle. "£600,000."

The bidding war intensified. Penelope, undeterred, upped the ante. "£800,000."

The room fell silent, all eyes on Madison. She faltered, then shook her head, conceding defeat.

Lord Montgomery grinned. "Do I hear £900,000? £850,000, perhaps?"

Before anyone else could respond, Penelope raised her paddle one last time. "£1,000,000."

A collective gasp swept the room, followed by thunderous applause as the gavel struck. "Sold! To Lady Penelope Hastings for £1,000,000!"

Ethan looked stunned as he descended from the stage. As he passed our table, his eyes briefly met mine, his expression unreadable. My heart raced, though I wasn't sure if it was from the spectacle or Eleanor's earlier words.

The night was far from over, but one thing was certain—this auction had changed everything.

As the applause for Ethan's auction began to fade, the room settled back into a hum of murmurs and anticipation. Lord Montgomery was still on the stage, effortlessly commanding attention as he began introducing the next participant.

As the applause for Ethan's auction began to fade, the room settled back into a hum of murmurs and anticipation. Lord Montgomery remained on stage, a master of maintaining the audience's attention, his rich baritone carrying easily across the grand ballroom.

"And now," he began, pausing dramatically as he scanned the expectant crowd, "we have someone truly extraordinary. Ladies and gentlemen, allow me to present a woman who needs no introduction—but deserves one nonetheless."

The air in the room shifted, a palpable ripple of curiosity and excitement sweeping through the crowd. Everyone leaned forward slightly, their gazes fixed on the stage.

"She has graced the covers of *Vogue,* captivated audiences on countless runways, and turned the fashion world on its head. Designers clamor for her endorsement, socialites and A-listers envy her style, and the world's most influential figures compete for her attention. But tonight," Montgomery said, his smile deepening, "she is here for something far more meaningful. Joining us at the very last minute, a gesture as gracious as it is glamorous, I give you the incomparable... Samantha Harrington."

The doors at the back of the ballroom opened, and all heads turned in unison. There she stood—a vision of effortless elegance. Samantha Harrington stepped into the room as if she owned it, her confidence radiating with every measured step. She was a striking figure, draped in a floor-length, deep red silk gown that seemed to shimmer with every subtle movement. The plunging neckline, thigh-high slit, and intricate gold embroidery along the edges highlighted her statuesque frame, while the fitted bodice accentuated her athletically curvy figure. Long, wavy brown hair cascaded over her shoulders, catching the light as she moved, and her piercing hazel eyes scanned the room with a sharp, almost regal gaze. Her bold red lips and soft smokey eye makeup were a masterclass in refinement, completing the picture of absolute perfection.

There was a collective intake of breath, followed by an audible murmur as the crowd took her in. Even among the elite gathered here tonight, Samantha stood out—an untouchable star among mere mortals.

"She's exquisite," someone whispered nearby, voicing the sentiment that seemed to hang in the air.

As Samantha reached the stage, she paused briefly to smile at the crowd, a smile that somehow managed to feel personal despite the sheer number of people present. Montgomery extended a hand to help her ascend the steps, and as she took it, he continued his introduction.

"Miss Harrington is not only a global fashion icon but also a passionate advocate for numerous charitable causes. Tonight, she lends her considerable star power to this event, proving once again that beauty and compassion are a truly unstoppable combination. Samantha, thank you for joining us."

The applause erupted, a thunderous acknowledgment of her presence. Samantha inclined her head graciously, the smile still playing on her lips as she took her place at the center of the stage.

"Ladies and gentlemen," Montgomery concluded, "let the bidding begin."

I glanced around the room. Even the most composed attendees were unable to hide their awe. Men and women alike seemed transfixed, caught between admiration and envy. Beside me, I caught Louis raising a brow in approval, clearly impressed.

The bidding began at £25,000, but it was clear from the start that this would be no ordinary auction. A gentleman from the far-left table raised his paddle immediately, followed by a flurry of bids from several other tables. The numbers climbed quickly, each bid punctuated by gasps and murmurs.

"£100,000!" called a man I recognized as a media mogul.

CHAPTER TWENTY-ONE

"£150,000!" countered a confident voice from the back of the room.

Samantha stood tall, her expression calm but with the faintest hint of amusement in her eyes. She was in complete control, as if she were watching a game she knew she'd already won.

"£200,000," announced another bidder, a glamorous woman seated near the center.

The competition grew fiercer. By the time the bidding hit £350,000, the atmosphere was electric, with participants leaning forward in their seats and whispering furiously among themselves.

"£400,000!" called the media mogul again, his voice edged with determination.

Lord Montgomery grinned. "Do I hear £450,000?"

"£450,000!" came another voice, this time from a well-dressed woman who had been eyeing Samantha with admiration all evening.

The gavel hovered as Montgomery teased the crowd. "And £500,000? Surely such elegance deserves no less."

After a tense moment, the media mogul raised his paddle once more. "£500,000."

From the back of the room, a quiet voice echoed in the crowd. "£1,000,000."

Lord Montgomery called out. "We have another million-dollar bid —going once, going twice, sold!"

People went silent. They all turned to look to see a young man in his early twenties, with tousled brown hair and a soft disposition. Samantha watched him, her face confused. Then, after a moment, her expression changed to one of shock. Recognition could be seen in her eyes. Then, like a package of Mentos and a bottle of Coke, the room erupted into applause as the gavel struck. Samantha descended the stage with the same poise she had entered, nodding graciously to her winning bidder as she passed.

As she found a seat, the whispers resumed, and I caught snippets of admiration from all around the room.

"She's magnificent."

"I've never seen anything like her."

"Worth every penny."

I couldn't help but smile. Samantha had always made an impression. Two million made on two people. It was absolutely unprecedented.

Still, as I glanced toward the table where Robert and his mother sat, I felt a flicker of unease. Eleanor's expression was unreadable, but the calculating gleam in her eyes was unmistakable. Whatever she was planning, I had no doubt it would involve more than just whispers in the ballroom.

Lord Montgomery stepped forward to center stage, his presence commanding the attention of the entire room. The lights glinted off the silver accents of his impeccably tailored tuxedo, and he lifted his glass of champagne with an easy confidence. He waited a moment, allowing the applause and murmurs to settle before addressing the crowd.

"Ladies and gentlemen," he began, his voice rich and deliberate, "thank you for your enthusiasm and generosity this evening. I must say, you've outdone yourselves already, but I believe we've only just begun."

The audience chuckled lightly, and Montgomery's smile widened as he paced slowly across the stage.

"Now, before we continue, I feel it necessary to clarify what you'll receive for your gracious donations. For each successful bid tonight, the winner will be granted a unique opportunity—a date with the individual of their winning bid. These dates will last for precisely 12 hours and will be arranged by the Manson Foundation."

A ripple of excitement coursed through the room, and Montgomery raised a hand to calm the renewed whispers.

"Rest assured, this is no ordinary date. Each experience will be designed to highlight the passions, interests, and talents of the participant who made such a generous donation to such a worthy cause. Whether it's an evening at the opera, an adventurous horseback ride, or a private culinary lesson with a world-class chef, our foundation will ensure it's a memory worth cherishing."

The audience buzzed with curiosity and intrigue as Montgomery continued, his tone growing more serious.

"As a further note, all dates will be documented by a discreet professional team—highlights, not the private details, mind you," he said with a wink, earning a wave of laughter. "These moments will be shared on our social media platforms to show the good work your contributions have made possible and to thank our participants for their generosity."

He paused, his gaze sweeping the crowd. "And let us not forget the heart of this evening's event—charity. Every penny raised tonight will go toward funding the foundation's critical work, from educational scholarships to housing initiatives and beyond. So, bid with your hearts—and, of course, your wallets."

The room erupted into applause, and Montgomery raised his glass in salute. "Now, without further ado, let us continue this unforgettable evening."

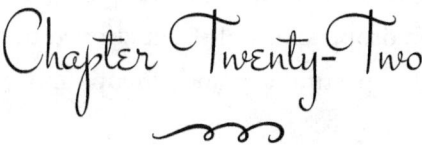

Chapter Twenty-Two

Samantha

I'd barely stepped out of the shower when my phone buzzed insistently on the bathroom counter. My first instinct was to ignore it, as I was already feeling a bit down. But when Louis's name lit up the screen, I paused.

He was with Aunt Victoria and Ethan at the Manson's ball. Seeing his name irritated me, as I was already annoyed at being left behind. I should have gone, even just to have the chance to dance with Ethan and hang out with my aunt.

I was acting so weird. I felt... attached to Ethan in a way that I really had no right to.

I looked at the phone again. Louis never called without a reason, especially in the middle of an event like the Manson Ball.

Could there be something wrong?

Wrapping a towel around me, I grabbed the phone. "Louis, what's going on? Everything okay?"

"Samantha," his familiar, smooth voice cut through the line, his tone a mixture of urgency and charm. "I need a favor."

I sighed, leaning against the counter. "A favor? This already sounds suspicious."

"Don't be dramatic," he said, but there was a smile in his voice. "Listen, Lady Marchand dropped out of the auction at the last minute. It's a disaster. Everyone's expecting a grand lineup, and we're one striking woman short."

I raised a brow, though he couldn't see it. "And you're telling me this because?"

"Because I need you," he said without hesitation. "They really should have asked you first, though they expected that you would decline. We need someone high profile, and let's be real, you've graced the cover of Vogue more times than I can count, and you'll completely overshadow Marchand anyway. You're not just the best option; you're the only real option."

"You know I hate these things, Louis," I reminded him, though secretly my mind was already racing, thinking, I don't like being left behind while Ethan was out with another woman, even if that woman was my favorite aunt.

"I know," he said quickly, his tone softening. "But they are desperate for a headliner, Sam. I know you don't care about their perception or reputation, but I know you care about causes, and this is a good one. It's for the Windsor Foundation and educational needs for the underprivileged. Think of the kids."

A groan escaped me as I pinched the bridge of my nose. Damn him for using charity as leverage. I was already thinking I was going to do it, but that cinched it for me. But there were some practical concerns. "Louis, I don't even know if I have a dress to wear, let alone if I can be ready in like 20 minutes."

"Leave that to the staff," he said with unwavering confidence. "The team is still there, and they will help you prepare. I've already told them. I've been informed you just got out of the shower."

I groaned. "Louis, how do you know I just got out of the shower?"

"Because I know everything, Dotti. You know that."

He continued, "You'll look stunning, as always. Please, Samantha. I wouldn't ask if it weren't important."

There was a pause, and I could hear faint sounds of chatter in the background—probably the ballroom. I made my choice. I exhaled. "Fine. But you owe me."

"Eternally," he promised, his relief palpable. "Get dressed and get here. You're the last in the lineup. You're up after Ethan."

"Ethan?" I froze mid-step toward my closet. "Ethan is participating? How? Wait. What? How did that happen?"

"Pretty much in the same manner that secured your participation," Louis said with a chuckle. "He's filling in for Lord Ashcroft."

Of course he was. My irritation flared. Lord Ashcroft was an asshat right up there with Roger, my ex. They were friends, actually. Ashcroft figured himself a modern-day Casanova. He hit on me constantly. "So I'm the backup to Marchand, and Ethan's Ashcroft's replacement? Fantastic. I hope you realize how absurd this sounds."

"Trust me, Samantha. It'll be worth it. Just hurry."

I hung up with a shake of my head and rushed to my closet. Fortunately, I had a gown stashed away—a last-minute backup I'd brought for a red carpet event. I was supposed to use it with Roger, but we ended up breaking up, and I didn't go to the event, which was a movie premiere if I remember correctly. The dress was a red silk masterpiece, stitched to perfection, with a plunging neckline, a thigh-high slit, and gold embroidery that caught the light. At least I wouldn't be underdressed for this circus.

The staff helped me get ready in record time. Hair styled. High heels strapped on. Stockings stretched over legs. I looked in the mirror and liked what I saw, all while Maya and Lily buzzed around me, excitedly taking pictures and offering their unsolicited opinions.

"You look fierce, Sam!" Maya gushed, holding up her phone to snap a photo. "This is going straight to Instagram."

"You're going to break the internet," Lily added, her grin mischievous. "Everyone is going to lose it when he sees this. Daddy loves the color red. Mom used to wear it for him. He will love you in it."

The mention of Ethan made my stomach tighten. Ethan liked red. Well, isn't that fortuitous? I was going to take his breath away.

By the time I stepped into the car that would take me to the main entrance of the Manson estate, I was as ready as I'd ever be. My hair flowed in soft waves over my shoulders, and my bold red lips added the perfect touch of drama. If nothing else, I'd make an entrance.

As I approached the ballroom, I heard the muffled sounds of applause and Lord Montgomery's unmistakable voice. They were in the middle of auctioning off Ethan's time.

Maybe I should slip in and bid. He wouldn't be able to avoid a date with me then.

Louis told me to wait, and he was going to have Lord Montgomery announce me, so I listened just outside the main ballroom. I could see through a slit in the double doors. The room was alive with murmurs and whispers. My gaze immediately found Ethan standing on the podium. Damn, he looked so handsome, even if he was clearly uncomfortable. Barely perceptible, there was a tension in his shoulders that hadn't been there before. And then I heard it.

"£1,000,000."

It was a voice I recognized. Penelope Hastings' declaration rang through my ears as clearly as if she'd spoken directly to me. My mouth fell open slightly. A million euros. Someone had paid a million euros for a date with Ethan Miller.

I didn't know whether to be impressed or infuriated. He said he wanted to avoid attention, and yet here he was, the star of the night.

I felt like throwing something.

As I waited for my cue, I caught a glimpse of Penelope, seated with her brother, Lord Hastings. I knew William fairly well—we'd been sort of friends—but Penelope was a different story. She was younger, and I didn't know her very well. I did know that she was enthusiastic and clearly smitten with Ethan. I doubted she even realized the spectacle she'd made of herself.

I could see she was getting an earful from William.

That's right, William, you tell her that she shouldn't get her hopes up. She was too young for Ethan and he was...

He was what? Mine? No... he wasn't.

I felt a twinge in my heart. I did not like it.

And then, it was my turn. Lord Montgomery's voice boomed across the ballroom as he began my introduction. I straightened my spine, smoothed the fabric of my gown, and prepared to make my entrance.

"...joining us at the very last minute, a gesture as gracious as it is glamorous, I give you the incomparable Samantha Harrington."

The doors opened, and the room fell silent.

As I stepped into the spotlight, every head turned. I could feel the weight of their gazes, the hum of admiration and envy that followed me like a shadow. I wasn't here for them, but I'd be lying if I said I didn't enjoy the moment.

The auction was a whirlwind. The bids came fast and furious, climbing higher than I'd anticipated. By the time we reached £500,000, I was sure the media mogul in the corner would claim victory. But then, from the back of the room, a quiet yet firm voice broke through.

"£1,000,000."

I froze. The room erupted into murmurs, and all eyes turned to the young man who had spoken. I recognized him, but it took me a moment to place him—yes—Allen, the quiet young man I'd met briefly at a charity gala last week.

Wow. Has it only been a week? Feels like a lifetime.

Allen and I made eye contact. His gaze was warm, and I remembered him being charming, intelligent, and a bit of an enigma.

As the gavel struck, signaling the end of the auction, I descended the stage, my thoughts racing. Why had Allen bid so much? What did he want? And why did Ethan look so thoroughly unimpressed?

As I stepped off the stage, I felt the weight of a hundred pairs of eyes still on me. The applause echoed in my ears as I made my way back to my seat. Allen was seated a few tables away, giving me a polite nod and a faint, enigmatic smile. I returned it briefly, though my thoughts were spinning. Of all the people to bid that much for me, Allen was one I hadn't expected. I'd barely exchanged more than a few pleasantries with him at past events.

Before I could dwell on it further, I reached my aunt's table, and Ethan appeared at my side, his tall frame blocking out part of the room's glow. He adjusted his tie almost absentmindedly, as if unsure how to start. Then, with a small, self-conscious smile, he spoke.

"You were stunning up there," he said, his voice warm but soft enough that it felt like he was speaking only to me.

I arched a brow, crossing my arms as I looked up at him. "Stunning? Coming from the man who just fetched a million euros, I'll take that as a compliment."

He let out a small laugh, his hand rubbing the back of his neck. "Says the woman who accomplished the same feat not two breaths later. I mean it. You look amazing. You were... well, you owned the room."

His sincerity caught me off guard, and for a moment, I couldn't come up with one of my usual witty retorts. Instead, I just nodded, a faint smile tugging at my lips. "Thank you, Ethan."

Victoria joined us then, her graceful presence impossible to miss. Her eyes flicked between Ethan and me, and she offered a knowing smile. "He's right, you know. You look extraordinary. I don't think anyone's going to forget your entrance tonight."

I shook my head lightly. "You two are terrible for my ego, you know that?"

Victoria chuckled, her hand brushing my arm briefly. "That's what makes me such a loving and gentle soul."

Before I could respond, a bright, somewhat grating voice interrupted us.

"Ethan!" Penelope Hastings came bounding over, her enthusiasm barely contained. She looked positively giddy, her cheeks flushed with excitement. "We should talk. I am so excited about our date!"

I exchanged a glance with Victoria, who raised an unimpressed brow. It was clear we were both thinking the same thing, and it wasn't very nice.

Ethan, ever the gentleman, turned to Penelope with a polite smile. "Penelope, I should really scold you. That was too much money for me..."

Penelope either didn't notice or chose to ignore the slight edge in his tone. Instead, she turned her attention to me, her eyes widening as if she'd only just realized I was there. "Oh! Samantha, you were incredible on stage. I mean, WOW. That dress! It's just... so you."

"Thanks, Penelope," I said with a tight smile. "You were very... enthusiastic during Ethan's auction."

She giggled, a sound that made my teeth clench. "Well, how could I not be? He's just so... perfect."

Victoria cleared her throat, stepping in before I could say something I might regret. "Penelope, shouldn't you be with your brother? He looked like he was heading this way."

"Oh, William's fine," she said dismissively. "He gave me a hard time too, but I told him, what is a massive trust fund for if not charity?"

She gave us a devilish grin. Ethan tried not to smile but did. It made my blood boil.

Lord Hastings appeared a moment later, his figure cutting through the crowd with ease. He approached with a calm, steady air, his sharp eyes taking in the scene with a flicker of amusement.

"Penelope," he said smoothly, his tone carrying a subtle reprimand. "I am pretty sure I just told you not to bother Lady Harrington and her date."

"And I told you that was a silly request. Besides, I just wanted to talk to Ethan and Samantha," she said, her tone defensive but still playful. "Isn't that allowed?"

William's gaze lingered on her for a moment before he sighed. He looked like he was going to say something to Penelope but stopped himself. Instead, he glanced at us. "Apologies. I hope she hasn't been too much trouble."

Victoria waved it off. "Not at all, Lord Hastings. Your lovely sister is always welcome. I can appreciate her admiration for Mr. Miller. It might even equal my own."

My jaw almost dropped. There were people around, and my aunt all but admitted she liked Ethan, though not in those words.

His lips twitched with the faintest hint of a smile. "You're very magnanimous, your Grace."

Before the conversation could continue, a sudden hush fell over the room. All eyes turned to the stage, where none other than Eleanor Haverford now stood, her icy poise radiating authority.

"Good evening," she began, her voice carrying effortlessly over the crowd. "I'd like to take a moment to thank everyone for their generosity tonight. This event is a testament to the strength and unity of our community."

Her words were polished and perfectly delivered, but something about her tone made my skin crawl. I glanced at Victoria, whose expression had tightened ever so slightly.

But then, something even more unexpected happened. As Eleanor continued speaking, another figure appeared on stage.

I blinked, my breath catching as I recognized her.

My jaw dropped—Lady Adela Pennington, Victoria's mother and my grandmother.

She stepped into the light, her presence regal and commanding in a way that matched Eleanor's. The room buzzed with murmurs of surprise.

Victoria's hand tightened on her champagne flute, her knuckles white. I didn't need to ask to know this wasn't part of the evening's plan. Whatever was happening, it wasn't good.

Chapter Twenty-Three

~∞~

Victoria

The murmurs in the room grew louder as Eleanor Haverford and my mother stood side by side on the stage, their commanding presence silencing even the most boisterous of guests. It wasn't often you saw two women of their stature sharing a spotlight, and judging by the looks of intrigue and unease that rippled through the crowd, I wasn't the only one wondering what on earth they were up to.

I felt my pulse quicken, my grip tightening around the stem of my champagne flute. Louis, seated beside me, leaned in slightly, his voice low. "This can't be good."

I didn't respond. My mind was racing, trying to piece together what my mother's sudden appearance could mean. She had always been a bit of an enigma—poised, calculating, and often distant. She rarely attended events like these, preferring to operate behind the scenes. It was something she had in common with Lady Haverford.

For her to step into the limelight tonight, alongside Eleanor of all people, was as shocking as it was concerning.

"Ladies and gentlemen," Eleanor began, her smooth, practiced voice cutting through the murmurs. "Thank you for your attention. Tonight, as we gather for such a noble cause, we are reminded of the power of unity and collaboration. It is in that spirit that I have the distinct pleasure of introducing someone very dear to me and, I believe, to many of you."

She gestured to my mother, who inclined her head gracefully. "Lady Adela Pennington, a woman of unparalleled vision and a true pillar of the aristocracy."

I paused. Someone dear to her? Huh? When did that happen?

The applause was polite but subdued, the audience clearly more interested in where this was going than in exchanging pleasantries. My mother stepped forward, her expression serene, her posture impeccable.

"Thank you, Lady Haverford," she said, her voice steady and refined. "It's a pleasure to be here tonight among so many esteemed friends and colleagues. As Lady Haverford mentioned, tonight is about unity—and not just in philanthropy but in our shared goals for the future."

My stomach sank. This wasn't just a simple appearance. This was orchestrated, planned down to the last word. I glanced at Louis, who gave me a look that said he was just as uneasy as I was.

"Over the years," my mother continued, "our families have worked tirelessly to uphold the values and traditions that define our legacy. But we also recognize the importance of progress, of adapting to the changing world while preserving what makes us unique."

She paused, her gaze sweeping the room before landing on me. The weight of her stare was almost unbearable, but I kept my expression neutral. Whatever game she was playing, I wouldn't give her the satisfaction of seeing me squirm.

"That is why," she said, her voice rising slightly, "Lady Haverford and I have been in discussions about a potential collaboration—a merger, if you will, between our respective family enterprises. Such a partnership would not only strengthen our economic foothold but also ensure the continued prosperity of future generations."

The murmurs grew louder, and I felt a cold knot forming in my chest. A merger? Between the Pennington and Haverford families? Was my older brother Thomas finally getting married?

No, that couldn't be it. The Pennington and the Haverford... it didn't make sense for them to join. They were in completely different industries and not particularly robust. Then I stopped and considered.

Because of me. It isn't about the Penningtons and Haverfords at all. It's about me and the Harringtons.

This was beyond anything I could have anticipated. My mind raced with questions, doubts, and a growing sense of dread.

Eleanor stepped forward again, her smile sharp and knowing. "It's no secret that our families have long shared mutual respect and admiration. This merger would be a natural progression of that relationship, one that would benefit not just our businesses but the broader community we serve."

I barely registered her words, my focus narrowing to the way she glanced in my direction, as if sizing me up. And then she said it—the words I'd been dreading, the bombshell I should have seen coming.

"Of course," she continued smoothly, "such a union wouldn't be complete without a personal alliance to solidify it. That is why Lady Pennington and I are thrilled to announce a formal arrangement between our families—specifically, between my son, Robert Haverford, and Lady Victoria Harrington."

The room erupted into gasps and whispers, the weight of the announcement rippling through the crowd like a stone thrown into still water. I felt the blood drain from my face, my heart hammering so loudly I was sure everyone around me could hear it.

Louis muttered a curse under his breath, his hand instinctively moving to my arm as if to steady me. "Victoria," he said quietly, his voice tight with anger. "They can't be serious."

I barely heard him. My mother's eyes were on me again, her expression calm, almost expectant. As if she were waiting for me to stand and graciously accept the proposal as though it were some grand honor.

Eleanor, ever the performer, turned her attention to the audience, addressing their shocked expressions with practiced ease. "We understand this may come as a surprise, but rest assured, every detail has been carefully considered. Robert and Victoria share a deep history, and we believe this union would be the perfect foundation for a prosperous future."

I wanted to scream, to shout that I had no interest in being used as a pawn in their carefully laid plans. But years of training, of being groomed to play this exact role, held me in place. I forced myself to breathe, to think. This wasn't the time or place for a confrontation. Not yet.

Eleanor glanced back at me, her smile widening. "Victoria, if you could join us on the stage."

All eyes were on me now, waiting for my response. Reporters were throwing out questions, asking for a statement and when the wedding would be. I could feel the weight of their expectations and questions pressing down on me, suffocating in its intensity. I turned to Louis, whose jaw was clenched so tightly I thought it might shatter. He gave me a barely perceptible nod, a silent reassurance that he was on my side.

I rose slowly, the rustle of my gown audible as the room went silent once again. The questions on the lips of the reporters died as I stood. For a moment, I said nothing, letting the tension in the room build. Then, with a practiced smile that didn't reach my eyes, I walked towards the stage.

Time seemed to stop. It was surreal, like one of those movies where raindrops or birds were just suspended.

The moment I touched the stairs, the sound and movement resounded.

The pictures, with accompanying flashes, resounded like a cacophony of gunfire, and the press pushed forward.

I didn't know until he was at my side. Robert grabbed my hand and put his other on the small of my back. He leaned in. "If you wouldn't be so stubborn and would just submit, you wouldn't be blindsided like this. I expect you will be more obedient when we are married."

I felt like I was slapped.

I inhaled deeply, steadying myself.

"Excuse me," I said, almost pushing Robert away from me. I walked up to my mother and took the microphone. It surprised her. It also surprised Lady Haverford. I took another deep breath before I spoke. "Thank you for your attention," I began, my voice carrying across the room with practiced elegance. "It seems tonight has been full of surprises, and I'm grateful for the opportunity to address you all."

A few polite chuckles broke the tension, but I pressed on, my gaze locking briefly with Eleanor's before I continued.

"Choice and circumstance," I said, pausing to let the words hang in the air. "Two forces that shape our lives in ways we often cannot predict. Tonight's announcement is one of circumstance—a calculated attempt to merge legacies, strengthen alliances, and ensure prosperity for generations to come. But what it lacks," I said, my voice growing firmer, "is choice."

A ripple of whispers ran through the crowd, but I didn't waver. "For all the power and influence we wield, love is not something that can be orchestrated in boardrooms or negotiated in tea rooms. It cannot be dictated or demanded. It must be chosen freely."

The room was silent now, the weight of my words pressing down on everyone present. My mother's face remained impassive, but I could see the faintest twitch in her jaw—a sign of her barely concealed irritation. Eleanor, on the other hand, looked utterly composed, her lips curving into a thin smile as if daring me to continue.

Robert wasn't as good at hiding his emotions. He looked downright livid.

I straightened, my gaze sweeping the room. "Many of you may be wondering if I have a statement regarding this... proposal. And the answer is yes." My lips curved into a smile—one that didn't quite reach my eyes. "I do have a statement."

With that, I dropped the microphone, my heels clicking against the polished wood of the stage as I descended the stairs. The crowd watched in stunned silence, their whispers a growing tide as I made my way through the ballroom. It felt as though time itself had slowed, the weight of my decision propelling me forward.

And then I saw him. Ethan stood at our table, his eyes wide with a mix of surprise and disbelief as I approached. His broad shoulders straightened as if bracing himself for whatever was about to happen. For a moment, I hesitated, the enormity of what I was about to do crashing over me. But then I remembered Eleanor's smug expression, my mother's cold detachment, and Robert's audacity.

They wanted to blindside me. Take away my choice. I was about to make it very clear where I stood.

Ethan's eyes locked with mine, and I saw the flicker of understanding in his gaze—just before I closed the distance between us. Without a word, I reached up, wrapping my arms around his neck and pulled him close.

I kissed Ethan Miller right on his gorgeous mouth.

The room's silence deepened in shock so profound you would have thought it was a funeral. It was silent. Deeply silent. Deadly silent. Until it wasn't.

The room erupted in gasps and murmurs and the furious flashing of cameras and outrage. I was displaying deep affection in a very public manner. But I didn't care. The world narrowed to just the two of us, me and Ethan, his lips warm and firm against mine, his hands instinctively settling on my waist and my tongue flicking in his mouth. The kiss wasn't just a declaration; it was a rebellion, a stake in the ground that said I would not be controlled.

When we finally broke apart, his eyes searched mine, a mixture of confusion and awe clouding his expression. "Victoria, what—" he began, but I pressed a finger to his lips.

"Not now," I said softly, a small, genuine smile breaking through. "A moment just... give me the moment."

About the Author

J.C. Anderson is an author inspired by the vibrant world of online storytelling and serial fiction. With a deep appreciation for character-driven narratives and rich, imaginative worlds, J.C. crafts stories that blend romance, drama, and heartfelt connections.

Rough Edges, J.C.'s latest work, draws inspiration from the online storytelling community, where dynamic, serialized tales thrive. Combining sharp dialogue, compelling relationships, and slice-of-life charm, the story invites readers to immerse themselves in a journey of unexpected love, personal growth, and second chances.

www.ingramcontent.com/pod-product-compliance
Lightning Source LLC
Chambersburg PA
CBHW050341030726
47503CB00008B/2562